NOWHERE ELSE

FELICIA DAVIN

ETYMON PRESS

If school was hell, this one's for you.

CONTENTS

CONTENT WARNINGS

A recently traumatized main character has self-destructive urges related to jumping back into the void where he was trapped prior to the story. This is mainly in the first three chapters, especially chapter one. This book also contains minor physical violence, brief mentions of emotional abuse/neglect, and explicit sex.

[1]

L'APPEL DU VIDE

"LANGE, IF I COME INTO THE ROOM, ARE YOU GOING TO throw something at me?"

That voice belonged to his least intolerable visitor, Jacob McCreery. The other visitors, better described as jailers or babysitters, flinched and cringed. Not McCreery. He didn't tiptoe in and out of the room. He talked. Not much, and always with a sort of benevolent exasperation, but Lange could abide him more easily than the others.

He'd had to learn their names and faces—*relearn*, they insisted—as well as his own. Pointless as it was, he retained what they'd told him: he was called *Solomon Lange*, which he did not remember; he was a physicist, which seemed equally inconsequential; he'd been trapped in the Nowhere, which was incorrect.

He'd been free in the Nowhere. He was trapped here.

"Here" encompassed the entirety of the physical world. More specifically, it meant an empty grey bedroom in what had once been Quint Services Facility 17, a research station carved into an asteroid. Despite Lange's evident lack of interest, the crew had kept him informed: Oswin Lewis

Quint, trillionaire founder of Quint Services, had died on Earth last night. The government had seized everything—except Facility 17. It remained a secret. The crew members still living here were now in control of the place. There were only seven of them, which was good for Lange. Fewer obstacles between him and his destination.

Lange was going back to the Nowhere. Back to the pristine openness and emptiness, back to the infinite simultaneity, the numb serenity, away from this body and this room and this reality.

McCreery repeated his question. "You gonna throw something at me if I come in?"

"No," Lange said, still surprised by the low vibration of his own voice. He disliked the sensation. The void of the Nowhere was pure. In his body, there was a filthy, shifting array of hungers and itches and smells, and all of it sickened him. Confinement made him desperate, and when he was desperate, he threw things.

Or rather, things threw themselves.

McCreery had removed the desk and the chair from the room five or six days ago after an altercation where Lange had nearly crushed a man in a suit who'd come to prod at him. That had been Quint himself, apparently, lured by the prospect of studying Lange's telekinesis. Lange did not care to be studied. Quint had survived their encounter only by virtue of McCreery's intervention. Lange felt no remorse about his own actions; it was a small mercy that no one had asked him to express any. No one seemed to miss Quint at all.

Now the room contained only the narrow bed with its scratchy sheets where Lange was currently seated, barefoot and in pajamas, because McCreery and the others had emptied the closet and removed the dresser. They'd moved the cat food after a messy incident three days ago, but some-times the cats still came around.

Lange had yet to hurt the cats.

The same could not be said of the other people in this remote space facility. Lange hadn't seriously injured McCreery yet, which was why the man made the foolish choice of walking into the room. Lange had no wish to harm McCreery, but this brief moment of the unguarded door was his best chance to escape.

"I brought you a sandwich," McCreery said, offering a plate to Lange.

McCreery was large. Almost immovably so. Both tall and broad, his size was his most daunting quality. Lange could never have lifted him bodily.

McCreery fell somewhere between twenty-five and thirty-five years old. He was white, of a complexion that would probably freckle in the summer sun, but the uniform paleness of his skin suggested years spent in space. His nose had been broken at least once and his hair was a middling blond. A blunt instrument of a man. No subtlety, no sharp edges. Holding still suited him, and he proved surprisingly patient, but Lange made him wait for so long that a fine tremor ran through his outstretched arm.

McCreery said, "You haven't eaten since yesterday morning. Everyone's worried about you."

Doubtful. Their concern about Lange began and ended with his ability to do violence. His health was of no interest to anyone, including himself.

Lange pulled on the plate, an act that no longer required the use of his body. Mental visualization sufficed. Or it would have if McCreery hadn't tightened his grip on the dish. The unannounced telekinesis had caught him unaware. McCreery frowned, though Lange's beautifully executed motion should have been no cause for distress.

Lange was rather proud of it, in fact. His best yet. He gave the plate another tug and McCreery let go.

It hovered in the air, carrying an uninspiring stack of wheat bread, sliced cheddar, and salad greens. The food was irrelevant, but the white ceramic dish could do serious damage if telekinetically hurled at someone's face.

It took a moment to line up his mind and his body, but Lange managed to grab the plate with his hand. A curious appendage—dark brown with long, slender fingers, less responsive than expected. Still, he was able to cup his palm under the plate, catching the edge with his thumb. He lowered the plate to the floor, the sandwich untouched, making a show of his deliberate, jerky movements.

The distance didn't put the plate out of range of his abilities, but he hoped the gesture would serve as a sign that if it did shatter, that hadn't been his intention. The thought of a ceramic shard piercing any soft and frail part of the human body disgusted Lange. McCreery didn't need to bleed or die.

He just needed to stay out of the way.

Lange was about to strike when McCreery said, "I know," with great sympathy, which startled him.

McCreery cast his gaze toward the discarded sandwich and said, "I miss deli meat, too. But we're not getting regular shipments from Quint Services anymore, so just be grateful I was able to scrounge up some cheese. If one of those runners doesn't take pity on us, soon enough we'll all be surviving off whatever's in Emil's greenhouse."

Lange couldn't rely on his memory of life before the Nowhere, but it struck him as unusual for McCreery to talk so much at once. The others, when forced to visit him, chattered nervously in the face of Lange's silence, wondering all the while if he was going to fling them out of the room.

When, not *if*.

"What would it take for you to eat this sandwich? Or anything?" McCreery asked. "What do you *want*? I can't make any promises, but I'm a decent thief. Beer? Cigarettes? Something to read? Eat the sandwich and it's yours."

Lange stared at him. It was hard to imagine a man as big as McCreery exercising any kind of stealth. Harder still to imagine himself wanting anything as mundane as alcohol and reading material.

McCreery inclined his head, emphasizing the seriousness of his offer. "If you want more than that, I'm gonna need you to shower, too. Not to be a dick, but it's been a week since the decontamination and it's getting rank in here."

Lange ignored that. But perhaps McCreery was willing to help him. "I want to go back."

"To Earth? I don't know if I can swing that, not while you're still—" McCreery waved a hand in the air, a gesture presumably meant to indicate *unpredictably telekinetic* "— but I'll see what I can do."

"Not to Earth," Lange clarified. "I want to go back to the Nowhere."

"You what?" McCreery said, his question punctuated with an incredulous laugh. "Sorry, man, not happening. It almost killed you. And you were... really not yourself in there."

Yes, exactly. *Not being himself* was the goal.

McCreery continued, "I can't let you do that."

"Unfortunate," Lange said, and then he hurled McCreery across the room.

McCreery's shoulders slammed into the back wall.

Lange immobilized him there, his feet dangling, and was gratified when McCreery swore at him, because it meant two things: Lange hadn't killed him, but he couldn't get free.

It was difficult to hold McCreery in place, more so because he wouldn't stop struggling and saying, "Lange. Lange, don't do this. We need you here."

Lange stood precariously. He'd spent the solitude of the past few days taming his mind, but his body remained an unruly animal. He wobbled, his vision spotting black. His destination was only a few minutes' walk, but that was more unassisted walking than he'd done in weeks. No matter; he'd slough off this form soon enough. He forced himself to move toward the door.

The lab was just down the hallway. He could feel the gash in the fabric of reality trembling, even from here. The void called to him. *Shift weight to one foot, bend the other knee, lift the heel, put the foot forward in a step.* Again. He could do this. One step, and then another. He'd exited the room and made it a few steps into the hallway. That was progress.

McCreery thumped against the floor. Damn it. Lange hadn't meant to drop him, but walking required too much focus, and it was hard to control things he couldn't see.

McCreery wasn't quiet when he groaned and stood. "Lange," he yelled. "Get back here."

Lange should have knocked him out. He hadn't wanted to do permanent damage. There was no way he could outrun—out*walk*—McCreery. Was Lange strong enough to throw him again? Could he hold McCreery off with his mind alone?

Lange forced the door to slide shut, but it didn't slow McCreery, who burst into the hallway a moment later, muttering, "Jesus fucking Christ."

The one object Lange couldn't move was himself. He'd tried to transport himself both within this world and out of it, and his attempts had come to nothing. He wasn't a runner. He didn't have innate access to the Nowhere. His only method of arriving in the lab was his weak, useless legs, so he'd have to continue his painstaking progress while pushing McCreery back with his mind.

McCreery made a long stride down the hallway. Lange shoved him back, the rubber soles of McCreery's shoes screeching resistance against the floor. Lange couldn't hold him still, not while walking required so much effort. McCreery fought free an instant later. Another stride. Another shove backward. Then McCreery huffed, rolled his eyes, and took a running leap. He tackled Lange to the ground.

Lange threw him off, or tried to. McCreery wrapped his arms around Lange's chest so instead the two of them rolled together, landing with McCreery flat on his back and Lange on top of him, glaring at the ceiling. Hanging on was clever, Lange would give him that. It rendered Lange's one advantage unusable.

"You done now?" McCreery asked, and then, more worried, "You're okay, right?"

Lange grunted, because there was no strand of the multiverse in which he could bring himself to answer "yes" to either question.

McCreery possessed the core strength to boost himself upright without loosening his grip, which put Lange in the unspeakably awful position of sitting between his spread thighs. Lange was in no pain, which he regretted. Pain, at least, he understood. Its absence made everything—being *cradled*—so much worse.

No one had touched him so much since he'd returned,

everyone else too cowardly or too wise to try. Now he was surrounded, one of McCreery's thick arms banding his chest and McCreery's belly pressing into his back. Lange could smell both of them, his own unpleasantly ripe scent under the clean fragrance of McCreery's soap. The sensory input crashed over him like a wave of static, leaving him unable to think of anything but how confined he was. How utterly, wretchedly human. McCreery was warm. Lange's heart thudded in his chest, its rhythm erratic from panic and exhaustion. He slumped back against McCreery's chest, seething and humiliated.

"Should've eaten the sandwich," McCreery told him, his voice right next to Lange's ear, inescapable.

———

JAKE HAD WANTED to give Lange a hug a bunch of times since his return, but not like this.

He'd never acted on the urge. They weren't close. But Jake didn't have a clue what to do with somebody who'd survived something awful. Some stubborn, animal part of his brain kept proposing hugs as the answer.

Lange didn't want hugs, even if it seemed like he needed one, and that was reason enough not to do it. Also, Lange was furious most of the time and he could move things with his mind, in case Jake needed extra reminders not to fuck with him.

Touching was a desperate measure, but Lange planning to hurl himself into the breach qualified as desperate times. Welcome to your stay at the Last Resort, Mr. McCreery.

Thankfully, Lange didn't fight him as they peeled themselves off the hallway floor and made their way back. It was more like helping an unsteady elderly person to bed, except

Lange was... what, thirty-five? Jake had no idea. The dark brown skin of his face was unlined. His beard made it even harder to tell.

Lange looked different now. He was still a handsome Black man, but before getting trapped in the Nowhere, he'd been in good health. He'd also kept his hair and beard as short as they were in the professional photo on the back cover of *The Physics of the Nowhere*. Lange had seemed like a guy who cared about personal grooming. And not that Jake would know—his only goal when getting dressed was not being naked or cold—but Lange had struck him as stylish. They lived in a secret facility in a hollowed-out asteroid with no place fancy to go and no one to impress, and still everything Lange owned fit him just right. Button-down shirts, suits, other things that looked like they required laundry care Jake didn't know how to provide. He was pretty good at getting engine grease out of clothes, but Lange's suits wouldn't need that.

Lange had been like that before, anyway. Whatever happened to him in the Nowhere had swept being presentable right off his list of priorities. All that time in unfolded space had weakened him, and apparently given the guy some kind of need to hurl himself back in.

"What do you want to go back for, anyway?" Jake asked. "Didn't you spend all your time in there trying to cling to Kit so you could get out? You nearly killed him, you know."

Instead of answering, Lange reached for the abandoned sandwich and ate it in sullen silence. Thirty-five? More like fourteen.

"We need you to stay, Lange. You're the only one who can repair the breach," Jake said. Emil had been on him to bring this topic up.

Everybody had shunted their responsibilities onto Jake.

They all said shit like *oh you have such a way with him*, instead of *Lange scares me out of my goddamn mind*, which would have been honest, at least. They acted like Jake had an advanced degree in dealing with genius physicists who'd accidentally trapped themselves in a mysterious void and then reappeared with out-of-control superpowers, which was funny, because Jake felt like it was one of those dreams where he was taking the final exam for a class he hadn't even known he was in.

It was true he'd spent a lot of years working Search and Rescue, pulling injured, scared, or drunk people out of their malfunctioning spacecraft. He'd done some training in field medicine and become pretty good at projecting a calm, steady presence. None of the people he'd rescued had been telekinetic. Or geniuses.

Lange finished the sandwich. The plate rose out of his lap and hovered back down to the floor, clinking when it landed. Lange didn't want to touch it. He didn't want to touch anything. Jake caught him shuddering at the brush of his own clothing sometimes. He felt for the guy.

"It calls to me," Lange said, not looking at Jake.

"The breach in your lab?"

"The Nowhere."

"*L'appel du vide,*" Jake said. Jesus. Self-destructive urges on top of it all. Jake had been through some fucked-up shit in his life, but it was just bad parents, no friends, *regular* misery. Lange blew him out of the water. "That's French for 'the call of the void.'"

Lange raised an eyebrow.

"What? I read." Everyone here was all about not judging people based on appearance, except when it came to the idea that the big guy from the sticks had cracked open a book once or twice in his life. Well, *l'appel du vide,* that one he'd learned from a crossword puzzle. It still counted.

Jake let go of his indignation and brought the conversation back to what mattered. "I'm not much of an expert on unfolded space, though. That's all you. Your machine made a door into the Nowhere, and now we need you to close it."

"Fine," Lange said. "Take me there and I'll close it."

"Uh huh," Jake said. He crossed his arms over his chest. "Take you there and you'll throw yourself in, more like. How about I bring Dax in here and you tell them how to close it instead?"

Dax Strickland, the other physicist remaining at Facility 17, had been Lange's junior colleague. They were brilliant, but they hadn't been able to repair the damage done by the accident on their own.

Lange responded to the question with silence. Maybe it was stubbornness. Maybe he didn't know the answer.

"I'm sorry for how things went down just now. I don't want to do that again. You wanna apologize for throwing me at the wall?" Jake said, pressing his luck. He wasn't in the habit of asking, but *habit* didn't cover any part of this situation. Lange wasn't in his right mind. He wouldn't hurt anybody if he were in control of himself. At least, Jake wanted to believe that. An apology would be a sign. A real historic moment—Jake's first-ever apology from somebody who started a fight with him. They could throw a parade.

Lange offered him half a second of cold eye contact, then looked away. After long enough that Jake thought Lange would change the subject and move on, Lange said, "I regret harming you."

Maybe not parade-worthy, but better than expected. Still a damn long way from promising not to do it again, but just like with a shitty Christmas present, the thought counted. It was enough for Jake to say, "Good. You could shower and change your clothes and act just a little bit more like a human being. I'd accept that as a peace offering."

"I will shower and change. Acting is beyond the scope of my abilities."

"You know I meant *behaving*, not performing. You can get nitpicky with me when you smell better," Jake said, tossing a bath towel at Lange. The towel hung in the air, untouched, and Jake sighed. Lange was full of shit, acting like he wasn't human. So he could juggle with no hands these days, that didn't make a difference. His bad attitude alone qualified him.

He offered Lange a hand up from the bed. There had been toiletries in the room before the team had removed all the small, hard, throw-able objects. Later, Jake had removed all the large, hard, throw-able objects. There wasn't much to be done about Lange flinging *people*. Lange's previous efforts had been a little gentler. He'd just sort of slid the other team members backwards out of the room and forced the door closed. Jake was lucky enough to get special treatment, apparently. His bruised shoulders throbbed.

Lange had apologized, Jake reminded himself. He unclenched his jaw and clung to that.

Jake walked Lange to the facility's shared bathroom and neither of them said anything, which was fine. Silence was good for thinking about the upgrades Jake would make to Eliza. Version one of the probe moved on treads, but he wanted more versatility. Version two could hover, maybe.

If the team ever stopped asking him to check on Lange, Jake would have time to make the changes.

Sure, they'd all been switching off shifts outside Lange's door, worrying. But when it came time to talk to him, that fell to Jake.

Ridiculous. Jake didn't even know the guy. Felt a kind of frustrated sympathy for him, sure. Weird loner, better with science than people. Jake knew that song. It didn't make them friends.

He'd thought for a while that it might. Lange was interesting. Jake wasn't *interested* in him—Jake wasn't much for that kind of interest—but buried under that lethal coldness was a brilliant mind. Someone Jake might have enjoyed talking to. It wasn't that Lange had rejected his friendship. Jake had made a few tentative overtures in their first few months living in Facility 17, and then Lange had—well, not *died*, exactly. But he hadn't been around.

Lange was back now, and he was a mess, and Jake was even more of one, because sometimes he still wanted to be friends. He thought about hugs, for fuck's sake.

It was the social equivalent of standing on a high precipice and looking over the edge. A jump would end in brutal, painful disaster, but those moments of free fall in between—*no*. Jake was not fucking doing this. The void could stop calling him right the fuck now.

Jake found a clean washcloth and a bar of soap and turned to give them to Lange, who leaned against the wall, brooding, still fully dressed.

Someone quicker with a joke might have teased him—*I know it's been a while since you bathed, but the usual thing is to take your clothes off*—but Jake's throat closed up at the thought. Instead he warmed up the shower and said, "It's ready. I'll, uh, wait over here. Yell if you need anything."

Lange pushed off the wall, jerked his shirt over his head, then dropped it. Jake spun on his heel after catching a flash of brown torso. He probably should have watched Lange totter into the shower to make sure their best chance at fixing the universe didn't slip and break his neck, but he couldn't move. Jake didn't turn around again until he heard the metal stall door latch.

Lange had left the towel and the set of clean clothes hanging on hooks opposite the stall. His discarded clothes lay crumpled on the floor, next to the soap and washcloth Jake had given him. As Jake watched, the toiletries rose from the floor and floated under the stall door.

The power itself was weird, and weirder still was how quickly Lange had adapted to it. He no longer thought to reach for things with his hands. Since his return, Lange acted like his body was some alien punishment that had been forced on him. He didn't welcome sensations of any kind, even ones Jake thought of as pleasant—clean sheets, hot coffee, a friendly pat on the back. No wonder he'd put this off for so long. The shower was probably making him miserable.

Maybe he really does feel bad about hurting me, Jake thought, and then a spray of warm water jumped out of the stall and splattered his face. He blinked, water catching in his lashes and dripping down his nose to wet his shirt.

"Very funny."

"Oh, did that hit you?" Lange's delivery was as dry as ever. "I was experimenting."

Jake wiped a hand over his face, pushing his wet bangs up. "How about you finish up your *experiment* and we get back to solving the real problem? You know, the one where your machine ripped open the Nowhere and now it's spilling?"

The water cut off. Lange's towel levitated from the wall hook into the stall. "You'll have to take me to the lab. I can't solve a problem I can't see."

The lab. Not *my lab*. Lange kept doing things like that. Divorcing himself from his former life.

"Promise me you won't hurt anybody, including yourself. And jumping into the Nowhere counts as hurting yourself."

"Remaining here is far more painful."

"I guess I wouldn't know," Jake said, frowning. Lange was unhappy, but who wouldn't be, after being trapped in the Nowhere for weeks and then stuck in that empty room with nothing to do? He hadn't realized Lange was suffering. What a fucking mess.

"It is not my intention to hurt you or anyone else," Lange said after a long pause. "But in my... condition, my intentions are worth very little."

"No," Jake said. "They're worth a lot."

There was only the sound of water dripping onto the floor.

"Lange, I know things really suck right now, and I'm sorry. If you just hold off on hurling yourself into the void for a little while, I will work with you to make things suck less. You stick around and I will too. Okay?"

"You're the first person who's said that."

"What?"

"That things... suck. Everyone else has been determined to assure me that *everything's okay now*."

"Oh. Well. Clearly it's not." Was that gratitude in Lange's tone? Jake hadn't done anything but acknowledge reality. He took a breath. "Listen, you fix the world and I will help you fix yourself. Or at least, make sure you're not in pain anymore. I'm good at fixing stuff. It's why I'm on the team."

Jake was good with wiring. Pipes. Engines. Robots. Hardware. Anything mechanical, he could take it apart and put it back together better than he'd found it. People didn't work like that—and they never wanted him around, so he didn't know much. But his gut twisted at the idea that Lange was so miserable he wanted to throw himself back into the Nowhere, so Jake had to say *something*. Lange didn't deserve to live like that.

There was a long silence as Lange dressed inside the stall. Instead of responding to Jake's offer, he said, "You don't know for certain that I am capable of 'fixing the world.'"

"Yeah." Jake blew out a breath. "You know someone better qualified, you give them a call."

"I don't," Lange said. The door swung open, his cool regard zeroing in on Jake. "Neither do I know anyone capable of 'fixing' my problem."

Jake could only shrug. It had been easier to talk to Lange with his face out of sight. "Guess we're stuck with each other."

[2]
THE SOUND

LANGE HAD UNDERESTIMATED THE VALUE OF cleanliness. Having eaten and washed, he couldn't say he was enjoying himself, but the odor of his body no longer bothered him, and the sharp pain in his stomach had decreased. Not being filthy and hungry had improved his condition.

So had talking to McCreery.

Who knew it would mean so much to have the reality of his situation acknowledged? Absurd. It shouldn't matter if other people believed him or not; the truth was the truth.

He moved toward the lab with halting, unsteady steps. He'd declined McCreery's assistance. Lange didn't like any bodily reactions, but the increase in his heart rate when McCreery touched him was particularly distracting and unwelcome. Lange had other problems to solve.

Soon he'd be close to the breach. Already it hummed against his skin, its presence a promise. He could return to the Nowhere, where he belonged.

And yet—

Lange didn't care for the world. He didn't owe it anything. But McCreery had been kind to him despite everything. Whatever happened to Lange, McCreery would continue living here, in the world Lange had endangered. He ought to examine the problem, at least. Perhaps he could help.

The lab door, papered over with menacing red warning signs, slid open when McCreery touched it.

In order to plan his escape, Lange had spent his waking hours supplementing his fragmented memory by compiling a mental spreadsheet of the seven people living in Facility 17, so he was able to identify the person who met them in the lab as Dax Strickland.

- Features: young, white, redheaded, nonbinary, medium height and build.
- Profession: physicist.
- Loyalties or attachments within the crew: unknown.
- Frequency of appearance in his room: low (two known visits).
- Attitude: reserved.
- Ability to enter the Nowhere: none.
- Ability to hinder his plans: low.

It was possible Dax had come to his room more than two times. Lange had been numb and stupefied for the first few days, physically unresponsive but telekinetically volatile.

Strickland jerked a thumb at their chest, clad in plaid flannel. "I'm Dax, in case you don't remember. Doctor Strickland if you're going to throw anything at me."

Lange was too distracted by the constant high-pitched whine in the lab to respond. Two whines. No, three—though the third was faint. Couldn't the others hear the sound?

"Doctor Lange? You there?"

"It's been a hard day," McCreery said softly. Was that meant as a defense of Lange's silence?

"It's okay. Let's talk about what's going on here."

Strickland gestured at the lab space, which had been stripped bare of broken glass and overturned furniture—oh. A memory. Lange had been here before.

The *accident* everyone spoke of in hushed tones had occurred here. An explosion of sorts. Hence the wreckage he remembered.

There was no trace of that. The lab was an empty expanse of grey walls and flooring. The windows that would have looked out on the hallway had sheets of brown paper held in place with duct tape instead of panes of glass.

His eyes stung and he blinked to clear his vision and bring things back into focus, but it wasn't him. It was the space. Something was wrong here.

At the far end of the room, the two silver parentheses of the machine stood.

They whirred and keened, but Strickland and McCreery hadn't noticed the noise. Lange said, "Have you tried turning it off?"

"Is that a joke?"

"Doctor Lange doesn't make jokes," Strickland said, which made McCreery grimace for some reason. "And no, it's not still on. It went into automatic shutdown twenty-four hours after your accident, as designed. I only left it on that long because we were hoping you'd reappear."

That word again. *Accident.* It was true that turning on the machine had unforeseen consequences for Lange, but if it was an accident, it was a happy one. He'd learned what it was to live in the Nowhere, unencumbered by his body.

"'Have you tried turning it off,'" Strickland muttered, offended. "It's been weeks."

"But I can hear it," Lange said. The noise. It had to be the machine, didn't it?

"I don't hear anything," Strickland said, at the same time that McCreery made concerned eye contact and asked, "What are you hearing?"

"Three constant, whining sounds," Lange said. The loudest one hovered at the pitch of A flat, irritatingly dissonant with the G of the second loudest. At times, he could detect a C, but it was significantly quieter. The buzzing cluster of pitches didn't coalesce into a chord. Long-ingrained habit silenced these details, which McCreery and Strickland would only find puzzling. Lange couldn't remember much, but he knew that.

"Could it be the breach?" McCreery asked. "Maybe it's another ability you developed in the Nowhere, being able to hear whatever's wrong in here."

"Where's the origin of the sound?" Strickland asked.

Lange slid his gaze toward the opposite wall. The air shimmered. Yes. He was hearing the breach, or the Nowhere, or something related to those two.

Shouldn't it sound more enticing?

"You think whatever you're hearing is coming from the breach?" Strickland asked.

"Something like that," Lange said. "If I could get closer—"

"No," said McCreery, speaking at the same time that Strickland held up a hand.

"Wait right here. *Don't* move." They dashed out of the lab and returned holding three tennis balls. "Here's why going over there is a really bad idea."

Strickland dumped a tennis ball into their hand, then threw it toward the machine. Halfway between their position and the machine's, the tennis ball vanished.

Strickland waited a beat. The tennis ball didn't reappear. They threw a second one down the left side of the room. It disappeared even earlier in its trajectory, then popped out of the air on the right side of the room like it had tunneled through some invisible space.

The first one might never return, and yet the second one had. Fascinating.

Being in this room brought back memories of his grant proposals for the project. The original goal of the machine had been to establish a permanent door into the Nowhere, meant to allow more research into the void and perhaps to democratize access to instant travel. Most people couldn't enter the Nowhere. Those that could travel through it— runners—were a tiny fraction of the population, often feared and mistreated by those around them.

Lange hadn't thought he could change that, not really. But building a door had seemed worth a try.

Instead, the accident with the machine had produced this unstable breach, which was now affecting the space around it, as evidenced by the unexpected behavior of the tennis balls. A sort of oil-spill of unfolded space.

Strickland bowled the last tennis ball along the floor. Its path toward the machine was strange—straight enough, but its speed changed seemingly at random, as though it were passing through different terrain. But it never disappeared. It trundled along for ages, making it seem like the other side of the room was a kilometer away. The ball slowed to a stop just short of the base of the machine.

"So crawling along the floor would get us there," Lange said. He'd be able to hear the sounds more distinctly if he were closer. Then he'd understand them.

"Still risky," McCreery said. "If we need access to that half of the room, we can send Eliza."

"Eliza?" Strickland asked.

"Uh. One of my robots."

"You *name* them? Jake, that's so cute. Why haven't you ever mentioned it?"

Judging from McCreery's expression, he hadn't mentioned it because he was hoping to avoid a reaction like Strickland's. These observations and the subsequent realization gave Lange the sense of having solved a difficult equation at last.

"I'd hate for you to lose Eliza, though," Strickland continued. "I know you design them to go where we can't, so it's her job, but it would be a loss. The whole room is a mess—you'd have to track the path of that tennis ball *exactly* to get over there."

McCreery nodded, held up a hand, and left the room.

He returned with more tennis balls and a can of black paint. He dipped the first one in, coating it, and pitched it along the floor, trying to follow the path of the previous ball. It left a black trail as it rolled.

A trail that ended abruptly when the ball disappeared.

"Good call," Strickland said. "We'll be able to map out where some of the dangers are if we cover the room like that. I'll get the others, it'll go faster that way."

"Wait," Lange said. "There's no need for that."

The shimmer he could see between the parentheses of the machine repeated itself elsewhere in the room, two dozen fluttering distortions of the light that burned his eyes. But he could *see* them. They matched the incessant buzz and whine burrowing into his ears.

This place was uncomfortable enough without more people entering it.

McCreery and Strickland were watching him, waiting for him to explain himself. With his hands hanging at his sides, Lange lifted a second tennis ball from the canister Jake was holding, dipped it in the paint, and then set it rolling across the floor. Manipulating the ball required the most control he'd exercised yet. He bit his lip in concentration.

The ball swerved left around a distortion, a smear of black paint marking the border, and then Lange drove it straight for another few meters. It jerked and zigzagged along the floor until it reached the base of the machine.

"Wow," McCreery said. "So that's how we get there."

"That's *a* way, but we'll need another," Lange said. He sent a third tennis ball floating through the room, following the painted path, and left it hovering in the air a few centimeters off the ground. "There's a distortion just above where the ball is. Nothing taller can pass."

He moved the tennis ball, outlining the ragged shape of the distortion. Something about the gesture tripped a switch in his memory: a classroom, a board with a diagram, and a laser pointer in his hand.

Fast on the heels of that memory, another followed: he'd never liked or been good at teaching. Other people were far too frustrating.

This feeling, at least, marked an overlap between the person he'd been and whatever he was now.

Strickland and McCreery were both attentive, their

gazes trained on the floating tennis ball. The tip of Strickland's tongue caught between their teeth.

"You can see the distortions," McCreery said. "And you can use your ability to show us where they are without getting too close. Let me call Eliza and together, we can get her over there to collect some data."

Lange shook his head. "It has to be me."

McCreery's eyes narrowed in suspicion. "Why?"

"You can't hear what I'm hearing or see what I'm seeing. The robot won't be able to record it. I need to get closer."

"To do what?"

"To *listen*," Lange snapped, and as he did, the tennis ball he'd been hovering in the air plummeted into the distortion below it.

It popped out of sight like a stone dropped into a lake. Its disappearance crackled, interrupting the buzz in the room. Then the sound resumed.

McCreery and Strickland stared in wide-eyed horror, first at the place where the tennis ball had been, and then at Lange.

"Yeah, let's take a step back and think this through first," Strickland said, and the three of them retreated to another lab, one where Lange almost couldn't hear the sound.

———

JAKE FOLLOWED Lange and Dax to another lab, one free of freaky space-time distortions, even though there was no reason for him to hang around while they conferred over Dax's laptop together. He had no idea how to run the machine they'd built. His usefulness had hit its limit after the three of them had drawn up schematics for the lab itself, pushing Lange to identify where the distortions were so he wasn't the only person with that knowledge.

Those plans, drawn on paper, lay on the lab bench in front of Jake. Finished. The last useful thing he'd done, taunting him.

Dax's laptop screen was covered in line after line of coded equations. Jake didn't recognize most of the symbols. It might as well have been an alien language. Even Dax and Lange's spoken argument, though technically in English, was pretty hard to follow.

"I think what happened on the night of your accident is best understood as constructive interference," Dax was saying.

"Yes, obviously," Lange said. "That doesn't help us reverse it."

"Wait," Jake said. He'd understood those words. "The normal kind of constructive interference? Like when two waves come together into a bigger wave?"

"Yes," Dax said, at the same time that Lange said, "No."

"Uh. Okay."

"Basically nothing in the Nowhere works like you think it would," Dax said gently. "So yes, there *are* waves, or there are things we call waves, but no, they're not like the waves you're thinking of. They're not limited to being longitudinal or transverse, for example. But if you want to think of what happened on the night of Lange's accident as a rogue wave, you can. A freak occurrence that happened right as he tested the machine. He had really, really bad luck."

"That much I knew," Jake said, and opted to retreat from the conversation.

He couldn't bring himself to retreat from the room. He didn't trust Lange not to hurt himself.

By Lange's admission, he wanted to throw himself into

the breach. Dax didn't know that. What if Lange's urge to self-destruct ended up hurting them all? So now Jake was leaning against the lab bench, pretending he could help, listening to their conversation while waiting for Lange to let slip some clue that he was secretly sabotaging all of Dax's work. They'd turn the machine back on and the whole damn multiverse would disintegrate.

"This is elegant," Lange was saying, his gaze on some passage on the screen. His knowledge of the equations and the code had come back to him far more easily than his knowledge of his own life, and he'd been almost eager—as eager as he ever was, these days—to read through Dax's work.

"Thanks," Dax murmured. They were so pale that any tinge of color showed in their face, and the unexpected compliment made them glow pink.

Come to think of it, that comment was probably the nicest thing Lange had ever said in Jake's presence. Naturally, it wasn't about Jake.

"We have to rewrite this next part, though," Lange continued. "I can already see that it will worsen the dimensional shear. That's unacceptable."

"You think it's shear stress? Not tensional?"

"Look at the readings. We're obviously dealing with multiple kinds of stress," Lange said. The tablet Dax had left lying on the bench rose into the air and then dropped back down, the telekinetic equivalent of an impatient wave of the hand. Lange's eyes remained on the code. "It will take us hours to pick apart this mess."

"Right," Dax said, resigned. "Mess."

Well. That was why you couldn't rely on an asshole like Lange for your self-esteem. He'd just as soon cut you down as build you up. Jake should know better than to want

Lange's compliments. Lange couldn't even be nice to the second-smartest person in the room for more than three words in a row. Jake had no chance.

"What are you still doing here?" Lange asked, turning toward Jake. "Go... fix the plumbing. Make a robot. Whatever it is you do when you're not hovering."

Jake snatched the plans and left without a word. Fuck him, anyway. Jake would warn Dax later, when Lange wasn't around to be such a dick.

He went back to Lange's lab. The open can of black paint was still sitting on the floor, an accident waiting to happen. Way less of an accident than the invisible rest of the room, though.

That gave him an idea. He called Eliza to him and she came trundling in on her treads.

She was a squat, square little thing, mostly grey metal and exposed wires, with a platform, a camera, and four movable arms stacked on top. Jake was aware that regular people wouldn't find her adorable, so he didn't talk to regular people about her. They didn't deserve her, anyway. Eliza always came when he called, no matter what he needed, which was a rare quality in robots and humans.

Jake might not have telekinesis, but for his purposes, Eliza would work just as well. It didn't take very long to mount the paint can on top of her and affix a paintbrush to one of her arms.

He taught her to dip the brush into the paint, drag a streak along the floor behind her, and then reload the brush. The movement was new to her. Paint blobbed and dripped on the floor the first few tries, and he had to go get rags to clean it up, but after maybe eight or nine attempts and adjustments—not too bad, really—she had it.

Robots were sweet like that. If you were patient, they'd cooperate eventually.

Eliza beeped. She didn't talk, but she could make a small array of sounds. This was her "yes, I can do that" affirmation.

"You're well on your way to a career as a forger," he told her, and then felt bad. "Or a regular artist, I guess. Didn't mean to assume you couldn't make original work."

Jake spread out the plans on the floor and got to work, directing Eliza to outline all the invisible dangers, giving each one a wide berth. She couldn't delineate how high the distortions hung in the air, but she could at least tell people where they shouldn't walk. Her path meandered all over the room, a wild contour drawing springing up behind her.

"Good girl," Jake told her after she'd come back to him, inordinately proud of her for picking up a new skill. He rolled his shoulders, aching from his fight with Lange, and was startled to discover Lange and Dax standing behind him.

And here he was, crouching on the ground, talking to the robot he'd just used to turn the whole room into a cartoon maze. Shit.

"We're going to recalibrate the machine and turn it back on, see if we can close the breach," Dax said. "Have you been in here this whole time?"

Jake nodded.

Dax smiled. "Love what you've done with the place."

Lange was staring, motionless as usual. "You've missed a few."

"The ones in the air? Some of them overlap. I just tried to outline where people shouldn't walk." God, why was Jake defending his actions at all, let alone in such a mumble? Lange's opinion didn't matter. Jake had done something useful, and it would be useful whether Lange acknowledged it or not.

"It's a good idea."

Jake nearly fell out of his crouch and landed butt-first on the floor. He caught himself and then stood up, as if he could salvage the moment. "Pardon?"

"There's the obvious safety issue," Lange said. "The readings from the machine only give the size of the breach, not these smaller pockets of space, and besides, they don't have the same impact as your painting."

"Oh."

Dax had carried a tablet and two laptops into the room. "What happened to the table that used to be in here? Can we set it up again?"

"It's in storage," Jake said. "The two of us can go get it."

They both walked out of the lab toward the storage closet across the hall, with Lange following slowly. The closet door slid open, and before either of them could lay hands on the table, it levitated. Jake and Dax both wisely got out of the way. The table floated through the door and into the lab, twisted in the air so its legs were facing down, and then dropped. It was a gentler landing than Lange had managed previously. Jake's shoulders hurt at the thought.

"Right," Dax said, after shaking off the strangeness of that display and walking back into the lab. They hadn't seen Lange move things as often as Jake had. "And we should tell the others that we're going to run the machine."

"Why? They won't understand," Lange said.

"Yeah, but we're a team. This is a big decision," Dax said. "I'm going to get them."

Without Dax in the room, the silence between Jake and Lange might as well have been one of the distortions, stretching two meters into twenty.

"You still hearing noises?" Jake asked after a moment.

Lange nodded. "I still want to investigate."

"But you helped Dax rewrite the machine's software so it will *close* the breach," Jake said, pressing. *Please say that's what you did.* Lange was a lot of things, but he wasn't usually a liar.

"I did," Lange said. "I hope it will make the sound go away."

"It's unpleasant? The sound?"

Lange nodded again.

"And your grand plan to throw yourself back in?" Jake asked. He hated to bring it up, but there was no way around it. "If you close the breach, you lose your chance."

"It will close slowly," Lange said. "We determined that the risk of forcing it closed too fast is worse than the risk of allowing it to remain partially open for another few days."

Jesus. There were *more ways* they could fuck things up. "So you're still thinking about going back."

"It is impossible not to."

"I don't understand why you helped Dax. Why help any of us, if what you want is to go back into the Nowhere?"

"I—" Lange started, and then closed his mouth as the others came in.

————

WHY WAS HE HELPING? Lange could invent something about ethics. Duty. Altruism. Perhaps even remorse over his own actions. Any lie would sound less absurd than *because you told me to.*

That would be true whether Lange said it or not.

McCreery didn't need to know that. If he knew, he'd assume—perhaps rightly, which was troubling—that he could get other concessions out of Lange. He'd undoubt-edly use his power to try to get Lange to stay. Out of the question. Lange *had* to go back to the Nowhere. This wretched physiological confinement couldn't be all there was.

Strickland was explaining to the people who'd entered the room that they planned to turn the recalibrated machine on in the hope of reversing the damage it had done the first time.

Lange consulted his mental spreadsheet about the first person who'd entered the lab.

- Name: Emil Singh.
- Features: approximately thirty years old, of South Asian descent, black-haired, tall, athletic, cis man.
- Profession: unclear; de facto leader of remaining Facility 17 residents.
- Loyalties or attachments within the crew: romantic and sexual attachment to Kit, last name unknown.
- Frequency of visits to Lange's room: medium.
- Attitude: calm, friendly, authoritative.
- Ability to enter the Nowhere: none.
- Ability to hinder Lange's plans: medium.

"Thank you, Dax," Singh said once he'd received Strick-land's report.

"Festive new decorations aside, this place still gives me the fucking creeps," said Kit, last name unknown.

- Features: background unknown, likely alien parentage on one side (see: Ability to enter the

Nowhere), light brown skin, violet hair (dye,
black roots visible), young, short, thin, cis man.

- Profession: likely a courrier or a smuggler (see:
Ability to enter the Nowhere).
- Frequency of visits to Lange's room: zero.
- Attitude: wary.
- Ability to enter the Nowhere: innate.
- Ability to hinder Lange's plans: high.

As a born runner, Kit could use the Nowhere to teleport himself anywhere in or out of the world, in this reality or others, almost instantaneously. Why he was enduring the misery of embodiment instead of floating in the void remained a mystery. If Lange could blink himself into the Nowhere, he would already be gone. But Lange's only access to the Nowhere was the breach on the other side of the lab—a place Kit could stop him from going, should he decide to interfere.

Kit continued, "Whatever you need to do to fix the breach, do it."

He was strangely familiar. Lange couldn't look away, and it had nothing to do with the electric blue pattern on that jacket and the way it clashed with his hair. What was it McCreery had said? *You almost killed Kit.*

Lange didn't remember. As an explanation, it was both repellent and inadequate, only giving rise to more questions. Why would he have done that?

He didn't feel like a person who would have done that—but he didn't feel like a person at all.

There were three other people arrayed behind Singh and Kit. Two of them nodded at him. They were Clara Chávez (Latina, mid-twenties, cis female, lanky, athletic; profession: unknown; frequency of visits: medium; attitude: friendly; ability to enter the Nowhere: none; ability to hinder plans: low) and Lennox Beck (Black, mid-twenties, cis male, large, athletic, glasses; profession: aerospace engineer; frequency of visits: medium; attitude: friendly; ability to enter the Nowhere: unknown; ability to hinder plans: unknown). Chávez and Beck spent most of their free time together but were not romantically involved—Chávez was a lesbian—and he'd gathered from eavesdropping that their close friendship was founded on a mutual love of sports and card games. They laughed a lot. Lange's brain was in disarray and had made space for this irrelevant trivia.

Chávez and Beck smiled at him, which he had not done anything to merit. It stirred up a vague memory that they'd both attempted to befriend him, before. He'd been unresponsive. He'd expended his lifetime quota of trust and could not afford strangers.

The third person was Miriam Horowitz (white, mid-twenties, cis female, short, muscular; profession: security of some kind; frequency of visits: medium; attitude: vigilant; ability to enter the Nowhere: none; ability to hinder plans: medium). Lange appreciated the simplicity of their relationship: she did not smile at him and he was not expected to smile at her. He hypothesized that she never smiled at anyone.

Lange opted not to think further about these three people, in case it turned out he had also tried to kill them.

He didn't like the thought, which didn't make sense. None of his feelings made sense. It would be a relief to be rid of them.

"There's just one more thing," Strickland was saying. "Lange says he can hear something in the room. Possibly the breach. Kit, I wanted to ask you if you can hear it, too?"

"Hear *and* see," Lange clarified. "The breach and the smaller spatial distortions around it."

Kit shook his head. "This place makes my skin crawl, but it just looks like a room. When Lange and the cats were trapped, I could see them sometimes, but I don't see anything now. I never heard anything. Right now I don't hear anything but us and the ventilation system."

Beck nodded. "I know I'm not a born runner, but I could see the cats sometimes, too. Nothing now, though."

(Lange updated Beck's file. Ability to enter the Nowhere: contingent on injections of dimensional prions; implies an ancestor with innate ability. Ability to hinder plans: high.)

So neither runner could confirm his observations. Lange waited for the inevitable dismissal of his experience—unreliable, untrustworthy, *crazy*—but it never came.

"What do you think it means?" Singh asked him. "Do you want to wait? Observe it?"

"I want to record it before we turn the machine on to see if it changes," Lange said.

"How can you record something nobody else can hear?" Kit asked.

"By making note of the pitches," Lange said, declining to elaborate so he could press his advantage. "I want to know if I can determine their origin more precisely. I need to get closer to it."

"That's not a good idea," McCreery said, fixing Lange with a look. His brows had drawn together and there was tightness around his mouth. Lange could perhaps have interpreted this expression to identify the underlying emotion. He chose not to.

"Since my return, I have a sense of the Nowhere," Lange said, speaking over whatever McCreery planned to say next. "As Doctor Strickland said, I can tell where the pockets of disturbed space are. And now the floor is marked as well. I should be able to get across the room safely."

"Why don't you think it's a good idea, Jake?" Singh asked. They were all so familiar with each other, using names and nicknames. As if that wasn't enough, McCreery was naming his robots. Lange's spreadsheet was already complicated enough.

"Lange isn't rational right now," McCreery said flatly. "He's a danger to himself."

"Is that true?" Singh asked, his thick brows drawn together like McCreery's, his lips pursed, his brown eyes unwavering in their focus.

"It was. McCreery and I had an altercation this morning. I confided in him. He... changed my mind."

Every person in the lab went wide-eyed, McCreery most of all.

"If you insist on going closer," McCreery said, "I'm coming with you."

The others seemed to accept that, so Lange acceded to the condition. It was insulting that McCreery meant to follow him around like a sheepdog. Lange had been honest; he wanted to investigate the sound. His desire to dive back into the breach hadn't robbed him of curiosity.

Besides, he'd have time to revisit the breach later, without McCreery intervening.

It wasn't possible to cross the room at full height. The distortions shimmered high in the air, catching the light like oil slicks. Even on his hands and knees, he'd be too tall.

Lange got down on the floor and began to crawl along one of the paths, smearing the wet paint. If walking was exhausting, crawling was far worse.

The other side of the room is ten meters away, he told

himself, knowing it wasn't true. His eyes and his mind contradicted each other.

McCreery followed him, struggling far less with the exertion. From the sound of it, he held still much of the time, waiting for Lange to move.

Lange stayed low and made painful progress, his hands slick with sweat and tacky paint.

As the other side of the room drew closer, the breach tugged at him. It hung between the two curving sides of the machine, perceptible in blinks and brief glimpses, piercing the lab with its dissonance. Waiting to swallow him and everything else.

A chill raced over his skin.

He wanted to go back, didn't he?

Lange kept lifting his head to confront it, but there was only the wall of the lab. Clean and dull, with not one speck of paint.

McCreery's robot hadn't made it all the way across the room. The floor was covered in tracks, and every other wall had suffered a few splatters, but the wall beyond the machine was white.

No encroaching darkness. No vast empty nothing waiting to tear him apart.

His heart tripped over a beat. *What?* No—he remembered the Nowhere as peaceful. Pure. Weightless. Free. Compared to his itchy, achy, fleshy existence, it had been infinite. Perfect.

Why was it so hard to breathe?

Lange squeezed his eyes shut and stopped moving.

"Lange?"

McCreery's voice was soft, probably too soft for the others to hear. With the room stretched to several times its usual size, would the sound travel? Lange could only hear the scream of the breach now. The A flat. The G. The relentless dissonance had a shine to it, like the oily glimmers in the air.

He couldn't remember why he'd come here.

McCreery said his name again.

The sound—a *real* sound, a vibration that originated in McCreery's body and filtered all the way through Lange's ears to his brain, not the eerie echo of the universe falling apart—eased the tightness in his chest.

"I'm fine," he told McCreery, and kept crawling.

He must be delirious from exhaustion. His time in the Nowhere had been heavenly, and *this* was hellish. That was true. That had to be true. What could be worse than being condemned to frailty and suffering in this tragic, faulty, mortal body? Existence in the Nowhere had been better than the endless noise of clicking joints and burbling organs. Lange clung to that truth and dragged himself forward along the floor, ignoring the shifting edges of the distortions around him, ignoring the keen of the breach ahead.

He had reached the base of the machine. The space above him was clear of distortions, so he pulled himself up slowly, leaving dirty handprints on the cool metal. McCreery rose to his feet behind Lange, careful not to move too quickly.

Then Lange glanced beyond the machine. The breach, previously a nearly colorless shimmer in the air, yawned open. Between its ragged edges—the screaming A flat and the G close but refusing to mesh—lay a slash of darkness. A wound.

A memory: sharp pains all over his body, thousands of tiny hooks digging into him and turning him inside out, stretching him until he snapped. No, that wasn't right—he'd been crushed, smashed into a small, constricting space, and it had been suffocating and scratchy-dry—no, wet—and freezing—no, scorching. He'd been compacted and blown apart all at once, and again, and again, every instant. He'd died. But he'd lived. But he'd *died*.

A howl split the air.

[3]
LEAVE

JAKE HAD NEVER HEARD ANYBODY WAIL LIKE THAT. Nothing changed in the room, but Lange went boneless, his consciousness gone like he'd flipped a switch on himself. Fainted dead away. Jake caught him before he concussed himself and lowered them both to the ground.

"Lange. *Lange*. Solomon."

Lange blinked awake an instant later, thank fuck. He mumbled, "Only my family calls me that."

"You fainted," Jake said. "You alright?"

"No. I can't—we can't—we need to go."

"Breathe in," Jake said and counted to four out loud. "And out. And again." After that he stayed quiet, watching Lange re-establish steady breathing.

Something had really scared him, but Jake couldn't tell what. They'd gotten closer to the machine and the breach, supposedly. Jake couldn't sense the breach. The space between the two silver parentheses of the machine just looked like air to him, with a white wall beyond. That didn't mean he was eager to reach an arm out and test it. He believed the others. He believed Lange. The breach existed whether Jake could see it or not.

But Lange had wanted to go closer to the breach, hadn't he?

Jake didn't ask. Hard to say if Lange would share with the class. Sitting on the floor, his back leaning against the machine like he couldn't support himself otherwise—he couldn't, Jake knew, but it was rare to see him so open about it—Lange had set his face in an expression of grim determination. He marshaled the rhythm of his breath.

"You need to remember this," Lange said. "The A-flat pitch and the G are the loudest, but from here, I can also hear C. The C is different. It comes from somewhere else."

"Okay," Jake said. He didn't ask why Lange couldn't remember that on his own. It was only a few pieces of information, and it meant a lot more to Lange than it did to Jake.

Lange closed his eyes and hummed.

Jake very patiently didn't ask what the fuck he was doing.

"It's not so bad, with the E," Lange said, mostly to himself. "A flat major seventh."

"Okay," Jake said again. "So... you got what you came for?"

Lange had opened his eyes and his attention was now fixed on some nearby point. There was nothing there—nothing that Jake could see. Lange was still humming. Jake hadn't known it was possible to hum desperately.

Crumpled against the base of the machine, its long curve towering over him, Lange looked small. The smooth form of the machine had nothing in common with the robots Jake built, which might not be as elegant, but they were comprehensible. They had moving parts. You didn't have to be a rarefied genius to know what they could do and how they worked. The machine that Lange had designed was an unreadable monolith. Right now its casing was marred by a couple of Lange's sweaty handprints and a small streak of rust right where it met the floor—huh, Jake would have to check on that later—but the machine was otherwise as unblemished and mysterious as ever.

Lange, still humming, was easier to decipher.

Jake said, "I take it you don't want to jump back in?"

Lange lurched forward and grabbed a fistful of Jake's t-shirt. "No. *No*. It's too close. We need to—"

"I know, we need to go," Jake said. He gently worked Lange's hand free of its death grip and then wasn't sure what to do with it. It seemed rude to drop it, and Lange didn't pull away, so Jake just kept Lange's hand between both of his own. "I'm working on it. Can you crawl?"

Lange exhaled a shuddering breath, his shoulders slumping further.

"It was hard work," Jake said. He was in fine shape and it had sucked for him. It must have been awful for Lange. "How about walking? Can you walk?"

Lange made a noncommittal noise.

Jake hadn't expected much more than that. Since coming back, Lange walked like his movement algorithm was still in the trial-and-error phase. He deliberated over every movement, tottering from one foot to the other. They'd have to try something else. He stroked his thumb over Lange's knuckles. "You can see where... where things are wrong, right?"

"Sort of."

If Jake hadn't already known Lange was fucked up, that casual mumble would've been a blaring alarm. "Can you tell me where to go? If I stand up and carry you, I mean. I'll follow the marks on the floor and you can tell me where to duck. Is there a path?"

"Maybe."

Yes would have put his nerves at ease, but that was too much to ask. "Can you think of a better plan?"

Lange grimaced and shook his head. Jake got into a crouch and then scooped him up, coming slowly to his feet. "Okay. You're in charge. Tell me where to go."

In between the tracks Eliza had made, there was empty space. It looked like he could simply follow the lines on the ground, but Jake was conscious of all the things he didn't know. He'd hate to get his torso sucked into another dimension.

"Step forward, and then to the left," Lange said, and as Jake moved, he shouted, "Not that far to the left!"

Jake froze, one foot in the air, and returned carefully to his previous position. "Okay. Smaller steps, then. Left and then what?"

"Twist to the side so my feet are pointing forward. There's a narrow passage between two distortions. Keep your head down. We'll fit if you're careful."

"Well," Jake said, taking a deep breath. "Then I'll be careful."

———

TIME STRETCHED and clung to itself like taffy between his teeth. It probably hadn't been hours, but Jake was too exhausted to tell.

The last few meters of the room were impassable except at a crawl, but by then, Lange had calmed down and Jake trusted him to make it out, even if it took a painfully long time. Jake focused on Lange like *he* had telekinesis, like he could pull Lange out of there just by thinking about it.

He did pull Lange out once the other man got within arm's reach. Jake grasped his hands and dragged him out of the maze and then up to his feet. Less impressive than telekinesis, but it got the job done.

Everyone was staring at them.

"Turn the machine on. We're going to Lange's room," Jake said, before anyone could dictate otherwise. If Emil had really wanted to talk, he could've caught them in the hallway. They weren't exactly making a break for it. But no one followed.

The paint on Jake's clothes was drying into a stiff mess. He shouldn't have used all his bargaining power on making Lange take that shower earlier. What a waste. He'd never get another concession that big out of the guy, and besides, Lange didn't look like he could stay on two feet that much longer.

Lange took a slow step past his own door. "I need to wash my hands. Or perhaps my forearms."

Jake hadn't even had to trick him into it. He followed Lange to the bathroom, where they did the best they could at rinsing the paint off. The sink filled with soapy grey water and Lange sagged against the counter.

"Good enough," Jake said, shepherding Lange back to his room before he collapsed.

Lange stripped before getting into bed. Jake turned away, but not before getting an eyeful. He almost said *maybe a little warning next time*, but couldn't get the words out. And why did he care? Nakedness shouldn't bother him. It didn't mean anything.

By the time he turned around, Lange was dressed again and seated in bed.

Jake risked sitting down next to him. Nothing flew across the room and hit him in the face. Lange didn't fling him onto the floor.

"I know you probably don't want to talk about it," Jake said.

"Correct."

"When I walk out of this room, the others are going to ask me what happened. What do you want me to tell them?"

"I suppose some traumatic memories resurfaced."

So detached and hypothetical. Like he was describing an imaginary case study instead of the last few hours of his own life. But at least Jake had an answer now. Getting close to the breach had reminded Lange of his time in the Nowhere, and it hadn't been good. He didn't want to go back after all.

"I hear that happens sometimes. People block out what they went through because it was too awful. The brain protects itself." Jake stopped himself. He needed to tread lightly. "What do you want to do?"

"I want to lose consciousness and remain that way for as long as possible."

"Okay," Jake said. "I was thinking more longterm, but you're right. You should rest. We'll talk later."

Lange really did have extraordinary eyes. Deep brown and startlingly warm. Jake had never seen him look so forlorn.

"You did a good thing in there," Jake said. "A brave thing."

Lange looked at Jake like he wanted to believe that. Or *Jake* wanted to believe that Lange wanted... well. The moment was over already. Lange was shaking his head.

"I'm really sorry for everything you went through," Jake

said. With anybody else in the world, Jake might have put a comforting hand on their arm or their shoulder, but Lange wouldn't like that. Jake wasn't a touchy-feely guy, not usually, but Lange's aversion made him hyper-aware of all the things he couldn't do.

So all he did was add, "And everything you're still going through."

Lange jerked his gaze away and Jake felt something invisible push at his body. "Leave."

"Okay," Jake said, standing. He put his hands up, palms out, to demonstrate surrender.

"I neither desire nor require contact with other humans," Lange said, as if Jake hadn't had that point hammered home by the force shoving him out the door.

———

UNCONSCIOUSNESS ELUDED LANGE. The room was dark and silent after he exiled McCreery to the hallway, but not dark and silent enough. He lay still on the bed, as still as he could in his quivering, fitful flesh.

He had little enough control over his body, and none at all over his mind.

Already his thoughts had raced to their conclusion: his time in the Nowhere had been ceaseless suffering. Driven out of his mind with pain, he'd latched onto Kit. He'd wanted to escape, and he hadn't cared if escape meant dying.

He hadn't meant to cause harm. He hadn't meant anything. There had only been pain.

Hurting Kit wasn't the only terrible wrong he'd committed, but somehow it seemed the simplest. Certainly, it was the easiest to sum up. *You nearly killed Kit.*

He'd nearly killed all of them by opening the breach.

His unlikely survival—through the initial implosion, through all those days stranded in the Nowhere, until now —haunted him. It would have been so much easier to die.

He *had* died, he thought. He wouldn't ever be the other Solomon Lange, the one who'd lived his whole life before going into the breach. That man was gone.

Lying here in the dark was a different person, a new person, one he didn't know yet.

I have to be this person all the time now, he thought, and nearly laughed at how banal it sounded, the unbearable burden of his whole existence. *I have to live with this.*

He shouldn't have driven McCreery away. The man was a good distraction. Lange couldn't imagine calling out for him to return, even though he knew McCreery or one of the others was just outside the door. They granted him privacy, but they never really left him alone. As well they shouldn't, he supposed. He'd been a danger to himself and, inadvertently, to all of them.

McCreery would come if Lange called. It was one of very few things Lange was sure of. McCreery would come, and he would do his best to be kind no matter what. Lange didn't know what he would do if McCreery was kind to him right now, but he suspected there might be crying involved. The thought was enough to keep him from calling.

Paws thudded on the floor near the bed, and Lange recognized the low meow of Subrahmanyan Chandrasekhar. A moment later, the cat's full weight was pressing against his sternum as he settled into position.

Lange considered pushing him off. He was heavy and disruptive, one more reminder that Lange was stuck here in this body, never going back to the Nowhere. But there was comfort in that thought. As bad as it was to be here, it had been worse in the Nowhere.

He'd survived that. He could survive this, too.

The cat's purr rumbled against his chest. Lange lifted a hand and let it sink into the softness of the animal's fur. It was good to touch something pleasant, something warm and alive, something that tied him to the world and to his life. He *wanted* to pet his cat. This small first step in wanting something led the way to a second one: he wanted to call his parents.

———

AN UNEXPECTED CHEER went up as Jake exited Lange's room. When he reentered the lab, Lenny came to greet him.

"I got this, I'll sit outside his door and make sure he's okay," he said, patting Jake's shoulder and leaving the room before Jake could even thank him.

Everyone else was crowded around one of Dax's laptops.

"It's too soon to tell," Dax was saying. "We don't have enough data."

"But the readings are better," Emil said.

"*Marginally* better."

They'd turned on the machine, then. "How long will it take to close the breach?" Jake asked.

"I haven't established the rate of change yet," Dax said, adjusting their glasses, sounding tired of being asked questions they couldn't answer. "But we were aiming for a week. I'll have a better sense of things in a few hours—or tomorrow."

Emil nodded. "Still. It's progress."

"I wouldn't go that far. It's not a failure yet, but let's not call it success, either," Dax said.

"Okay." Emil turned to Jake. "How's Lange?"

"He's sleeping it off," Jake said.

"And you?"

"I'm fine."

"Do you know what happened to Lange? Did he hear... whatever it was he was hearing?"

Jake nodded slowly. "He told me what notes he was hearing. I think he wants to see if they'll change as the machine runs. As for what happened—earlier today, he wanted to go back."

"To the Nowhere?" Emil asked.

"Yes. He doesn't like it here. But something about getting close to the breach... well, when I asked him, he said 'traumatic memories resurfaced.' He wasn't interested in elaborating."

"So he remembered his time in the Nowhere," Chávez said. Beside her, Miriam raised her eyebrows and nodded. "And he'd repressed it before?"

"It must have been bad," Emil said, his expression drawn taut. He'd survived his own walk into the breach, but he'd been prepared in ways that Lange hadn't, and he'd only spent a brief time in the Nowhere. Lange had been trapped for almost two weeks. "I can imagine that recovery will be a long process."

"Guess that sorta explains why he doesn't really remember us, even those of us he maybe tried to murder a little bit," Kit said.

"I know it sucked for you, but can we not talk about it like that, please? He was suffering and he needed your help," Jake said.

"I don't mean to be too negative," Miriam said. "But

how *do* you recover from something like that? As far as we know, it's never happened to anybody in human history."

Jake shrugged. "Time and therapy would still probably work. And I think we have to get him out of here. Away from the breach. Down to the surface would be best."

"But we need him to fix his mistakes," Miriam said. "This isn't over. Dax, I know you're doing your best and you did make progress, but you shouldn't have to do all the work here."

"He can't fix anything in the state he's in," Jake shot back.

The room went silent. He'd never spoken like that to anyone on the team. And he'd chosen *Lange* of all subjects for his first time getting into an argument. Christ.

"You both make good points," Emil said, smoothing things over. "And we did make progress. We just need to keep an eye on it while it's closing."

"Caleb's double found us because of the breach. We're lucky he's the only thing so far," Miriam said. "*Closing* is not the same as *closed*. Something else could come through."

"If anybody else up here had been through what he's been through, you'd all be understanding," Jake said. "I know he's difficult, but try to put that aside. Whatever happened to him in the Nowhere, it really fucked him up. He probably won't be okay for *years*, or maybe ever. I'm just asking for a few days. A week."

Emil held up a hand to stop anyone else from speaking. "Alright. I hear you—both of you. We all agree it's important to close the breach as fast as possible, but I see Jake's point about giving Lange some time away from it. Let's revisit this in two days and see if the readings are good."

"And if they are?" Jake asked.

"Then he can go. Kit, do you think you could take Lange down to the surface?"

"He can't go through the Nowhere," Jake interjected. "He can't handle that."

"If you want me to act like a human being," said Lange, who had appeared in the doorway with Lenny shrugging apologetically behind him, "you should start treating me like one."

Fuck, how long had he been there? What had he overheard?

"Glad to see you're feeling okay," Emil said. "Please come in."

"McCreery is correct," Lange said, not moving.

There was a sentence to set the world on its head. Jake's stomach went tight.

"I still have a house on the surface," Lange continued. "And since McCreery is so certain that more time in the Nowhere will further *fuck me up*, he can fly me down himself."

———

HOURS LATER, Jake was fiddling with one of the many half-built robots strewn around his workshop when Emil knocked cautiously on the doorjamb.

"Come in," Jake said, setting the robot down on his workbench and stripping off his gloves. He hadn't really been making progress, anyway. He felt too shitty about trying to speak for Lange.

Emil came in, glanced around and realized there was no second chair, and moved as if he was going to lean one shoulder against the wall. He couldn't. The magnetized panel was covered in wrenches and pliers and screwdrivers.

The only stretch of wall not festooned with tools was the floor-to-ceiling window on Jake's left. With his work light on, the view was only darkness, but if Jake turned it off and let his eyes adjust, the field of stars was spectacular.

Instead of leaning against the wall, Emil ran a hand through his dark, already tousled hair, crossed his arms over his chest, then dropped them to his sides instead.

"I tried to talk to Lange," he said. "He told me to leave him alone. Lenny and Chávez are playing cards outside his door now."

"Sorry," Jake said, even though he hadn't done anything. Privately, he thought telling someone to fuck off was a huge step up from throwing them into a wall, and he was proud of Lange. Was that weird? It was probably weird.

"He used words instead of pushing me out the door, so it's progress," Emil said, echoing Jake's thoughts. "And I think if he's up, walking and talking, then he's doing well, all things considered."

"Yeah."

"You've helped him a lot," Emil said. "We asked a lot of you—too much, maybe—but you're the only one he'll talk to."

"Or I *was*, anyway." Screws and other hardware were scattered all over the workbench. The mess had never bothered him before. Jake grabbed a jar and started sorting. Each screw clinked into the pile below it, filling the jar and the silence.

"We've been friends a long time," Emil said. "You know you can talk to me about anything."

Jake supposed that was true, though he'd never tested it. He'd come to friendship late in life, when he'd moved to Franklin Station and started working Search and Rescue with Emil at the age of eighteen. Jake had done nothing to make their relationship happen except to shrug and go along with it whenever Emil invited him out for a beer after their shift towing broken-down spacecraft to safety. This accumulated time together transmuted, after crossing some unidentifiable threshold, into friendship. He'd lived it and still it bewildered him. There wasn't any good reason for Emil to want to spend time with him. But other people extended invitations to strangers so casually. They talked about their lives—their feelings—with such ease.

Jake had known Emil for twelve years. Hell, he'd followed Emil here, to this secret research facility in lunar orbit. It wasn't like he didn't trust Emil. Or any of the other people Emil had collected and brought to Facility 17, strangers turned coworkers turned sort of friends, too, maybe. Jake just wasn't much for talking, that's all.

So Jake had raised his voice in the meeting for the first time ever. They didn't have to open an investigation into it.

"I don't have anything to say," Jake said after a length of time that had probably been uncomfortable for Emil.

"Okay," Emil said slowly, like he was trying to give Jake a few more seconds to change his mind and spill his guts. "Today was rough, and it's been a hard few weeks. If you need a break—or if you don't feel prepared to fly him down—"

"I do," Jake said. "Feel prepared, I mean. I don't need a break."

He'd promised to help Lange. Flying him down to the surface was a concrete task. Lange had asked him for something specific and relatively easy, and goddammit, Jake was going to provide.

"Let me know if you need anything," Emil said. "I mean that."

And then he took pity on Jake and left.

Jake picked up the half-built robot he'd set down and went back to attaching manipulator arms to its squat body. By the time he heard the next knock, his workbench was cluttered with hardware again.

"Come in," he said, reluctantly setting his work down. It must be Emil again. The only other person who came around with any regularity was Lenny, because he'd worked as an aerospace engineer before coming here and he liked taking stuff apart and putting it back together as much as Jake did. But Emil had said Lenny was outside Lange's door playing cards with Chávez, so it couldn't be him.

The silence made him look up. Lange was standing in the doorway, or leaning against it, his posture heavy with fatigue. He'd changed into a different pair of soft grey sweatpants and a clean white shirt. His feet were bare. The large orange cat was twining around his ankles.

It was strange to see him outside the room. Every time Jake had offered to go somewhere with him—just a stroll to the kitchen or the greenhouse, anything to get him out of bed—Lange had refused. And here he was, unaccompanied. What had he said to Chávez and Lenny, that they'd let him come here alone? Jake hoped Lange hadn't knocked their heads together or pinned them to the hallway floor.

"What—" Jake started.

"I told them I wanted to speak with you," Lange said.

And they'd treated him like a capable adult. Right.

"I'm sorry for how I talked about you earlier," Jake said. "I shouldn't have tried to decide things for you. If you want to yell at me, you can. Actually, if you want to telekinetically slam me into a wall again, you can do that, but we should probably pick a room with fewer sharp objects."

Lange blinked. "I don't want either of those things."

Wow. Jake wasn't sure what was happening, but he didn't want to ask and fuck it up.

"I was angry, and I don't want you to do it again, but you weren't wrong," Lange continued. "I need to get out of here and I can't go through the Nowhere. Both of those things are true. And I know I've been... difficult, and I appreciate you keeping me alive through my... distress and—"

"If you're gearing up to apologize for generally being, uh, out to lunch, and also kind of a dick, you don't have to," Jake interrupted. "You went through some shit. I get it. I mean, I guess I *don't* get it because I don't know what you went through, but I get that it was bad. Makes sense that you weren't totally present this past week."

"I wasn't going to apologize," Lange said haltingly. "Is this one of those moments where I'm meant to understand that your dismissal of the apology I didn't provide is, in fact, a request for an apology?"

"Uh... no?"

"Oh," Lange said. "Good."

Lange remained in the doorway, silent. Jake got the feeling that neither of them could navigate their way out of this maze.

At last, Lange said, "Today's discovery changed my perspective, and I have decided to conduct myself differently."

"Okay."

Lange scanned the array of tools on the walls, the discarded bits of wire and metal on the workbench, and the towering piles of junk on the floor and said, with subdued horror, "This is where you work?"

Jake knew, from packing up Lange's room, that the man was beyond neat. The only thing messy about him was his inscrutable handwriting. His closet had been sorted by type and by color, for fuck's sake. Jake couldn't be mad that Lange was judging him because he was so relieved to have such a nice, harmless thing to talk about.

"You don't like mess," Jake said. He'd spent his conversation with Emil nervously sorting hardware, but now he had a perverse urge to tip over one of the jars of screws just to see what face Lange would make.

"I suppose not," Lange said.

It was sort of sweet that Jake's might-need-that-some-day-you-never-know collection of old parts had caused Lange to rediscover this lost piece of himself. Jake hadn't known his piles of junk could do something like that, which was one more good reason to keep them around. You never knew.

The orange cat left Lange's ankles and came to sniff Jake's shoes. It headbutted his shin and rubbed its face and body all over his legs for a long, mesmerizing moment. Jake had no idea if this was normal cat behavior. The animal's affection, if that's what it was, felt excessive. He didn't know what to do with it, but he reached down and scratched behind its ears. The cat purred louder, slinking between his legs for more, and then it flopped on the floor and showed its extravagantly fluffy belly.

"He doesn't do that for everyone," Lange said.

Jake retracted his hand from the cat's fur like he'd been caught committing a crime. "Um. Did you need something?"

"Yes, actually. They said you were the one who moved my things. I want my tablet. I'd like to talk to my family."

"Oh," Jake said, even more embarrassed. He'd never meant to make Lange feel like he couldn't have access to his belongings. He just hadn't wanted anyone to get hit in the face. Worse, Jake had assumed Lange was like him, with nobody to talk to down on the surface, and he'd been wrong. "Shit. Of course. I put all your stuff in one of the empty rooms upstairs. I'll show you where it is."

The cat followed them all the way there.

[4]

FUGUE

His parents had called him Solomon in their call last night. Of course they had. It was his name. But it had been strange to hear it, nevertheless, since he'd been stuck here with people who didn't have permission to address him that way, and he hadn't been thinking of himself as Solomon. It had been hard enough to think of himself as a person, let alone one with a whole lifetime's worth of memories. Hearing his parents' voices had called up a tide.

A message could travel from Earth to lunar orbit and back in about two-and-a-half seconds, so live conversation was possible, if stilted. He hadn't felt ready for that. Instead he'd sent them a recording, and they'd responded promptly with one of their own.

His mother had also called him "Sol." And asked why his recording didn't have video enabled. And reiterated many times over that she loved him and that he should come home.

He hadn't explained it to her, the accident and its after-math. He'd said that he'd missed their calls because he'd been "caught up in work," which was technically true. Regardless, she'd known something was wrong. His assurances that he was fine had done nothing to persuade her, and she had only stopped worrying aloud when his father had intervened on his behalf.

The only thing stronger than his desire to go see them was his fear of hurting them. They were in their sixties, happily retired, frequently visited by family members, including Lange's many small cousins. It would be emotional, seeing all those people again. Overwhelming. If he accidentally pulled or pushed or hurt one of them—no, he couldn't. He wouldn't go until he could be sure it was safe.

What he needed was some time to himself.

Lange hadn't known he wanted to get away from the breach until he'd heard McCreery say it, and then it had been the only thing he could think about. As the next two days' readings indicated that the breach was decreasing in size, a strange loosening happened in his chest. In his jaw.

It still sounded hellish in the lab, the screeching wrongness of the A flat and the G jostling each other for space, but it was quieter. Perhaps the sound would die off as the breach closed.

Lange left the lab lighter. As they suited up and loaded the pod with luggage, emergency gear, and perishables, McCreery's various objections and conditions slid off him. Lange had to get in touch with "people" once they'd arrived. He couldn't be left alone, but it would not be McCreery who acted as sheepdog. McCreery was willing to take Lange down to the surface, and possibly to fetch him back to the facility, but he had no intention of staying.

"That's fine," Lange said. He brought the ventilated carriers into the bay, floating them toward the pod one after the other. It didn't matter how gentle he was. There were still cries of protest emanating from inside. "And I won't be alone."

"No. Absolutely not," McCreery said. "You want me to put *three cats* in this pod with us? Nobody's gonna enjoy that."

"They go where I go," Lange said.

"They don't have suits. It's breaking safety protocol."

Lange had already said his piece. It had taken him two hours and forty-five minutes to cajole Niels Bohr, Lise Meitner, and Subrahmanyan Chandrasekhar into their carriers. Afraid of injuring them with his ability, he'd resorted to using his hands. He was exhausted and clawed all over. But the cats themselves had failed to resist his will; McCreery's protests were laughable in comparison.

All three cats were still yowling. Lange strapped the carriers down in the back of the pod without another word and then got into his seat behind McCreery's. This elicited a defeated sigh, almost inaudible amid the feline wails.

The cats made conversation difficult. They meowed until long after the engine had switched from thrusting to coasting. The change in gravity, like their imprisonment in carriers, was cause for complaint. It took another hour until they settled.

Lange had never minded silence, and he was pleased that McCreery wasn't interested in interrupting this one. It was the correct accompaniment for gazing at the distant stars. Lange had infinite patience for such observations.

He'd created a false memory of his time in the Nowhere. He hadn't meant to, but his mind had protected itself from the truth. He'd remembered it like this: tranquil drifting through the dark.

The Nowhere hadn't been tranquil. Lange squeezed his

eyes shut, but ghost pain lanced through him anyway. His heart seized.

"Lange," McCreery said. "You okay back there?"

"Fine."

"Now that the cats are asleep and we're coasting, I can hear you breathing. Nothing else to listen to."

Lange had no interest in analyzing his own respiration. It was troublesome enough to have a body, especially one so weak, but to know that other people were studying it was worse. McCreery listening to his breathing like he was a faulty engine was too much to bear. Lange forced down his unpleasant feelings and changed the subject as sharply as possible. "I can hear you turning pages. I didn't take you for someone who'd insist on paper books."

"Eh." McCreery shifted in his seat, suit rubbing against the straps. Lange couldn't see much of him, but he imagined a shrug. "I read whatever's around, mostly. But this is a book of puzzles. I like to be able to scribble on it with a pencil."

"Puzzles?" Lange wasn't sure what he had expected. Technical nonfiction about machines, perhaps. Robots. That was all he really knew about McCreery. Lange had never considered what else the man might be interested in. Even before his time in the Nowhere, other people had been like aliens for Lange, their interests and desires a code with no cipher. Now he was alienated even from himself.

"Crosswords," McCreery specified. "You want to help?"

"Memory loss," Lange reminded him. "And I suspect my knowledge of popular culture has always been limited."

"I bet you can help me with some of it," McCreery said. "Here. Five across is 'unit of energy.'"

"That could be anything. Joule. Kilojoule. Hartree."

"It's only three letters."

"Try 'erg,'" Lange said.

"That works," McCreery said. "That means five down starts with E. It's a first name. The clue is 'Zinnia Jackson songwriter, blank Holl—'"

Lange didn't need to be told how many letters were in Evelyn Holland's first name. "Evelyn."

"For someone with limited pop culture knowledge, you were pretty damn quick on that one."

It wasn't pop culture knowledge for Lange, but he couldn't bring himself to say so. The memories were fresh, elicited by the sound of her name and the sound of his mother's voice on the video recording she'd sent, and they were too precious to share just yet.

The first time he'd met Zinnia Jackson, he'd been intimidated. Not because her reputation as a singer preceded her, but because he'd been about six years old at the time and painfully shy. Even without her gowns and feathers and sequins, she was always in the spotlight. She had light brown skin and dark red curls and when animated, she laughed with unrestrained joy. Her voice swooped from the height to the depth of her five-octave range in conversation as well as in song.

Adults usually ignored him, beyond asking how old he was and if he was in school, and he liked it that way. That summer, as his mother and Zinnia wrote and recorded demos for an album that would later go platinum, he'd spent a lot of time lying on his belly in a carpeted hallway just outside the recording booth, scribbling pictures of Saturn and rocketships in washable marker. Strains of melody had emanated through the door, interspersed with his mother's warm, smooth contralto.

"Zin. *Zinnia*. Stop this. That take was perfect. The last six takes have been perfect. I know you know this."

He remembered that so easily because his mother had

often said "Zin" and "Sol" in the same tone: *I love you, but I'm warning you*. It had inspired solidarity between them.

In retrospect, it was unexpected that a globally famous, furiously driven perfectionist diva had time in between sessions to crouch down and interview her creative partner's six-year-old son about his passion for space, but Zin had been a dedicated listener. Other than his parents, she was the only grown up who always wanted to hear what he had to say. It had won him over quickly. He could remember sitting in her lap, which was as expansive and luxurious as the rest of her, her arm wrapped around him so he was snuggled into the soft contours of her body. She'd asked him, "Solomon, did you know your mama is the smartest woman in the whole world?"

"Yes," he'd said, because nothing could have been more obvious to him at age six. At age thirty-five with a half-dozen prestigious prizes awarded to his research, he was still certain of it.

"You make sure everybody knows that Evelyn Holland writes the best songs," Zinnia had continued.

"And that you're the best singer."

Never modest, she'd said, "Oh, everybody already knows that," and then laughed and kissed his head.

He hadn't seen Zin in more than twenty years, since she'd withdrawn from public life and stopped recording, but he knew she still called his mother every week.

It had been hard, declining his mother's invitation to come home. Evelyn Holland had a quieter, more serious presence than the star whose discography she'd composed and produced. He missed her so much. His eyes stung. Coming back from the Nowhere had left him raw and full of feelings, and calling his family had made everything worse. Ridiculous. Unbearable. Right now his mother was probably peering over her reading glasses at one of her students at the community music center, making it clear she knew they hadn't practiced. She was in Milwaukee and she was perfectly fine. There was no reason to get emotional.

The few tears he'd produced floated up from his lashes. He closed his eyes and willed his body to stop this nonsense. It was good McCreery was seated in front of him and couldn't see.

"Keep going," Lange said.

McCreery's pencil was scratching against the page. "I'm glad you knew that one. I don't think I would have gotten it by myself. Emil is a huge Zinnia Jackson fan, did you know that? He probably would have known her songwriter's name. Even though we've worked together long enough that I've heard him put on every single album, I never really got into it. But if you're into her stuff, maybe—"

Could a man not have a sudden revelation of childhood memories in peace? McCreery's turn toward chattiness made Lange grit his teeth. Lange couldn't handle talking about any of this. "Tell me the next clue."

"Uh. Okay. Six down is 'see stars,' which I think in this case gives us 'reel.' Seven down is 'macroeconomics stat,' so that's 'GDP.' Those all make sense, right?"

"Yes." McCreery's protests aside, he clearly didn't need Lange's help. Yet he'd asked for it anyway.

McCreery narrated the puzzle. "Oh, the double L formed by 'Evelyn' and 'reel' is the ending for 'Carroll,' author of *Through the Looking-Glass*, so now we've got that, too. And underneath 'erg,' I've got V-E-D. Oh, the clue's 'inamorata,' that means 'beloved.' How about 'Johann Sebastian Bach creation'? It's five—"

"Fugue."

"Fits," McCreery said, approval in his tone. "How'd you know that?"

Rubbed raw, Lange almost said *everyone knows that, how it is possible not to know that*, but he bit his tongue. It was self-preservation rather than niceness. They had three hours remaining in this pod. It would be best if McCreery didn't eject him into space. "I like all kinds of music. I play. Or played. I don't suppose I could now."

He glanced down at his gloved fingers, which would no doubt be useless at fretting and plucking.

"What'd you play? I'm sure you could pick it up again with practice."

"Guitar. Underneath the V-E-D of 'beloved,' you should have E-E-P, yes? What's the clue for that?"

"Damn, you're holding all that in your head?" McCreery asked. "I'm good at crosswords, but I still need to look at them."

Lange braced for further discussion of all the ways in which he was an aberration.

Instead, McCreery let it go. "I didn't know that about you playing guitar. Did you take lessons as a kid? Is that why you knew that songwriter thing? The clue is 'not easily understood,' by the way."

"Deep," Lange said. If they discussed any of that, he risked producing more tears. "That was too quick to be satisfying. Give me another."

"I like music but I don't know how to play anything," McCreery said. He waited, his silence an obvious invitation for Lange to contribute a personal tidbit of his own.

It took eighteen seconds for him to give up and provide the next clue. Lange counted.

———

LANGE'S SILENCE lost its edge and lulled him to sleep soon enough. He woke when McCreery turned on the thruster to guide their craft into low Earth orbit, then let his attention drift. He amused himself with the math: they'd slowed from 27 kilometers per second to a mere 7.8 kilometers per second, a change that he could calculate but not feel.

He felt it when they entered the atmosphere.

The cats felt it, too, screeching in protest as the ship rattled. The roar of the atmosphere soon drowned them out. The air inside the ship heated and Lange was forced against the straps of his harness.

He didn't hear the console beeping, but a warning light blared orange. McCreery was in front of him, piloting the craft, and at first, Lange couldn't tell which warning light.

Then he heard McCreery yelling over the din.

"The heat shield is cracked!"

Ah. The orange light was the temperature sensor.

Not that Lange needed a machine to sense the temperature; his body was adequate to the task. It was hot in the craft. If the heat shield fell off the underside of the pod, they'd burn up.

The cats. McCreery. Incinerated. His whole body rebelled at the idea, his spine straightening and his insides twisting. He couldn't let it happen.

Lange closed his eyes and thought of the ceramic panel insulated with a layer of aerogel that was bolted to the exterior of the pod. The two materials were distinct in his senses, the aerogel an empty framework, the ceramic impossibly heavy. He could feel the fine crack running through it, threatening to split it in two.

"Lange! Lange, did you hear me?"

"Yes, the heat shield is cracked," Lange said, and then

repeated himself at a louder volume until he was sure McCreery had heard. "Maintain attitude control."

The heat shield only protected one side of the pod, so if they flipped, Lange's efforts would be wasted. At this velocity, the heat caused by the friction of the atmosphere meant certain death.

McCreery shouted, "It won't matter how good of a pilot I am if we lose that—holy shit, are you *holding* it?"

"Maintain attitude control, McCreery," Lange repeated.

"If you got the heat shield, I got this," McCreery called back, his unhinged laughter only a ghost of a sound within the roar. "We're not gonna roll over and die. Not today."

That was the last of their conversation for what felt like hours. Lange thought only of the heat shield, its single solid panel vibrating violently, but not breaking. His head ached. Perspiration left damp tracks down the inside of his suit.

Something coppery trickled over his lips—a nosebleed.

They slowed and slowed until their velocity could no longer be measured in kilometers per second, the noise and heat thinning, but the ride grew no smoother.

The woods came into sight as a swath of green interspersed with white, larger and larger in his view until they were individual pines tipped with snow.

"Gonna be a rough landing," McCreery yelled.

With fatigue bearing down on him, Lange almost didn't have the energy to brace himself. His fingers slipped inside his gloves as he tried to grip the straps holding him in his seat. The air thundered around the pod, buffeting its sides, and Lange clenched his teeth and forced aside all the sensations rattling in his body so he could concentrate on the heat shield. Their little pod jolted and lurched until it slammed into the ground.

[5]
CABIN

JAKE RAISED THE POD'S CANOPY AS SOON AS THEY'D stopped moving, letting the trapped heat dissipate. His whole body throbbed with the impact of the landing. He unbuckled his harness, tossed his sweaty helmet to the floor, and jumped out of the cockpit. The cool air from the woods was a shock to his lungs, but a welcome one.

"Lange? You okay?"

Lange's eyes were closed. Condensation fogged his helmet.

Jake hoisted himself back into the pod and leaned over Lange. It was tight quarters back there since the narrow pod only had two seats. It got tighter when Jake bent to unclip Lange's helmet to make sure the guy was still breathing. He was, though he didn't look great. A sluggish trickle of blood ran from one nostril. Jake wasn't sure Lange was conscious until he opened his eyes, which he did as though his eyelids weighed five hundred kilos each—that would put their total at roughly the weight of the heat shield, which Lange had *held together with his mind.*

Jesus.

"You were amazing," Jake told him. "You saved us. Are you okay?"

Lange's weak nod wasn't convincing. His eyelashes were all wet and clumped together. His face was such a mess that Jake couldn't tell sweat tracks from tear tracks, and it seemed rude to ask for specifics. Hell, Jake had just about cried during that descent. Had just about pissed himself.

"You're really okay?" Jake asked again.

"No," Lange said. "But we're not dead."

Jake reached for the buckles on Lange's harness, hesitated, and then went for it. Lange hadn't objected to the removal of his helmet, and he seemed too dazed to get himself free.

"Let's get you out of here and then just take a minute."

He helped Lange out of the pod—Lange accepted his gloved hand without recoiling—and then put the cat carriers and Eliza on the earth and just left them there. He and Lange sat on the muddy ground, far enough from the pod to feel safe, slouched over, heart rates slowing.

The caterwauling from the cats would have been unbearable in any other situation, but right now it made Jake feel alive.

Which he was.

He'd brought the pod down in the flattest, most open space he could find. Wooded mountainsides surrounded them. The pod was damaged and the cabin Lange had sworn he owned was nowhere in sight, and Jake couldn't care because he was too thrilled to be breathing.

He stood and stretched. Snow crunched under his feet every time he moved. "Okay. Who're we calling? Whoever's coming to stay with you can come get us."

Lange's brown eyes focused on some distant point in the

pines. He scanned their surroundings as if he'd never seen any of this before—not merely like they were lost in the woods, which Jake hoped they weren't, but like he'd never been on the surface or seen a pine tree.

Jake tamped down the first flutters of panic. Fear was no good to him now. They might not have burned up in the atmosphere, but they weren't safe. Not yet.

"Lange. You *do* have someone who knows you're here, right?"

"Yes," Lange said, finally coming out of his daze. "I called my parents, who undoubtedly told the rest of my family, and I also called my aunt Cora."

"And?"

"My parents live in Milwaukee and they're both sixty-seven years old, McCreery. No, I didn't ask them to travel to the Alaskan wilderness to babysit me. My cousins have jobs and children and lives. I don't intend to trouble them with this. Cora lives an hour from here. I will get in touch with her if I need something."

If they weren't coming, there must be someone else Lange could call. A friend. An amicable neighbor. An ex who didn't hate him. A polite coworker. A letter carrier he tipped really well.

As Jake went through his increasingly desperate mental list, his shoulders slumped. He paused to wonder who *he* would call, if he needed someone to stay with him for a few days while he was recovering from an inexplicable near-death accident that had left him telekinetic.

Emil, maybe. Someone else on the Facility 17 team. The list wasn't long.

Fuck. *Jake* was the polite coworker. He repressed a sigh. "You told me you wouldn't be alone."

"I never specified," Lange said. He got to his feet. "You

asked if I would be alone and I said no, which is the truth. The cats will be with me. That's how I prefer it."

"I asked about people," Jake said, already too tired to have this argument. He couldn't be angry at Lange for lying by omission about the depressingly friendless state of his life. The whole thing was too damn sad. And truth be told, he'd been eager to believe Lange's answer. Let somebody else deal with this shit for a while.

So of course he'd stranded himself in the remote wilderness with the guy. Of course.

Nope. No more of that. He'd have plenty of time to regret his choices *after* they found shelter.

Jake said, "Where are we headed? Which way's your place? You remember, I hope."

Lange nodded, thank fuck, and then tilted his head toward the woods.

"Fine. I can get two of these carriers if you can get the third. We can hike back for the rest of the stuff, assuming your cabin's not too far. I don't think I can fix this pod today —not with the sun about to set—but I promise I'll get out of your hair tomorrow."

"It's not necessary to haul the carriers. The cats will follow me."

Jake didn't believe that, but soon enough, the evidence was right in front of his eyes. The cats trotted at Lange's heels, occasionally ranging farther, but always circling back. Jake asked Eliza to follow him, and Lange led their strange little party through the woods, setting a slow pace that left Jake far too much time to contemplate how close they'd come to dying.

"It was incredible, what you did up there," Jake said.

"You're overly impressed."

"I'd've been so fucked without you. Dead for sure. And

instead you saved us both with your telekinesis. I'm the exact right amount of impressed."

Lange hummed, probably in disagreement.

"Let me be grateful," Jake insisted one last time before changing the subject. "Is it far to your place? Why do you have a place in Alaska anyway? Did you grow up here?"

"I estimate a half-hour walk," Lange said, and Jake thought he was going to quit there, whether from stubbornness or because his memory was unreliable. Though he'd remembered his family well enough. Then Lange added, "I grew up in Milwaukee."

"You're used to the cold, then." Asking more questions was a risk, so Jake settled on the impersonal and inoffensive, "It's beautiful here."

Lange nodded. He didn't smile. They continued up the path. While it alternated patches of mud and snow, it was also wide enough to drive a vehicle on. It zigzagged through the trees and up the mountainside and could only be the product of years of maintenance. No one else lived out here, not that Jake could see. Lange must have spent time clearing this. It was hard to imagine him out here, at least in this life, and yet here he was.

The air was cold and clean. Late-afternoon October sunlight wove through the weft of the trees.

"It would've been a shame to destroy it," Lange said at length.

"The forest?"

"Existence."

"Oh," Jake said. He tried to work out if that was the first time he'd heard Lange express anything resembling remorse about the accident—or any halfway nice sentiment about *existence*, as he'd put it. Remarking on his change in attitude would make him clam up, so Jake said, "You think that's what would've happened with the breach? It would've destroyed everything?"

"I wouldn't want to make a formal prediction without the data in front of me," Lange said. "And it depends what we mean by 'destroy,' of course. But I think our lives would have been rendered unrecognizable, if they'd lasted."

"Well," Jake said, disturbed even though he'd known those things already. "Good thing you averted *that*."

Lange said nothing.

They emerged into a clearing. Lange had said "cabin," so Jake ought to have expected the small, square, wooden house in the middle of the pines, with a porch stacked with firewood under a blue tarp and an old truck parked next to it. That was exactly what the word "cabin" indicated.

He glanced at Lange and then back at the house. Cabin. Lange. *Cabin.* Christ, this was weird.

"You live here?"

"I used to," Lange said, pulling off a glove and half-unzipping his spacesuit to pull an old brass house key out of an inner pocket. "I suppose I still do."

———

THE WOODS HAD TURNED a tap in his mind, starting a trickle of memories, and the sight of the cabin opened the flow.

Lange had been braced for a rush of awful things, but what he remembered was surprisingly pleasant. He had always liked coming here. This place belonged to him. No one had ever stayed here other than him and the cats. He hadn't built it with his own two hands, as Jake probably would have if he owned a cabin, but he'd designed it.

There was a layer of snow on the porch steps. Some

half-dormant part of his mind told him October was early for snow, even at this altitude, but the weather was always unpredictable here. At the top of the stairs, he shook the snow off his boots, stomping on the doormat out of habit. His key fit the lock. The bolt slid back almost soundlessly, and the door swung open without a creak.

The cats preceded him, eager to get inside. The unheated cabin had little warmth to offer, but there was firewood stacked on the porch and a wood-burning stove in the living room. The cats seemed to remember that the warmth would originate there, since all three of them curled up expectantly on the red rug in front of the stove.

Habit took over for Lange, too. He sat on the bench to the left of the door and took off his dirty boots, which put him more or less in the kitchen. The bedroom and bathroom were behind closed doors, situated at the back of the house, and the main space of the cabin was undifferentiated. The kitchen counter and cabinets ran along one wall of the room, and opposite them was a wall of bookshelves, interrupted only by the cast-iron stove.

The smell of woodsmoke was layered into the whole place, a faint varnish over the walls and the floorboards. Lange was surprised to find he liked it. Smells had previously only irritated him, but perhaps there hadn't been anything worth smelling in Facility 17.

The cabin was lightly furnished, but it felt nothing like the empty room at Facility 17. That rug in front of the stove, the telescope in the corner, the full bookshelves, the pair of binoculars—these were comforts, not necessities. Someone had chosen that color, that pattern, all those books.

Not someone. Him. Everything here was his choice.

Surrounded by these carefully organized paperbacks and the windows pouring clear sunlight into the room, he was at ease in a way he hadn't realized was possible. Someone lived here, and he wasn't afraid of them.

A single armchair was angled toward the stove, and there was a table with four chairs on the kitchen side of the room. Those chairs had never been occupied by anyone other than Lange and the cats, and the cats were just as happy to sit on the floor, so it had perhaps been optimistic on his part to buy the full set.

Everywhere, there were signs of a man who lived alone. The armchair wasn't part of a pair and wasn't accompanied by a couch.

Belatedly, it occurred to him that there was nowhere for McCreery to sleep.

"The fuel cell's off," Lange said, glancing back at McCreery who was still standing by the door. He'd closed it behind him, very politely, even though there was no warm air to keep inside. "It needs to be turned on. And we'll have to put some wood in the stove."

"Where's the fuel cell? I'll handle it."

"Behind the house," Lange said, and McCreery went out the door.

Lange went into his bedroom, undisturbed since he'd last used it six months ago. It felt like a museum dedicated to the person he'd been, the walls lined with books he had only a vague notion of having read. He liked the pattern of repeating red-and-gold diamonds in the kilim on the floor, but couldn't remember where it had come from. He wished it had a caption next to it: *purchased in Milwaukee in 2087*, or *a gift from a dear friend*—except it definitely wouldn't say that. He remembered at least that much.

He opened the dresser and found clothes that appealed to him equally well, as though a personal shopper had stocked it while keeping his size and taste in mind. That was, he supposed, the case.

Inspired, he pulled out some clothes, went into the bathroom, and rinsed off as best he could—the water wouldn't be hot until the fuel cell was on. As bracing as the cold shower was, the almond scent of his body wash brought back more pleasant memories. There were more products in the medicine cabinet, including a trimmer and an electric razor. He touched his beard. Maybe tomorrow, when there was hot water.

It was good to be out of his spacesuit and marginally less filthy. He put on a sweater and jeans. McCreery would probably be surprised that he'd voluntarily bathed and changed clothes, but Lange had resigned himself to living in this body. He might as well be comfortable. It was something he used to value.

Lange returned to the living room and sat in the armchair. It was a relief to have McCreery gone for a moment, not because he was irritating, but because he represented an anomaly: the only person in the universe, outside of Lange's family, who wasn't irritating. Inexplicable. Lange had spent years warding himself against new people, who only ever wanted him for what he could do for them, and McCreery had slipped right past him.

McCreery's presence distorted everything, as though he had his own gravity, pulling everything in Lange's mind askew. He was an obstacle to clear, objective perception—in an unfortunately literal sense, since he took up a lot of space and Lange couldn't ever seem to stop *looking* at him.

Without McCreery around, Lange was able to float some wood from the porch toward the stove. He was fatigued from holding the heat shield together, but this task felt easy in comparison. It didn't make his head throb in the same way. The front door presented only a minor delay, which was how Lange discovered he could manipulate more than one object at a time.

Fascinating.

"Did you open the door with your mind? While moving the logs? Jesus."

The logs in question thudded to the floor and Lange had to take a deep breath before he could resume loading the stove. Surely it violated the laws of nature for McCreery to move so silently.

McCreery flipped on the overhead light—he'd been successful with the fuel cell, of course—and sat on the bench to remove his boots, still in his suit. "I assume the cabinets are empty. Want me to drive that truck to the nearest store?"

"It's too far to go tonight," Lange said. McCreery had not commented on the shower or the change of clothes, and there was no reason to be disappointed about that. "There are canned goods."

"That's good. We should get in touch with the team, I guess. Tell them we made it but I won't be back until tomorrow. And do you think I should move the pod? Will it be okay out there?"

The questions struck him as bizarre and irrelevant until he realized that McCreery was *nervous*. McCreery had been calm and unaffected by entering Lange's room when Lange was borderline hallucinatory and throwing furniture —hadn't even been all that fazed when Lange had thrown *him*—and he'd piloted their spacecraft through that harrowing descent with success. Yet coming to the cabin had frayed his nerves.

Lange might have laughed if only he could figure out what the joke was.

It didn't make sense. Lange had become less threatening, and therefore McCreery should feel less threatened by him. They had, in fact, solved an urgent and potentially fatal problem together less than two hours ago. Lange did not often feel camaraderie, but it was his understanding that collaboratively solving problems was a ready source of the feeling for other people. Lange himself could not deny a certain pleasure in their collective accomplishment, and McCreery was firmly in the category of *other people*, so it followed that he should no longer be anxious around Lange. There should be warmth between them.

It was so frustrating when an equation didn't work out.

"Lange? Should I move the pod?"

"The pod might acquire a dusting of snow, but it will remain otherwise unmolested," he told McCreery. "There is no one around for kilometers. It was why this place appealed to me."

McCreery got up and began searching the kitchen cabinets. From his armchair, Lange opened the one whose contents were pertinent, careful not to slap McCreery in the face with the door.

"Right," McCreery said, startled by the motion of the cabinet. He recovered and started sorting through the cans. "What kind of soup do you want?"

The can of minestrone that McCreery heated up wouldn't ever earn anyone's five-star rating, yet it was the first meal Lange could remember appreciating since his return. He ate it without protest.

"Could your aunt get here to be with you, if you needed her?" McCreery asked after a few minutes.

Lange had been enjoying the silence. Too bad.

"I don't feel good about leaving you here alone,"

McCreery continued. "Someone needs to be able to get to you."

"She could get here. Or someone could," Lange said. He wouldn't ask her to, but she *could* get here. Anyone could get here. The world was a lot smaller since the discovery of the Nowhere. Of course, you had to be a runner or know a runner to travel instantaneously, and runners were a tiny fraction of the population, but it was all still technically possible.

McCreery eyed him, but said nothing.

Ridiculous to worry so much. Lange was fine. Would be fine.

After a moment, McCreery spoke again, taking care with his words. "I know this is none of my business, but... maybe talk to someone. A therapist, I mean. About getting trapped in the Nowhere."

It was hard to conceive of a therapist—or anyone—who'd comprehend, but the path of least resistance was evident, so Lange took it. "I will."

"You're not just saying that to get me to leave you alone?"

Damn it. "How should I prove it to you? Do you want to come to the appointment? Hold my hand?"

McCreery's frown felt like a victory—Lange had succeeded in putting him off—until it felt like a loss. Ridiculous. There was no reason to feel that way.

Lange conducted a thought experiment: an alternate reality in which McCreery had said *yes, actually, I do want to hold your hand*. When it came time to picture his own response, the hypothetical universe collapsed.

"I'll sleep on the floor," McCreery said, changing the subject. "I know lately you have a thing about, uh, sensory input."

"Also, I threw you into a wall," Lange said for the sake of accuracy.

"Yeah, that too."

They had already discussed the incident. There was no need to say more. "I shouldn't have done it."

"Still feel bad about it?" McCreery asked.

"Yes," Lange said, the truth of his feelings surfacing quickly. "I do."

"Good."

McCreery didn't offer him further absolution, so there was a beat of silence. Lange got up to wash the dishes—with his hands, because he suspected McCreery would approve.

Eventually, Lange said, "You can take one of the pillows from the bed. There is an extra blanket in the bottom drawer of the dresser in the bedroom."

All that information had come to him with so little struggle. He found himself staring at McCreery, waiting for praise, and then remembered that knowing the contents of one's own house wasn't noteworthy or impressive. Neither was washing the dishes with one's hands. Such achievements were unlikely to elicit anything like *you were amazing* or *it was incredible, what you did up there.* Lange shouldn't have dismissed McCreery's earlier compliments, but he hadn't known he wanted more until none were forthcoming. He averted his eyes.

McCreery had treated him well, all things considered, and instead of returning the favor, he was wishing for more.

When McCreery emerged from the bedroom with a pillow and a blanket, Lange said, "You should take the bed."

McCreery scoffed. "Sure. Your princess-and-the-pea ass'll sleep great on the floor."

"It's only one night," Lange said.

"Exactly. And I've slept in worse places, Lange, don't worry about me."

"What worse places?"

The question surprised both of them. After a moment, McCreery laid that gaze on him, heavy as a hand. "Your floor's inside and free of rats. I'm good, I promise. Go to bed."

[6]
MANUAL

I<small>T WAS STRANGE TO FEEL SUMMARILY DISMISSED INSIDE</small> his own home, and stranger still to feel... whatever this was.

Lange undressed and lay down in his bed thinking of the moment in the pod when McCreery had asked him about his interest in music. He'd refused to answer.

And now McCreery had refused to answer one of *his* questions. It shouldn't have mattered, because Lange did not care about McCreery and whatever sort of life he'd lived before they'd met. The question was an error, a string of words that had escaped his mouth by accident, and the answer was irrelevant. Still, it was disagreeable to receive no response.

He had made McCreery feel this way. Undoubtedly, with his other actions, Lange had made McCreery feel far worse.

And yet McCreery had not returned the unkindness. He remained tolerable. Likable, even. Frustratingly so, since Lange had now developed a desire for his attention.

A desire that was currently unsatisfied.

Lange hadn't wanted anything earthly since his return. This new feeling was physical, almost like a stomach-clenching hunger pang, but he knew a trip to the kitchen wouldn't solve this. Something hummed inside him. He lay perfectly still in resistance, and it did not go quiet. Sensation stole over his skin, hot and tight, heightening his awareness of his body. Between his legs, his member swelled.

With it came memories. Clothed only in the smooth sheets, it was easy to remember what he used to do here. How it used to make him feel.

He ran his hands down his chest, over the ridges of his hipbones, to the tops of his thighs, and shivered—but not with revulsion. It was novel, the idea that being embodied might carry its own rewards. Until now, all touch had been constrained to its function, and he'd completed the bare minimum of showers and changes of clothes. What had McCreery said? *You have a thing about, uh, sensory input.*

Lange had spent a lot of time angry and afraid of his body, but his nervous system was something of a miracle: the way he could feel his palms, but also the coarse hair of his thighs and the warmth coursing under his skin. A closed circuit.

Not all sensory input was bad.

One fingertip drawn slowly over his skin provided a wealth of data, effortlessly cataloguing the heat and texture of everything underneath. Was he ready for more than that? He wanted to be.

He'd grown fully hard. His meandering hands had coaxed his arousal into something heavy and aching, yearning to be touched. Warm, wet drips were already gathering on his stomach.

The mechanics of the act were simple. (They would be

slightly more complex if he slid open the drawer of his nightstand, whose contents he recalled with striking clarity. Lange filed that thought under *future experiments*.) What had eluded him, until now, was the appeal. Masturbation was one more tiresome bodily habit, like eating or sleeping, to which he would eventually succumb.

Lange trailed his fingers up the length of his dick and hissed out a breath. *Fuck.* He'd been wrong about a lot of things. It was good to touch himself. Better than anything else in his new existence.

Taking himself in hand provoked a loud, shuddering breath. The sound reverberated in the still room. Shit. The door. He'd left it cracked open so the cats could come and go.

He hadn't intended to do anything other than sleep. Intentional or not, his hand was moving now, gliding up and down. It would be easier to shut the door than to stop. One sustained moment of focus on his part could swing the door closed, silently enough not to disturb McCreery.

Lange didn't move it.

McCreery wouldn't come in. He'd ignore any sounds he heard, very politely, just as he'd averted his eyes when Lange had showered and changed near him. The care that McCreery took with everything, the way he was quiet and gentle and patient, was alluring and infuriating at once. With few exceptions, he'd asked "Is it okay if I touch you here?" before every instance of contact. The man was unfailingly appropriate.

Lange liked that he asked—and hated it.

Oh.

He wanted McCreery to be inappropriate with him.

Or perhaps it was the other way around. It was easier to

imagine that, and Lange's thoughts slid in that direction as his hand slid down. McCreery was kind, compassionate, and above all, he loved to solve a problem. Lange could be that problem.

Lange could throw the sheets off, groan, and drop back into the pillows.

"Lange?" McCreery would call. "You okay?"

"No," Lange would say, surly and despairing.

McCreery would enter the room cautiously, and when he caught sight of Lange naked, he would *both* put a hand over his face *and* turn around. The hand would muffle the sound of him saying, "What the *fuck*, Lange."

"This keeps happening," Lange would say. "It won't go away."

"Jesus fucking Christ," McCreery would mutter. "What did you call me in here for? Instructions?"

McCreery would pose the question sarcastically, but Lange would say yes without a trace of irony.

"Eleven-year-olds regularly figure this one out on their own, Lange. I'm pretty sure you can handle it."

"I can't," Lange would say, and it would be just pathetic enough to keep McCreery from leaving. Asking for help was galling in real life and easy in fantasy.

McCreery would huff and swear again. "Fine. Wrap your hand around your dick and pull. There's your goddamn owner's manual. I'm leaving now."

Lange would yelp in pain and McCreery would cringe in sympathy, his shoulders lifting sharply.

"Be *gentle*, you fucking doorknob."

"My fine motor control isn't what it once was."

That would do it. McCreery would turn at last, his face flushed with a mixture of mortification and frustration and —Lange might as well indulge himself—arousal.

McCreery would stomp over to the bed and sit down next to Lange. "Is your hand wet?"

"What?"

Exasperated, he would say, "You can't just yank on it when everything's dry. Come on."

In the fantasy, it wouldn't occur to McCreery to check the drawer of Lange's well-stocked nightstand for lube. Instead, he would take Lange's hand—he would *not* ask permission—and raise it to his mouth to run his tongue over the palm in generous, wet strokes. Lange shivered. If McCreery was going to do something, Lange felt sure, he would commit to doing it right.

And then he would replace Lange's hand on his dick, adjusting his grip just so. He would keep his own hand there, wrapped around Lange's, guiding it up and down. His touch would be warm.

"See? It's easy," he would murmur, all his irritation softened into something else. His big hand engulfing Lange's, staying steady even as Lange's breathing grew shorter and shallower. "You got this. Good, just like that."

McCreery would risk looking at him. He did it all the time, checking to make sure Lange was still with him, still listening, still okay, and if so, he'd smile. Not a big grin, nothing so loud, but something small and reassuring and pleased. It did good things to his face, that little smile. Seeing it was a rare reward.

Lange thrust into his own hand and came hard. His whole body had tightened and then suddenly released, and now he felt... liquid, almost. Like he could melt into the mattress.

It wasn't so bad to have a body.

He blotted at the mess with a tissue and then lay in bed

and drifted toward sleep. He should be nicer to McCreery, he thought.

It might be easier to return to Facility 17 and close the breach. In both cases, he had no idea where to begin.

[7]
BAD IDEA

IT WAS STILL DARK WHEN JAKE GAVE UP. HE'D SPENT A restless night on the floor in front of the wood stove, surfacing from sleep at every creak of the cabin and every movement from one of the damn cats. All three of them had visited him, walking on him or sniffing him, and at one point one even curled up and slept next to him. He hadn't welcomed the intrusion at first, but once the cat had settled, it had been kind of nice.

Plus, the cat's presence was a distraction from the other noises he'd heard. Noises he wished had been less identifiable. Noises that were absolutely none of his business.

Jake had been caught between thinking *good for him* and wondering if maybe Lange would be less of a dick now that he'd relieved some tension. Probably not.

He reached down to scratch the cat—the big orange one, Chandrasekhar—behind the ears. The animal tightened the circle of its body, tucked into the crook between his stomach and his bent legs, and began to purr. Jake felt the rumble before he heard it.

It was probably nice to have a person sleep next to you like that, too, not that Jake would know.

He got up, leaving Chandrasekhar to sleep in the nest of his blanket, and went poking around the kitchen as silently as possible. There were more canned goods, but little else. He had some emergency rations in the pod, but this wasn't technically an emergency, and he knew better than to eat those right away. Repairs always took twice as long as expected.

Because Lange's cabin was so tidy—just like his room at Facility 17 had been, before Jake had packed it up—Jake didn't have to search for the truck keys. They were on a hook next to the door. If Jake left now, the sun would come up on the drive and he'd get to the nearest town just as stores were opening. He could pick up some epoxy for the heat shield in addition to food. He didn't know what Lange liked to eat, but Lange probably didn't know either. If Jake left him alone in that cabin with no food, there was no telling how well he'd fend for himself tomorrow or next week.

The trip took three hours. Lange was still asleep—or at least, in bed—when Jake got back. The note Jake had left on the counter was untouched. He stocked the pantry as quietly as possible, ate breakfast, updated the note, and then hiked down to the pod.

Absorbed in fixing the heat shield, Jake didn't realize Lange had come to find him until he backed up into the man. Eliza beeped a warning, but she was too late. Jake stepped right on Lange's foot. He stumbled and would have fallen, but Lange caught him telekinetically, so he ended up with his feet hovering above the ground. It was disorienting and *then* Lange spun him around so they were facing each other. Jesus.

"Your hair," Jake said, which was *really* not the most important aspect of this situation.

Lange ran a hand over his head like he needed a reminder that he'd buzzed it, leaving it just a little longer on top than on the sides. He'd neatened up his beard, too, so it angled sharply down his face, emphasizing his cheekbones. It was weird to see Lange looking like the professional photo on the back cover of his book.

Crap, Jake was staring. "Also, good morning. You can, uh, put me down now."

"Oh," Lange said, like he hadn't realized he was levitating a human being fifteen centimeters off the ground. Like he'd moved Jake—who was both taller and heavier than him—without really thinking about it.

Lange deposited him on the ground with precision and gentleness.

"I came to see if you needed help," Lange said.

Today was full of surprises.

"You're too late, I just finished," Jake said. He'd have to do a pre-flight check, and a test flight, but he'd been through everything else. His apologetic smile was a reflex. Lange wouldn't give a shit.

After a hesitation, Lange said, "So it's fixed? You're leav—"

"You know," Jake interrupted. "The hardware store owner gave me a hard time this morning. She said 'who are you and why are you driving Solomon's truck?' But you told me that only your family called you Solomon."

"She *is* family," Lange said, unfazed.

Jake blinked. He hadn't expected Lange's family to include a seventy-something Native woman in rural Alaska, but Lange had mentioned that one of the people he'd called lived an hour away.

"You met my aunt Cora," Lange continued. "She's not related to me, legally or biologically, but I've known her for most of my life. My other aunt and uncle were atmospheric chemists. Their research required visits to remote locations, so they came here for work regularly. They were worried about feeling isolated up here, about being the only Black people, but Cora and her family made them feel welcome."

"And you?"

"My aunt and uncle used to take us with them in the summer. My cousins hated it—no one to socialize with—but for me, it felt peaceful. I spent a lot of time helping them with their research. I came back on my own, and later I helped Cora's grandson with his homework a few times. She's never forgotten that."

"You what?" Jake couldn't picture that at all. First, it was the idea of Lange with a child of any age, and second, it was the idea of a child of any age being tutored in school-level math and science by a world-class, award-winning genius who was also an infamous recluse. Items one and two on his list were the same. Jake's brain wasn't working quite right.

"He was twelve. The questions were easy," Lange said, as though Jake's bewilderment had anything to do with the contents of the kid's homework. Then Lange made pointed eye contact. "Before this digression, we were discussing whether you plan to leave."

"You picked me up. What else can you move?" Jake asked, dodging the question about his departure. For a moment there, Lange had looked unnervingly... pleading. Big brown eyes or not, that shouldn't be possible. It was *Lange*. Mean, recalcitrant, occasionally terrifying Lange. Jake had probably hallucinated it.

He'd probably *projected* it, being as foolishly worried

about leaving Lange alone as he was. Aunt Cora or no Aunt Cora, Lange was alone here. One seventy-something woman an hour away couldn't do much in an emergency. God, Jake couldn't have picked a more difficult person to care about.

Lange was squinting at him, so Jake doubled down and asked more questions. "When you move something, does mass matter? Or volume?"

"I haven't found a limit yet," Lange said.

"How many things can you move at once?"

"At least three," Lange said. That seemed correct, since Jake had seen him open the cabin door and bring in two logs.

Jake grinned, nudged the tool roll he'd left on the ground with the toe of his boot, and said, "Wanna try four?"

Lange nodded, pleased to be asked. Jake supposed experimenting was familiar territory for both of them, even if Lange dealt in theory far beyond what Jake could understand.

Jake patted his pockets until he came up with a pad and a pencil. He'd pulled a crate of emergency supplies out of the pod before the repairs and it was still on the ground, so he sat on it.

"Okay. What do you wanna test first?"

"Number of objects."

One by one, a drill, a screwdriver, and a wrench slid out of the tool roll and hovered in the air. It was kind of creepy, watching things move when nobody was touching them, but Jake couldn't help the buzz of excitement that ran through him, either.

"Cool. So that's three."

Lange added a second screwdriver. Jake made note of that, and by the time he'd looked up again, the whole roll was empty and there were sixteen objects floating in the air.

"Impressive," he said, and braced for Lange to tell him that it wasn't.

Instead, Lange beamed at him. The bright, excited expression rendered him almost unrecognizable, and for a second, it cut the signal to Jake's brain. Reconciling the wide, shallow curve of that smile and the crinkled corners of those eyes with the idea of Solomon Lange took real effort. But there hadn't been much joy in Lange's life, these past few weeks. No reason to smile. The novelty captivated Jake. That was it.

Lange raised his brows. Waiting for more.

"What can you do with them?" Jake said, finding his voice. They obviously had to keep experimenting, since it was making Lange so happy. "Could you actually unscrew something? And simultaneously use the drill? Or is it like when people can't rub their belly and pat their head at the same time?"

Lange frowned like he'd never heard of any such thing. Then the drill rose out of the cloud of tools, slow and unsteady. As its trigger depressed and the motor turned on, the remaining fifteen tools clanged against each other in their fall.

"Okay," Jake said, not sure why he was bothering to sound reassuring. It wasn't like Lange had failed a test. "So that's a limit, of sorts. But could you pick up all the tools and move the whole group around?"

This proved easier and also significantly scarier if Jake imagined himself in the path of sixteen unforgivingly solid objects hurtling through the air.

Finer control proved elusive, and those experiments dampened Lange's good mood, so Jake switched subjects.

"You held the heat shield together yesterday. That's, what, a thousand kilos? You think that's your upper limit?"

"I wasn't lifting its whole weight," Lange said, as though that lessened the impact of him saving both their lives. "Merely keeping it in place. And it was an extraordinary circumstance."

"Still," Jake said. "Besides, knowing how much you can lift seems useful, right?"

Lange said nothing and for a long moment, nothing happened. It was impossible to say what he was focusing on. Jake didn't know where to look.

Then the pod creaked. It didn't move, just sat there in the frost and the mud. Of course it didn't move. That thing weighed five thousand kilos, easy.

"Holy shit." Jake laughed out loud. "Maybe set your sights a little lower."

Lange exhaled roughly and his whole body slumped. "I wasn't trying to move the whole pod, just the heat shield. I can't do it. It's beyond me."

"Yeah, well, it's beyond the rest of us, too," Jake said. "I'm amazed you had any impact at all. As for the heat shield, you did it when it mattered. But let's maybe not experiment any further on my method of getting home."

"Mm."

Lange had perked up since they'd been messing around down here, but he looked a little drawn now, his eyes less alert and sweat at his hairline. Lange hadn't exerted himself in weeks and yesterday he'd nearly passed out from saving them and now Jake had worn him out again. Shit. Lange should probably be resting.

"How do you feel?" Jake asked. "You didn't hurt yourself, did you?"

"No," Lange said, scowling like he didn't need to be

asked any such thing. Like he wasn't the guy Jake had recently coaxed into eating a sandwich and showering. Like he hadn't given himself a magic nosebleed yesterday. "The telekinesis is tiring, but painless."

"We should test your stamina at some point," Jake said. "Maybe not today. We've already done so much. Let's go back to the house."

Lange's eyes lit up, and Jake had no idea what he'd done to make that happen.

———

THE HIKE BACK to the cabin had left Lange embarrassingly winded. He hadn't protested when McCreery insisted he sit at the kitchen table. He'd been relieved to deposit himself into a chair with minimal wobbling.

McCreery hadn't said much on the walk, but that was his way. It might not be significant. He was cooking in silence now, slicing an onion with a dexterity that revealed long practice. Lange's eyes stung. Watching McCreery's knife clip the hemisphere into translucent white arcs, he remembered something. This wasn't the first time McCreery had cooked for him.

Months ago at Facility 17, they'd encountered each other in the middle of a sleepless shift. Lange's wandering had taken him through the halls, and he'd discovered the lights already on in the kitchen. McCreery had been standing at the stove making a perfectly square and golden grilled cheese sandwich.

He'd reacted to Lange's entry only by saying, "Want one?"

Lange had said yes. The hour or the fatigue—or possibly the scent—had weakened his usual defenses. Whatever it was, he'd accepted McCreery's offer and had ended up seated at the long metal table with the grilled cheese on a plate in front of him.

Moments later, McCreery had sat down across from him with an identical plate. He'd smiled, which Lange knew was the prelude to small talk, which might lead to companionship, which might lead to emotional investment, which he avoided at all costs. Lange had made a mistake, coming here and sitting down.

Fixing it would be simple enough. He had only to execute his usual tactic. He knew many ways to drive people away, but one of the fastest was to weaponize his own life.

He deployed this tactic with precision. He was, of course, capable of being polite and professional; that had been a survival requirement, and he knew exactly when and with whom it was necessary. And sometimes professional etiquette sufficed to keep people at a distance. Even so, it was defense.

Some situations required offense, so he had looked right at McCreery and said, "No one befriends me or offers me anything unless they want to use me."

When he said something uncomfortable, the overly friendly stranger he was talking to would look stricken and mumble an apology and then the conversation would halt. Future interactions would be as brief as possible, because Lange said true, upsetting things that no one knew how to respond to. People avoided that. Social overtures would dwindle to nothing after a while, and he would remain safe. Not from people using him, but that couldn't be avoided, and when it had to happen, he preferred his transactions bare of the guise of friendship.

McCreery *had* looked stricken, so Lange had thought

things were off to their usual start. But instead of stumbling through an apology and retreating, he'd said, "So what's this grilled cheese worth, then?"

"Not even a tenth-grade algebra assignment," Lange snapped, though it wasn't true. Back in high school, he'd thought the people asking him for favors were his friends. He hadn't known to charge them.

"Ouch," McCreery had said. "I guess it's a good thing for both of us that I dropped out. Maybe you're using me."

Lange had scowled—also an excellent tactic for keeping would-be friends away—and said, "Why?"

"I make a good grilled cheese. You'd know if you'd eaten any of it."

"No, why did you drop out?"

"Didn't wanna be there, and nobody else wanted me there, either," McCreery had said. "I'm not as useful as you, I guess."

"Oh," Lange had said, stunned—and irritated that someone else could use his own tactic on him. Now *he* had to be the one to offer sympathy and withdraw.

"That's shitty, about people using you," McCreery had said. "I'm sorry. If it helps, I don't have any pressing multidimensional physics problems for you to solve. Or any algebra homework."

McCreery didn't need anything from him. Perhaps there was nothing to guard against. Cautiously, Lange had cleared his throat and said, "Likewise, I am... sorry that you felt unwanted in your youth. Or, ah, a moment ago."

No matter the words, this was not an exchange of platitudes. This was personal, and earnest, and Lange had to turn away from McCreery, who had tricked him into having a real conversation. About his feelings. Worse, his fears.

And Lange couldn't even blame him for that, because *Lange had brought it up in the first place.*

Lange had swallowed around a lump in his throat and collected himself.

He'd been outmaneuvered in a handful of sentences. No, that made it sound like McCreery had been calculating, when really he'd been anything but. No one had ever taken Lange's deliberate rudeness in stride like that. Lange had risked a glance across the table, where McCreery was eating his grilled cheese like nothing unusual had happened.

Lange ate his own sandwich. It was, as promised, good. Crisp and buttery and gooey inside. It shouldn't have moved him, this small and simple comfort, but it was too late for that.

After some time, McCreery had said, "So you wanna go another round of awful shit we've lived through, or you wanna talk about something else?"

"Why are you in the kitchen in the middle of the night making grilled cheese?" Lange had asked, the question tantamount to admitting that he wanted to talk about something else. That he wanted to *talk*. Remarkable. Embarrassing. He should have wanted to flee the room.

McCreery had shrugged. "Couldn't sleep. I used to work the late shift at an all-night diner, so it felt natural to come in here."

Lange had asked him about the diner, and then they'd talked about the work, and the food, and tricks for falling asleep, and the whole thing had been shockingly pleasant.

They had not discussed what was keeping them awake. In Lange's case, the answer had been the machine.

Perhaps in some other timeline, he'd said so, and then McCreery had convinced him not to rip a hole in reality.

He grimaced and tried not to think about that. It

couldn't be undone; it could only be repaired. He had to live in this timeline, the one where he'd fucked up.

Right here, in the cabin with McCreery, that didn't feel like such a punishment.

Lange relished the opportunity to study McCreery without being observed in return. His hands worked with a speed and precision that Lange couldn't imagine matching.

McCreery wasn't beautiful, his buzzed hair somewhere between brown and blond, his features some bland mixture of western European heritage, but the way he moved was fascinating. Everything about him was deliberate. Was it because he was so big?

His bulk wasn't decorative, but useful. Even a little intimidating, though he'd probably never intentionally threatened anyone. With a body like that, he could be as quiet and solitary as he liked, and still no one would trouble him.

Perhaps I wouldn't have honed my tongue quite so sharp if I'd had shoulders like that. A worthless hypothesis. Too many variables. Untestable.

The top of McCreery's half-unzipped flight suit hung down around his waist. The shirt underneath was grey cotton that had been washed within an inch of its life, the thin fabric stretching over the softness of his middle and baring his thick arms. McCreery looked, Lange thought, like he would give pleasingly solid hugs.

No. Absurd. Lange didn't want hugs. Affection was a trap. He wanted orgasms, which McCreery also looked like he could provide.

"Lange," McCreery said, interrupting his unruly thoughts. "Are you pulling on me?"

Lange made a choked sound that would have to serve as

a reply. Upon reflection, it was... not impossible that the answer to McCreery's question was yes.

"Because I've had to work really hard just to stand here, these past few minutes. It feels like the floor keeps slipping under me, or like the stove keeps getting farther away. I've been resisting, but it *really* feels like some invisible force is pulling me toward you."

No point in dissembling, then. "I find you distracting."

McCreery paused, the wooden spoon in his hand no longer stirring the pot of tomato sauce, but pointed aimlessly upward. He cleared his throat. He didn't make eye contact. "Yeah, about that—"

"We should have sex."

McCreery looked at him just long enough for Lange to catch the whites of his eyes. His face turned a dull red. He stirred the sauce with furious concentration. "I don't—that's a bad idea, Lange."

"Why?" Lange asked. "I remember sex. I've had a lot of it."

"Wha—you have?"

"I assume you're surprised because I'm not good with people," Lange said. "But I have very symmetrical features, and in my former life, I had impeccable personal hygiene."

"Yeah, I've seen your bathroom," McCreery said, sounding a little dazed. "You're hot and you smell good— that's all that's necessary?"

Lange didn't require confirmation. It was nevertheless satisfying to hear McCreery say *you're hot*. The words suffused him with pleasure in a way no mere statement of fact should have, simply because McCreery had said them. The skeptical question that had followed meant nothing.

Lange answered, "I didn't say I'd had a lot of relationships. I said I'd had a lot of sex. Mostly, but not solely, with men. That's a combination of personal preference and the availability of the kind of unattached encounter I prefer—"

"Yeah, okay," McCreery interrupted. "Don't need your whole CV."

"I'm qualified, I assure you."

"Not the issue," McCreery said. "What you were doing just now, pulling on me. Was that on purpose?"

All his possible answers seemed equally undesirable, so Lange told the truth. "No."

"Yeah. Like I said, bad idea."

It was, unfortunately, a good point. Lange would develop perfect control in time, he had no doubt, but he didn't possess it now, not to the degree needed. After a moment, he said, "That wasn't an outright refusal."

"Well, it sure as hell wasn't a 'yes.' We're not talking about this anymore."

"I apologize for broaching the issue," Lange said stiffly. "My previous rejections have all involved putting physical distance between myself and the other party. I don't know what to do when that's not possible. Should I now make an empty promise that this won't make things 'weird' between us?"

"Not if it's empty," McCreery muttered. "Jesus Christ, Lange, 'weird' is our default. I'm not gonna fuck you. Change the subject."

"An interesting assumption on your part."

"Lange," McCreery said, loud and exasperated.

In the ensuing silence, McCreery dumped a pound of pasta into the pot of boiling water on the stove. There was no longer a need for him to pay close attention to his cooking, and there hadn't been for some time—*watched pots*, and so on—but he hadn't turned around. There was tension in his posture that hadn't been there before, and Lange felt a pang of guilt.

"I did take music lessons as a child, of a sort. My mother taught me," Lange said, offering the answer to McCreery's long-ago question like an olive branch. "She can play anything—any instrument, any genre, any work. She can sing, too. For me, it was only ever the guitar."

McCreery didn't comment on the non sequitur; he was the one who'd requested the change of subject, after all. His shoulders dropped minutely.

McCreery didn't ask any questions about Lange's mother, and Lange couldn't say if that was a relief or not.

Lange had never asked McCreery about his family. At least, Lange couldn't recall asking when they'd been in the Facility 17 kitchen that night, and his memory was devoid of other details. McCreery hadn't mentioned them, not even in passing. It felt unwise to bring it up.

"Do you remember how to play the guitar?" McCreery asked, turning to face him at last.

"I think so," Lange said. "I've never been as good as her."

"There's a guitar case in the corner over there," McCreery said.

The instrument had been untouched for months. It would need care before it could be played. Lange curled and uncurled his fingers, splaying his hands on the table. "I doubt there's much overlap between what my mind remembers and what my hands can do."

"Practice makes perfect, so I hear."

"I couldn't. Not in front of you."

McCreery snorted. "And yet you proposed—"

"I thought we weren't speaking of that," Lange said.

"Right," McCreery said. "Go get that book of crossword puzzles. God knows we need it."

Discussion of crossword clues—*impersonal* crossword clues, mercifully—saved Lange from further conversational missteps over lunch. Afterward, McCreery made a show of going by himself to check the pod for damages, leaving Lange alone in the cabin. Lange picked up the instrument and began to tune it.

[8]

FRIENDS

JAKE TOOK ELIZA BACK DOWN TO THE CLEARING WITH him and spent a peaceful hour with only the sound of her whirring and beeping. There was nothing wrong with the pod.

He almost wished Lange had damaged it in their tele-kinetic experiment. Then Jake would have something to do.

And no choice but to stay.

"What the hell is wrong with me?" he asked Eliza, who was sitting at his feet under the perfectly functional console.

He hadn't given her the ability to speak—too weird, choosing a human voice—and her language processing was internal, not hooked up to a bank of servers with all of recorded speech at her disposal. Most of the time she just beeped in affirmation. But she recognized when she'd been asked something. His tablet buzzed with a message.

I do not understand the question, she'd written.

"Yeah, me either," he said. A moment later, he put in a call to the team at Facility 17. It was work, just a regular check-in, but all the same, it'd be a relief to have a conversation that wasn't a hundred different layers of discomfort and desire.

"How are things going up there?" he asked.

"Good." After the short delay from lunar orbit, it was Emil's voice on the other end of the line. "They're good. I'm as surprised as you are."

"That's a nice change of pace."

"Yeah," Emil said. "The breach has slowly but steadily decreased in size. What about you? You heading back up now?"

Jake had checked in yesterday after their landing to confirm that they'd made it despite their troubles. He'd said he thought he could finish his repairs by today, so naturally they were expecting him to come back.

He was expecting that himself. What was he doing down here except enduring a series of awkward conversations and another night on the cabin floor?

Fuck, he'd extended this pause too long. This conversation was choppy enough without him overthinking everything.

"Do you need me up there?" Jake asked.

"There's a leak in the greenhouse I think you and your robots could fix, but it's not urgent. Wouldn't mind having you examine the outside of the facility, just in case, but like I said, none of that's time-sensitive. Are you thinking of staying?"

Fuck, he wanted to lie and he didn't know how.

"I, um—if you're okay up there without me, maybe I'll take a little more time," Jake said, his face heating. Good thing it was a voice-only communication.

"That's kind of you," Emil said.

Jake hadn't specified *why* he was staying. He could have food poisoning for all Emil knew. He should have said that.

Be back soon, just don't wanna shit myself in the pod, you know how it is. Less embarrassing than the truth.

"You'll be okay to get back up here when you need to?" Emil asked. "If the pod's beyond repair, Kit can come get you."

"The pod's fine," Jake said. He dragged a hand down his face. What he wouldn't give to be a better liar or a worse mechanic.

"Okay. Keep checking in regularly. Let us know if you need anything."

"Yeah. Hope things stay good up there," Jake said. They signed off and he stared down at Eliza. "I guess we have to go back now."

The whole walk back, he tried to organize his thoughts and work out what he would say to Lange. He didn't know if he'd set the right boundary.

Every attempt to clarify what he wanted sank back into the morass of feelings lurking in the bottom of his brain. Jake rarely thought about the stuff that everybody else obsessed over. Smiles, eyes, hands, hips, whatever. Sex. Back in high school, people had asked him who he thought was hot, and that little social ritual had felt like a puzzle he couldn't solve. Other people seemed to be able to look at a stranger and think *wow yes them*, and that had never once happened to him.

He only ever thought of that fact with relief. Falling in lust with a stranger sounded like a hell of a lot of trouble.

Sex had crossed his mind on a handful of occasions— always with someone he knew as a friend—but he'd never acted on the impulse. Curiosity, physical loneliness, those weren't reasons to risk a friendship. Until a couple of hours ago, he'd always assumed that nobody would be interested.

He was quiet and weird and not particularly good-looking, and on top of all that, he had no experience.

I find you distracting. We should have sex.

Lange probably had no idea that Jake was still reeling from those two little sentences. It was hard to imagine approaching sex so casually.

Fuck. Jake had been content without all this. He had two good hands and was inclined to DIY projects in all other areas of his life. He could take care of himself. Being demisexual was luck, and being single was a choice. None of this was a problem.

The problem was that Jake had noticed Lange.

Sort of the same way he noticed, now, trudging through the woods, that the sky had thickened with grey and white clouds. A snowstorm was coming. Nothing to be done about it.

Lange had smiled at him and he had thought *oh no*.

Attraction didn't feel much like a lifetime's worth of pop songs had told him it would. It felt, actually, very similar to Lange telekinetically pulling on him. Except Lange hadn't been doing that when they'd been outside this morning. *Jake* was the origin.

He liked Lange.

He was sexually attracted to Lange.

It made no goddamn sense. Lange, of all people. He was handsome, of course, but that had never mattered before. And brilliant, but that shouldn't count for anything. Jake knew plenty of smart people and none of them had ever done it for him.

God, he wished they had. *Anyone* else would have been simpler. Jake could toss a dart at the people in line for a docking permit at Franklin Station and have an easier time of it than he'd get with Solomon Lange. Their relationship was complicated enough already. *And* Lange had been a dick even before his return from the Nowhere. *And* Jake didn't know what the fuck he was doing when it came to sex or romance, and if he wanted either, he'd have to talk about his feelings—*with Lange*, who had enough to deal with already—and that was no guarantee the whole thing wouldn't go to shit anyway.

Fuck. Why did his body only want to play this game on hard mode?

"I wish *you* could reboot *me*," he told Eliza.

She beeped in sympathy.

Snow began to fall, littering the two of them and the surrounding trees with huge, lavish flakes. They melted on contact with his bare skin, leaving him to blink droplets out of his eyelashes.

He'd lived in space so long, he'd sort of forgotten about weather. Earth weather, not solar flares and micrometeoroids. Would've been nice if the snow had started a little earlier. Then Jake could have told Emil he was stuck on the surface waiting out the storm, instead of... whatever he was doing.

A sound was coming out of the cabin. No—music. Halting fragments of melody interspersed with long silences. Even from out here, Jake could tell they were frustrated. He guessed Lange's playing hadn't sounded like that in his other life.

Jake hated to interrupt, but it was snowing hard. He picked a silence, stomped up the porch stairs, and wiped his boots on the mat, a lot more carefully than necessary. Eliza rolled back and forth to clean her treads.

"Good girl," Jake told her, theatrically loud.

When he opened the door, Lange had, at least, not hidden the guitar like it was evidence of illicit behavior.

He'd simply stopped playing. He was sitting cross-legged on the floor in front of the wood stove.

"I called a therapist," Lange said. "We arranged a remote appointment."

"Okay." Jake knew a peace offering when he saw one, but he braced himself for the next thing out of Lange's mouth to be *I did what you wanted, now can we have sex?*

When it didn't come, Jake let out a breath and took off his boots.

"You are under no obligation to stay here," Lange continued. "At present I'm neither helpless nor a danger to myself. You're free to leave."

"You want me to go?"

Lange paused, his hand falling to the guitar strings. "No."

"You... want me to stay?"

"That would be a logical inference," Lange said, and then, thank fuck, he stared right at Jake and said, "Yes, I want you to stay."

That was a fucking revelation. It struck Jake speechless for a second.

Misreading his silence, Lange added, "If you want to, that is. As I said, you don't have to."

Jake didn't know what to do with this—this invitation. He jerked his thumb over his shoulder. The window behind him was probably splattered with snowmelt by now. "It's snowing."

"Ah," Lange said.

Shit. Jake had taken the coward's way out. "And I already told the team I'd stay longer. I don't mind keeping you company. It's probably good for both of us."

Lange's fingers moved against the strings. He muted the

accidental sound almost as soon as he made it. "I agree that your presence is good for me."

"Don't give me all the credit. You've been a lot better since we arrived."

"Yes. But I fail to see how *you* would benefit, though you are welcome to stay."

"Well," Jake said slowly, unwilling to respond to a question that hadn't been asked and uncertain if he even knew the answer, "you're pretty good at crosswords."

"True, but irrelevant," Lange said. "Absent other evidence, I am forced to the improbable conclusion that you like me."

"Yeah, it's weird for me too."

"But you don't want—"

Jake cut that sentence off with a hand gesture. Lange might be ready to go there, but he wasn't. "Can't we be friends?"

"I don't know how to do that."

"Honestly, I'm not sure I do either," Jake said. "But it can't be any harder than surviving a descent to the surface with a cracked heat shield. Between the two of us, we can figure it out."

———

WITH THAT TENUOUS AGREEMENT, Jake and Lange spent the afternoon in surreal domesticity, periodically restocking the wood stove and clearing the drive of snow. They settled on Lange's ability as the safest and most interesting topic of conversation, designing a new series of tests. Lange cleared some of the snow without a shovel, but he was unable to stop the snow falling from the sky. Jake made a solemn and disappointed noise when Lange reported that to him, and then had to duck a snowball, which didn't work because Lange's throws could change course mid-air. Likewise, all of Jake's snowballs failed to make contact.

It would've been good sportsmanship to let *one* make contact—there was nothing wrong with Jake's aim—but when Jake explained that, Lange said, "Wouldn't it also constitute good sportsmanship for you to lose without complaint?"

"Was that a joke?"

"No," Lange said, but one corner of his mouth pulled slightly to the side. It wouldn't count as a smile for anybody else. Jake recorded it in his memory as a milestone anyway.

Lange had turned away too fast for any lingering glances. He walked back toward the house, the snow shovel hovering at his heels like a faithful pet.

Jake nailed him in the back with a snowball.

Lange didn't turn around. A second later, a whole pine tree's worth of snow got dumped on Jake's head.

"Fuck," Jake said, or tried to say. It was more like *fuh* and then the sound of him spitting out snow.

Lange peeked over his shoulder, and Jake definitely didn't imagine *that* smile. The little shit.

Jake brushed himself off, returned to the cabin—he had to carry his own shovel using his hands—and followed Lange inside. Lange set his boots aside and sat on the floor near the wood stove, where the cats had made a nest of Jake's bedding. Jake joined them on the floor.

"Did you do that a lot as a kid in Milwaukee?" he asked before he could think better of it. "Play in the snow, I mean. It's okay if you don't remember. Or if you don't want to talk about it."

"I did," Lange said. "My cousins and I used to play

outside every winter. Sometimes our parents would help us construct forts."

"It sounds nice, having your cousins around like that," Jake said, aware he was treading into dangerous territory. He didn't know much about families, at least not happy ones.

"Most of my family is there. My mother probably should have moved to Nashville for her career, but she worked remotely because she didn't want to leave. We lived right down the street from her sister," Lange said. His gaze was fixed on the wood stove, and his hands were absently stroking Niels Bohr's fur. "My father's from there too. He was a high school science teacher before he retired."

Jake forced himself to look away from Lange's hands on the cat. It was a bad idea to think about physical affection. It made him burn with a kind of tingly, all-over tightness, like his skin ached everywhere he wasn't being touched.

He wished he could mute the sound of purring. Attraction was awful. It had scooped out half his brain and replaced it with this twitchy restlessness. It was making him jealous of a cat.

Jake cast around for something to say that had nothing to do with his thoughts. What had Lange just said? His dad was a teacher.

"Did you like school?"

Lange let out a bark of laughter. "I spent all my time in class bored and furious about being bored. School was hell."

"Well, yeah," Jake said, because *school was hell* described his experience, even though it had been drastically different. "But I just thought—you're so smart—"

"So are you," Lange said with apparent and shocking sincerity.

It took Jake a moment to recover from that. The number of

people who had recognized his intelligence over the course of his life was still vanishingly small, and Lange had been pretty fucking rude about the robots. Jake had sort of assumed that Lange didn't think of *anybody* as smart. If you were standing on the peak of a mountain, you couldn't distinguish height differences among people who were down in the valley.

"Don't tell me you liked school," Lange said. "You dropped out."

Lange remembered that? Jake said, "We moved around a lot. I was always the new kid. I tried to keep my head down and be quiet, but—I don't know. I got into a lot of fights."

"I got into a lot of fights with teachers," Lange said wryly. "In my defense, they were always wrong."

"I'm sure they were."

Niels Bohr got up to stretch, arching his black back and reaching forward to knead Jake's bedding with his white paws. Lange stretched, too, raising his arms above his head and then bringing them down so he could roll his shoulders, looking more at ease in his body. He unfolded his crossed legs and Jake thought for a moment that their conversation was over, but instead what happened was that Lange lay down on his stomach in front of the wood stove. He pillowed his head on his arms.

The position put him closer to Jake, his head and shoulders now within easy reach. Lange was lying on top of a corner of the rumpled blanket Jake had been sleeping on, which was almost like he was in Jake's bed, such as it was. Jake couldn't afford to think about that.

Niels Bohr curled up in the small of Lange's back and purred. Smug asshole cat.

Lange said, "School wasn't as bad when I was younger.

My cousins liked me. And I had my parents watching out for me. My father couldn't start arguments with his colleagues, but Mama—nothing could stop her."

"Your parents sound great," Jake said, trying to keep the envy out of his voice.

"They were. They are. I wish—" Lange stopped for a long time. He watched the fire. "I was afraid I'd hurt them, if I went back like this. I'm sorry, that's a terrible thing to say to you. I shouldn't have hurt *you*. And I shouldn't have kept you here, made you responsible for me. That wasn't right. I... don't really know how to live like this. That's not an excuse."

"Hey, it's okay."

Words were never really adequate, because nothing was, and Jake couldn't fight off his urge to comfort Lange. A hand on the shoulder, that was pretty standard stuff. Lange wouldn't hate it. Probably. Jake was leaning back, propped up on both hands, and he went so far as to sit up straight and lift one.

Lange caught him in the act, his dark gaze more alert than his posture suggested. Jake froze.

"You can," Lange said.

Jake lowered his hand to Lange's shoulder like either of them might detonate at the slightest wrong move. When that didn't happen, he relaxed a fraction, letting the weight of his hand settle there. He rubbed a small circle into Lange's shoulder.

"I get why you were worried about hurting them, but for what it's worth, I don't think you would," Jake said. "Not now, anyway. You've been doing a lot better."

Lange relaxed. "Your touch helps me."

"Helps you what?"

"It's like an anchor," Lange said. "It helps me stay here. It helps me feel right. This is my body, where I live."

"Oh," Jake said, unprepared for this intimacy—unprepared for how much he loved it. It fulfilled a craving he hadn't known he had. "I get that, I think. It helps me, too."

"And I like talking to you. Even about this. It's good to talk about this," Lange said, like he'd only just put that together and couldn't quite believe it. "It hurts, but it's good."

"Yeah."

The smile Lange offered him was sad, but it was there. "Being alive is like that."

"That's a better review than you gave it a few days ago," Jake said. "And yeah, I'd say that's about the shape of things."

Jake wanted Lange to keep talking, even if it was about his parents. Jake didn't have any stories about his own mom, except the one where she'd ditched him when he was a baby, and the stories he could tell about his dad were all pretty goddamn grim. Lange could bring him some souvenir from this country he'd never get to visit. "You said your mom did music, right? What kind?"

"She wrote everything. Pop, R&B, country, electro-ballads. She would tell you 'anything that pays the bills,'" Lange said, amused. "She always underplays her talents. My dad never lets her get away with it. He loves showing off her awards."

Awards. Electro-ballads. Jake hadn't expected their conversation to go in this direction, but it wasn't the first time Lange had known something surprising about pop culture. When they'd done the first crossword together, he'd known the name of Zinnia Jackson's songwriter. Evelyn Holland. Maybe it hadn't been a lucky guess.

"Lange," Jake said. "Is your mom Evelyn Holland? Like in the first crossword we did?"

Lange huffed out a laugh and lifted his head from his arms. "Are you offering me a helpful hint about my own mother's identity?"

"Shut up," Jake said, his embarrassment tempered by the knowledge that he'd made Lange *laugh*. "I mean, that's her, though, right?"

"Yes, Evelyn Holland from the crossword is my mother," Lange said. "I'm gonna tell her that's the only way you knew her name. She'll get a kick out of that."

The thought of Lange talking to his mother about Jake—how the hell would he explain their relationship?—made Jake uncomfortably warm, and yet he didn't hate it.

Lange stilled, the last little tremors of his amusement dying down, and then said, "Well, maybe some day, anyway."

"You haven't told them what happened," Jake guessed.

"I will eventually," Lange said. "If we live."

"Yeah," Jake said, at a loss.

"I wish I could play you something my mother wrote," Lange said suddenly, twisting so he could sit up. "On the guitar, that is. Not with a recording."

"Why can't you?"

Lange closed his eyes. "My fine motor control isn't what it once was."

"So?" Jake asked. They'd had plenty of conversations about what Lange could and couldn't do, and usually Lange was frustrated and cranky, but not embarrassed. If that's what this reaction was, even. The way Lange was pressing his lips together, it almost seemed like he wanted to laugh.

Jake didn't poke at it. He plowed ahead. "Who said you have to use your hands?"

———

PLAYING the guitar with telekinesis turned out to be just as hard as playing it the regular way, or so Jake assumed, since he couldn't do either. But the experiment entertained both of them. By the end, Lange could play "Twinkle, Twinkle Little Star" with either method, and he had laughed at Jake's dumb "look Ma, no hands" joke, and that was good.

"It's important to me to perfect my control," Lange said, setting the guitar down. As Jake was nodding and on the verge of agreeing, Lange added, "So I don't hurt you. It's important to me not to hurt you."

"Yeah, that's important to me too," Jake said, as lightly as he could. "Probably it would be good if your goal was not to hurt *anyone*, though."

"Of course. That is also one of my goals."

Jake clamped down on the things he wanted to blurt out, like *are you still thinking about having sex with me*, because any variation on that question was an admission that *Jake* was still thinking about it. Better to take this special consideration as a sign of friendship, which was the relationship they'd agreed on. Still, it was fine to feel flattered, he reasoned. Having your heart rate accelerate and your mouth go dry because somebody admitted they liked you best was just normal friendship stuff.

It had never happened to Jake before, but he didn't exactly have a wealth of friendship experience to draw on.

Shit. Time to change the subject.

"Can I ask you about your research?" Worst possible subject change, Jesus fucking Christ. "Uh. We don't have to talk about that, if you don't want to."

"Ask," Lange said, and even though they were still

sitting on the floor next to the wood stove, the air between them had cooled.

"I guess I just wondered—why change the Nowhere so regular people could walk into it?"

"Greater access to instantaneous travel could save lives. That's merely one advantage among an expansion of possibilities so immense it's almost impossible to imagine."

"Yeah, I get that, or at least I think I do. But the bulk of the other research is focused on changing people, not changing space."

"One could argue that my research was also focused on changing people. I just didn't know it until it nearly killed me and I came back permanently physically and psychologically altered."

"I'm sorry. I shouldn't have brought this up."

Undeterred, Lange said, "If you're asking why I didn't *start* with human experimentation, one reason is because it's so often unconscionable, as our ex-colleagues demonstrated."

"But *you* wouldn't have kidnapped and tortured anyone," Jake objected.

"Except myself, by accident," Lange said. "Another reason is that my work has always been on the nature of folded and unfolded space, not on the nature of human beings. Your *why* question is the simplest thing about my research: I wanted to learn more about the Nowhere."

"And when you want to learn more about something, you take it apart," Jake said. "That, I get. Will you tell me about the machine?"

"I've never been good at explaining my work to people outside my field," Lange said, and probably *people outside my field* meant *everyone except Dax*, and Dax didn't need anything explained to them.

"You wrote a popular book about this," Jake pointed out.

"I'm told my first draft was incomprehensible," Lange said. "And the book doesn't discuss the machine."

"I know I won't get it, not all of it, not the way you do, but tell me anyway. Do a bad job. I give you permission," Jake said, and the corner of Lange's mouth quirked. "I like to know how things work. Whatever you say will interest me, I promise."

"The easiest way to understand it is by thinking about sound," Lange said. He picked up the guitar again and plucked the bottom string with his thumb. "I strike one string and the string beside it vibrates, even though I never touched it. That's what the machine does to matter."

"And if everything's in tune, a regular person can pass into the Nowhere?"

Lange nodded. "Though in my case, entering turned out to be easier than exiting."

"And even the part where you entered didn't go to plan, right? Dax said you had bad luck. And Emil, well, he said the whole room sort of imploded and exploded at the same time."

"The Nowhere is not static, nor is it truly empty," Lange said. "It moves. I caught it at a bad time."

"And you didn't have a sensor that could pick up on that? You and Dax talked about readings."

"I watched the readings very carefully. They were normal," Lange said. "Rogue waves are often preceded by a period of order—but not every period of order precedes a rogue wave. They are unpredictable."

"Shit," Jake said. "And is that why the breach is unstable?"

"Part of it," Lange said. "I intended to make a door, you know. Not something that would remain permanently open. I thought it would close itself as soon as the machine turned off. A door can open and close. A breach, on the other hand... I hope the changes Dax and I made to the machine are slowly sealing it."

"So far, so good, last we heard," Jake said, but it worried him anyway. Maybe it was just the guilt of being down here, safe and cozy, enjoying Lange's company a little too much.

Their conversation had forced him to think of the Nowhere for what it was: an enormous, pulsing cloud that touched all of reality and moved in incomprehensible, deadly ways. It had spilled into Lange's lab, stretching and pinching and twisting the space. Like the ocean, it was both the medium through which dangerous things traveled and a danger itself. Something could pass through. Another wave could come. No matter how cheerful Emil had sounded on their call, other than reporting that greenhouse leak, Jake couldn't shut out Miriam's voice saying "*closing* isn't the same as *closed*."

COMPLETELY UNRELATED TO SPACE

THE CHILL OF TALKING ABOUT THE BREACH PASSED, and their rapport remained easy through the rest of the evening. Jake's night on the floor was uncomfortable but worth it, because they made it through all of the next day without incident. Lange even had a remote appointment with his therapist.

On Tuesday evening, Jake lay down to sleep on the floor in an unexpectedly good mood. He could do this, he thought. He could be friends with Lange and ignore any other feelings he was having. He was okay. Lange was going to be okay.

A crash woke him up in the middle of the night. It sounded like a fucking stampede. He bolted for Lange's door. It was ajar, but Jake held the doorknob with one hand and knocked with the other, not wanting it to swing open and surprise Lange.

"Lange?"

"I apologize for waking you," Lange said from inside the room. "It was the bookshelf."

That explained what Jake had heard: thud after thud of

dozens of books falling, followed by the shelves themselves. The room must be a mess. It didn't explain *why*, but Jake repressed that question.

"Are you hurt?"

"No."

"Can I come in?"

"I suppose," Lange said.

Jake was in the clothes he'd had on under his spacesuit, an undershirt and form-fitting shorts, and it didn't occur to him that Lange wouldn't be dressed similarly until he had to avert his eyes from the proof. Lange was sitting up in bed with the blankets pulled to his waist, his slender brown torso exposed to the cool air. Jake didn't want to speculate about whether the lower half of his body was as bare as the upper half.

It probably was, though. *Damn it, stop that.*

Two large bookshelves leaned precariously atop haphazard mounds of books. Jake bent to pick up a stray paperback from the floor, and then paused with the book in his hands, wondering where to put it. *A Field Guide to Arctic Alaska*, it said. There were some pine trees and a bird on the cover.

Jake ran his fingers down the cracks in the spine. "Do you want to tell me what happened?"

"I don't even want to tell myself what happened."

Jake set the paperback down on the edge of the bed, carefully not looking at Lange on the other side. He crouched and took hold of one of the shelves. "I'll just... pick these up, then."

The shelf was half as heavy as it should have been. Lange was helping him. They righted both shelves and then Jake began clearing the books from the floor. He was almost tired enough to accept it when books jumped into the air around him, or maybe he'd just spent so much time with Lange that he was getting used to it.

A book missed its mark, too tall for the shelf it was aimed at, and dropped to the floor. Jake noticed a second book trembling, and risked a glance back at Lange.

He was still very probably naked, but if Jake forced himself not to think about that, he could notice other things: how rigid and miserable and grim Lange looked, the way he was holding himself motionless, the sweat at his temples. The blankets were wrinkled in a way that suggested the clenching of clammy palms.

A nightmare. Jake would bet on it. It was bad fucking news for both of them if Lange was tipping over bookshelves in his sleep, and Jake had no idea what to do about it.

He reached for the nearest floating book, one that was wobbling alarmingly, and took hold of its glossy paperback cover like he was scooping up a wounded bird. *Principles of Topology* was printed in white on the red spine. Jake guided the volume toward the shelf. Maybe Lange shouldn't be doing telekinetic shit right now. "This can wait until tomorrow."

"And what do you suggest we do instead?"

The question was petulant, not suggestive, which was a relief. Jake wished, briefly, that he could be a person who didn't find relief in that.

He was also a little bit disappointed, but he slammed the door on that thought.

"What do you want to do?" he asked Lange cautiously. "Do you want to go back to sleep?"

Lange moved then, a single turn of his face away from Jake.

Jake knew a *no* when he saw one. "How about watching

something? Doesn't look like you have a wall display, but I have a tablet."

"Is that what you would do?"

Jake inferred the end of that question as *if you'd had a nightmare and were afraid to go back to sleep*. "Yeah. Or read, maybe."

Lange eyed the half-cleared wreckage of his personal library.

"I'll get the tablet," Jake said and left.

When he came back into the room, Lange had put some clothes on, thank fuck. Jake reached across the huge expanse of bed between them and handed him the tablet.

"Uh," he said, unsure how to make his exit. "I hope it helps."

"You're not staying?"

Lange didn't often sound like that. Uncertain. Scared.

Shit. Lange had gotten dressed *for him*. He'd considered Jake's comfort. And he'd done it while he was a giant mess. He wanted Jake to stay pretty goddamn badly.

Jake only felt a little foolish, crawling onto the bed. He kept a healthy distance—and the bed covers—between himself and Lange, but the tablet screen was small, so seeing required him to get a little closer.

Something about Lange scrolling through all the stuff Jake had watched recently embarrassed him, even though it was just a bunch of sci-fi and a couple of comedies. Okay, one movie was less comedy and more romance. The bright colors of that one's little icon stood out. It shouldn't have felt so revealing. It wasn't like Jake had been watching porn.

Given what Lange had said about his sexual history, he probably watched—*nope*. Not thinking about that.

Thankfully, Lange's only comment on Jake's entertainment habits was, "You like science fiction."

"Don't you? What else would make you want to move to space?"

"A well-funded research opportunity."

Probably not the best topic of conversation. Jake steered them back toward movies instead of reality. "You don't like sci-fi at all?"

"They get everything wrong," Lange said.

"Well, sure, but it's cool," Jake said, which slid right off Lange. Jake had a lot more to say in defense of science fiction, but it occurred to him that it was still too close to home. Nothing set in space would soothe Lange's fears. "What do you like to watch?"

"I don't engage with much fiction of any kind, and I prefer my non-fiction in written form."

Right. Jake should have expected that. If Lange had said that when they'd been in Facility 17, he might have interpreted it as *fuck off*, but now he was pretty sure Lange was asking for help. Well, not so much asking as telling, but still. All that aloof haughtiness was masking an *I don't know what to do*.

"There's this cooking show that Lenny and Chávez love," Jake said, having cast around for something completely unrelated to space—or sex.

"Cooking," Lange repeated skeptically.

"Or baking, I guess? I think they make cakes. I've never watched it." Jake was already reaching over to select the first episode. "Hey, even if you hate it, it'll be a good distraction, right?"

Their arms brushed as Jake finished—he'd overestimated the distance between them—and Jake stiffened and scooted over. "Sorry."

The dispassionate glance Lange directed at him was

more embarrassing than any accidental touch. "Your virtue is safe."

"Fuck off."

"I like *sex*, McCreery. Not assaulting the unwilling. You've made your unwillingness clear."

"Not so long ago, you would really have hated that contact," Jake pointed out, because it was easier to make this about Lange's comfort than his own. He hoped Lange wouldn't bring up their earlier touching as a counterpoint. They hadn't been *in bed* then. Or they had, sort of, but—it was different. "The show is starting."

It was good to have something else to focus on—or it would have been, if Jake had been capable of focusing on anything other than Lange right next to him. Not touching, but close enough that Jake could feel how much warmer he was than the rest of the room. It had been a mistake not to get under the blankets.

Lange had characterized him as *unwilling*, and the whole problem was that he wasn't. He'd never been willing before. It scared the shit out of him.

Did Lange's comment about his "virtue" mean Lange knew—

The big orange cat jumped onto the bed and curled up next to Jake's hip. Jake shifted to make space for him, bumping into Lange again.

"You're cold," Lange observed, and damn him, he was right. This far from the wood stove, Jake didn't have nearly enough clothes on. "It's unpleasant to be cold. One of many disagreeable aspects of being embodied."

Lange made space so Jake could get under the blankets, and Jake shoved his legs under without thinking too hard about what he was doing. They rearranged themselves so

Jake could see the display in Lange's lap if he craned his neck a little, and resumed watching the episode.

During the second episode, the tuxedo cat joined them, making himself at home on Lange's other side. Lange shifted to accommodate the animal, and then he and Jake were shoulder to shoulder, and it felt... good. Too good.

He wanted to lean his thigh against Lange's, or drape his arm around Lange and pull him in. To feel the weight of his body. To smell him.

How *did* people do this? Jake had barely managed to put his hand on Lange's shoulder earlier, and now they were in bed, and not fully clothed, and the idea of verbalizing his desire was mortifying. And *desire* was the right word for it, even if all he wanted now was to cuddle. It didn't feel chaste; it felt overpowering.

If Lange had asked him to summarize the plot of what they were watching, Jake couldn't have come up with two words to string together, even though every single episode could be described as *the contestants bake something*. His whole brain was dedicated to assessing the space between them, pinpointing every place they were in contact, calculating the likelihood that Lange would comment or react negatively if Jake got closer. If he could have moved Lange with his mind, it would already have happened. *There* was a deeply embarrassing thought. Fuck.

"McCreery."

"Jake," he blurted. "My name is Jake."

"I know your name," Lange said. "Are you not enjoying this show? You seem ill at ease."

Well, he'd fucked this up. "Sorry. You're the one who had the nightmare. You shouldn't have to comfort me."

There was a long moment of only the TV contestants

chatting, and then Lange paused the episode. "Is that what you want? Comfort?"

Jake reached over and pressed play. "I'm good. Don't worry about it."

Lange looked right at him, which was a lot like being punched, except *good*, and Jake couldn't explain that. How had he been looking at Lange all this time and not seeing him? The lustre of his dark brown skin in the blue light of the screen. The sharpness of his jaw, the fullness of his lips. That beard. Those brows. The symmetry. It was like somebody had designed his face with exactly the right distribution of straight lines and curves, like he was the expression of some perfect mathematical formula.

The rest of him wasn't too bad, either.

Watch the show, he told himself, and tore his gaze away. With what little attention he possessed, he bore witness to the meticulous creation of a tiered cake. He petted the cat at his side and *almost* stopped yearning.

And then Lange began to nod off.

His head dipped. He swayed. Jake froze. If he let Lange fall fully asleep, he could slip out afterward. It would be cruel to wake Lange just as he was finally relaxing.

When Lange leaned against him at last, he slid down until his head lolled against Jake's chest. It required no thought to wrap an arm around his shoulders to steady him. He weighed less than Jake expected—not crushingly heavy, not enough for how big the moment felt—and more. It was the heat, he thought, or maybe the solidity and the texture of him, the knob of bone at the end of his shoulder, the way Jake's fingers sank into the firm flesh of his upper arm. His ribs expanded and contracted with breath.

Jake had never been this close to anyone. Not like this.

And God, a few days ago Lange would have murdered

anyone who touched him. He definitely hadn't smelled like soap or fresh laundry then. Yet here he was, nestled against Jake, sighing contentedly in his sleep.

Oh. Shit. Jake had been planning to disentangle himself.

The thought made him tighten his arm ever so slightly. It would be impossible to get out without waking Lange. He'd already had a bad night. Lange needed this.

And if it was exactly what Jake wanted, well, that was a stroke of luck. And it had never happened before, so he had to memorize how it felt. Enjoying it didn't mean he was taking advantage. The only harm done was that now, every other night for the rest of his life, he'd know what he was missing.

[10]
FALSE PREMISE

FOR A SECOND AFTER WAKING, SOL WAS HAPPY.

It lasted only a second, and then he knew, with a dread that hardened into certainty, that something was wrong. He should not have allowed himself to fall asleep in such a way —he wished he could return to ignorance of how much he liked the heavy embrace of McCreery's body, a sensation he could not remember ever having experienced, one he was now condemned to long for—but that was negligible.

There was someone in the cabin.

McCreery was still remarkably deep in sleep, so it was trivial to extricate himself. It was not yet light outside the windows and the house was silent. Solomon couldn't say what had alerted him to the intruder. A disturbance in space, perhaps. A shift in the accounting of presences and absences, something his body now tracked even as he slept.

He crept to the bedroom door, suspended open by a gap the width of a house cat, and paused. The unseen person on the other side was small, he felt. Solomon mentally located one of the kitchen chairs and lifted it into the air, letting it hover. Just in case.

The knock, when it came, was tentative.

Solomon stepped aside and swung the door open in one movement.

The person's eyes glinted in the darkness like a cat's. Solomon's heart seized, and a blink later, the puzzle pieces aligned: standard humans from this world did not have a reflective surface to their eyes, therefore the person across from him wasn't one, therefore it was a stranger or... *Kit*. A runner.

Solomon had been the first to hypothesize that runners could travel through the Nowhere because they had one parent from this reality and one parent from elsewhere. This wasn't to say runners weren't human, exactly. Many, many strands of the multiverse were populated with humans, even some who were identical to the ones here. But the multiverse was infinite, and it contained infinite variations on what it meant to be human.

Some could move things with their mind, for example. Others could teleport.

The knowledge calmed Solomon's fears, but he didn't relax. Kit had good reason to hate him.

Kit had come via the Nowhere.

Solomon did not shudder at the thought of the void. The tapetum lucidum suggested that Kit had good night vision; he would have seen.

Discreetly, Solomon set the kitchen chair back in place next to the table. He gestured at the living room, and Kit let him pass. Solomon closed the door quietly behind him. He didn't turn on the lights, testing his hypothesis that Kit could see him.

"I'm actually looking for Jake," Kit said. He followed Solomon a few steps into the living room with no trouble. "We need him."

"He's asleep," Solomon said, defensive of McCreery's rest. The man had suffered through two-and-a-half nights on the floor. He deserved to stay in Solomon's bed.

"Yeah, as you can probably tell from the fact that I jumped into your living room in the pre-dawn hours, it's kind of an emergency."

"Kind of," Solomon repeated. "It's not the breach, then."

"Yesterday we had a leak in the greenhouse. Now we have a burst pipe or something. It's a mess in there."

"That sounds like a flaw in the greenhouse design, not an emergency."

"Are you blaming Emil—" Kit interrupted himself, forcing an inhalation and then a slow, exaggerated exhalation. "Jesus fucking Christ, Lange, can you stop being a dick and use that huge brain you supposedly have for *one* second?"

Solomon had, unfortunately, ruled out his own suggestion even as he'd spoken the words. There was nothing wrong with the greenhouse design; he wasn't sure why he'd said it, except to make Kit angry enough to leave. That hadn't worked, and now he had to confront the obvious. The expensive, newly constructed facility was unlikely to experience sudden and massive plumbing problems without interference.

Something had damaged the pipes.

"You haven't seen it," Solomon said. "Whatever caused this problem."

"Emil thinks it would be safer if we investigated the area with one of Jake's robotic probes, in case whatever's in the pipes is... infectious or whatever."

"'Infectious' implies you think the cause is animate."

"I don't think anything, Lange. I'd know a lot more if

you'd wake up your fuckbuddy in there so he can do his job."

"We were not having sex," Solomon said, only because he thought McCreery would appreciate the clarification.

"As long as you didn't kill him, I don't care what you were doing," Kit said. "And if you won't go get him, I will."

Solomon should have expected the topic to come up. "I am sorry. I regret that I hurt you. I don't intend to hurt you or anyone else again."

Kit narrowed his eyes. "But you didn't ever *intend* to, did you?"

"No. I was—" something caught in his throat when he tried to speak about that painful, fragmented time "—not rational."

"Yeah," Kit said emphatically. He didn't say *apology accepted*, as McCreery had, but some things were too much to hope for.

How absurd that Solomon had once mistaken his body for the worst of his burdens; it was his actions that weighed on him. Nothing could lift that.

Solomon tried to breathe the way McCreery had in sleep, deep and slow. His guilt would keep, and right now there was bad news to face. But he could handle this. They could handle this together. "It is unwise for me to travel via the Nowhere. I will wake McCreery and we will return to the facility in the pod."

"Who said anything about both of you returning?" Kit asked. "I came here to get Jake. We don't need you."

That might have stung, had Solomon not already arrived at a different, more troubling conclusion. "Unfortunately for all of us, I think you do."

———

WHEN JAKE DRIFTED out of sleep, there was white sunlight reflecting off the snow outside the windows, a third cat in the bed, and no Lange. He knew he hadn't dreamed last night only because there was no other explanation for why he'd be in Lange's bed. And there were still dozens of books on the floor.

Lange came in while Jake was studying the cat asleep next to his feet—the one that had appeared some time in the night in total silence. It was a tabby and, if he recalled correctly, the only female of the three.

"This one doesn't like me," Jake said. "She glares a lot."

"That's not a glare, that's just her face," Lange said. "Lise Meitner wouldn't have slept next to you if she didn't like you."

"Oh." Jake swallowed. He'd been so swept up in last night that he hadn't accounted for the inevitable awkwardness of waking up in Lange's bed. They had to fit this into the framework of their strange new relationship. *Friendship*. Allegedly.

Lange saved him from answering in the worst possible way. "I made coffee. You should probably drink some, because we have to go back up. There's a problem with the breach."

"What?" Jake sat straight up. "Fuck. That's bad. What happened? Is everyone okay?"

Lange handed him the mug and went through his questions methodically. "As far as I know, no one is hurt. They want you to go back up because there has been a flood in the greenhouse and your robots were deemed the safest method of investigating the area."

"Shit. It's not as bad as it could be, but I don't like it. What makes you so sure it's related to the breach?"

"Process of elimination, mostly."

"Mostly?"

"The C," Lange said.

It took Jake a moment to parse that statement as anything other than *the sea*, and either way it barely made sense. Lange must be talking about the sounds he'd heard coming from the breach. Jake opened his mouth, unsure what question would come out. He had too goddamn many.

Lange spoke first. "We have to go. I'm going to feed the cats."

"You're going to leave them here?" Jake risked petting Lise Meitner. She would have fucked him up for trying if she'd been awake. In sleep, she purred.

"The trip down distressed them so much, I can't make them go back up. And I don't want them in danger," Lange said. "One of the runners will feed them if we're gone long."

"You know people who can travel across the universe in the blink of an eye and all you want from them is to feed your cats."

"It's a better use of their talents than Quint would have made," Lange said, and Jake couldn't disagree with that.

He'd been in the military, so he was no stranger to working for a massive institution whose goals were at odds with his values, but having worked for Quint was such a gut-punch of guilt. Jake hadn't known about Quint's secret prison cell, but shit. He'd worked for a guy who'd built a *secret prison cell*.

That didn't say much for his judgment.

He got up. It took no time to get ready since he had nothing with him. The only preparation Lange made was to leave extra food for the cats—and to give each of them an elaborate and solemn goodbye, which Jake had to stop watching because it was making his face do things he couldn't control.

Half an hour later, they were hiking down to the pod, leaving boot prints and robot treads in the slushy snow. Lange had brought his guitar, which Jake wished was just an attempt to reconnect with his old life and not a link to the eerie music of the breach.

The woods were quiet. No birdsong. Jake thought of finding *A Field Guide to Arctic Alaska* among Lange's books as their path wove through the pines.

The pod was covered with snow. Jake began to clear it with his hands, and then the layer coating the fuselage simply slid to the ground.

"Thanks," Jake said. He lifted the canopy, reached inside, and picked his helmet up from where he'd dropped it on the floor after their near-crash landing. He'd *wanted* to leave then. That felt like a long time ago.

Jake swallowed. "You know, I—I liked it here more than I expected to."

What a useless thing to say. He shoved his helmet on and turned away from Lange. "You ready to go back up?"

"Of course not," Lange said. He took the helmet that Jake passed him.

"Can I ask you something?" Jake said, stopping before he got into the pod. "If you're so outdoorsy, didn't you hate living in space?"

"False premise."

"You're trying to say you're not outdoorsy?"

"What I like about nature is the sense of peace I get from observing something outside myself," Lange said. "That feeling is readily available in space."

"Okay, I get that."

After a pause, Lange said, his voice soft, "It was the first technique I learned, as a lonely, depressed teenager, that worked. It sounds so simple as to be useless: 'look at a bird.'

But when you're suffering, sometimes picking something from your surroundings to stare at is the only thing you can do. And sometimes it helps."

"Yeah, I—I think that's why I took up building stuff. Fiddling. Using my hands."

Lange accepted this blundering confession, which was maybe thirty percent of what Jake wanted to convey, with grace. He'd fixed his attention on the tree line, sparing Jake the ordeal of being looked at. "I came to like the wilderness for its own sake, I think. As you did."

It wasn't the wilderness Jake liked, but if he said so, they might have to reexamine their delicate new *friendship*. Talk about a false premise. So instead he ran through his pre-flight check, turned on the antigrav, and launched the pod into space.

11

LEAK

SOLOMON HAD BURNED HOT AND COLD WITH ANXIETY since the asteroid that housed Facility 17 had come into view. Now that they were standing in the dripping greenhouse, the useless and overpowering sensation would not leave him.

He could hear the A flat and the G of the breach.

No. No matter how eerie, he refused to let the dissonance of the lab haunt him. He would simply focus his attention elsewhere. He was here in the greenhouse. With McCreery.

The air smelled like dirt. Cloudy, brown water sluiced off the plantings and table edges to pool ankle-deep under the hole in the ceiling. A length of green, patinated copper pipe hung down like a dead limb. The remaining plumbing was too shadowed to see.

The hole was in the white plastic part of the ceiling, which extended halfway across the room before meeting the windowed steel construction that comprised the majority of the greenhouse. Every windowpane was covered with a

UV-filtering blind that turned the near-constant sunlight red.

"It was sudden," Singh was explaining. "One day it was a small leak and then a flood came pouring through the ceiling. I've never seen a pipe break like that."

McCreery nodded and tapped at his tablet to direct the robot up the wall and toward the problem. He didn't speak to the robot when other people were watching; he'd been embarrassed when Solomon and Dax had caught him in the lab.

The robot's treads had been magnetized, so it managed to climb the interior wall and the ceiling with no difficulty. Once it reached the site of the damage, McCreery paused to study his tablet, which was showing whatever the robot's camera picked up. He offered it to Singh, and the two of them bent their heads over it.

Solomon didn't like their closeness. The feeling itself was uncomfortable, and so was the recursion: he didn't like not liking it. He shifted his weight, focused on the droplets of water falling by ones and by twos, and tried not to think about McCreery or the sound.

"I think these other pipes are damaged," McCreery was saying. "It's almost like they were corroded."

"What could do that?" Singh asked.

Instead of answering, McCreery walked over to Solomon and held out the tablet, saying, "Lange, take a look at this."

It startled him to be included, and to have McCreery's shoulder brush his own, but nothing was as much of a shock as McCreery saying, in a low voice, "You doing okay?"

"What will you do if I say no?" Solomon murmured.

"Dunno. Depends what you want, I guess."

What Sol wanted was to be back in the cabin with

McCreery, preferably in bed, not here in this damned facility where every breath was a labor. He wanted not to feel responsibility dragging down his shoulders when he looked at the hole in the greenhouse ceiling.

And he wanted very much for the tablet screen in McCreery's hands not to show any evidence of the breach's influence.

He wasn't going to get any of those things.

"Worry about this, not me." Solomon tapped the screen, which now showed the dangling pipe in close-up.

McCreery switched from the live video feed to a control screen. A moment later, one of the robot's metal arms extended to take hold of the pipe. The thirty-centimeter-long piece broke away entirely, loosing water onto the tables and floor below. The robot brought the fragment closer to its lens, manipulating it so the camera stared down its hollow length. As green down the inside as it was on the outside, the pipe looked like a normal piece of copper tubing to Solomon—excepting its ragged edges.

The robot raised its camera and swiveled it. Solomon braced for some horrible revelation, but the tablet screen showed only the cramped, wet interior of the ceiling, the pipes grey in the darkness.

His mind spun possible theories. Some kind of emanation from the breach, something he couldn't see or sense, might be the cause. Radiation. A local spatial distortion. Or perhaps time was passing faster in this one spot, causing the pipes to degrade? He needed to narrow the possibilities.

McCreery switched the camera off and the screen went dark. The robot retreated from the hole and rolled back down the wall until it stopped at McCreery's feet, still carrying the length of pipe. McCreery's fingers moved over the tablet. The robot put a second arm on the length of pipe and snapped it in half.

"She shouldn't be able to do that, not so easily," McCreery said. "Something weakened those pipes. We should watch for leaks in other parts of the facility."

Why had the leak emerged in this spot and not elsewhere? Was it random?

McCreery pulled his spacesuit gloves out of his pocket, put them on, and crouched down. He lifted one piece of pipe out of the robot's grip and said, "This is way lighter than it should be. And there's some kind of residue coating it."

Sol's heart seized at the sight of McCreery examining the pipe. Even an arm's length away was too close to his face. There was no telling what he was breathing in.

Equally worrisome, Solomon doubted that an emanation from the breach would leave residue. But a biotic explanation presented itself.

An alien.

A living being did not necessarily have motives, but his shift from a physical explanation to a biotic one raised the question. Why would an alien come through the breach and cause a leak?

A strange method of sabotage, if that's what it was. If one wanted to cause destruction by weakening metal, surely the greenhouse's steel provided a more logical target. Breaking the greenhouse windows wasn't the most efficient method of killing everyone in the facility, if that was the goal, but it would drastically interfere with their safety. And if whatever was in the facility corroded copper or other metals, it could do far, far more damage to the asteroid that housed them.

Not wanting to incite panic or draw attention to his

own grim reasoning, Solomon only said, "We should be wearing protective gear."

Singh nodded. "Good point. Let's get that sample to one of the labs. We're short on personnel due to, uh, putting our two senior scientists in prison, but I'll do what I can."

"McCreery and I have the least exposure, if there is a contaminant in the air. We can suit up and gather data using McCreery's robot." Solomon took a deep breath. "We'll start with my lab. You and the others should keep close watch on yourselves for any possible symptoms."

Singh drew his brows together. "Did you just—never mind. Thank you for volunteering."

"It's necessary. I am responsible for what has happened here and for what might happen next. This facility contains the breach. We can't evacuate until it's closed. And we should consider keeping it open, since we may need to send something back through it."

"Evacuation will be a last resort, but we will if we have to," Singh said. His tone was agreeable, but it was clearly a disagreement. And an assertion of his authority.

Solomon bristled. Did these people want him to accept responsibility or not? "You cannot—"

"Hey, let's maybe cross that bridge when we come to it, okay?" McCreery said. "Nobody's hurt. It's just a leak. As soon as we figure out what's causing it, I'll start work on repairs to the water recycling in here. Not saying we shouldn't be cautious or think ahead, but... one step at a time. Let's find out what we're dealing with here."

"Right," Singh said and followed McCreery and the robot out the door.

Solomon shut it behind them, blinking at the change in color. Unlike the red interior of the greenhouse, the hallway was cold, fluorescent white—until the low hum of electricity coalesced into a buzz and the lights went out.

———

JAKE DIDN'T EVEN HAVE time to turn on his tablet's flashlight before the hallway lights came back on. Still, that split second of darkness had set his heart racing.

"There's a backup fuel cell," he said, not sure who he was reassuring. The backup didn't matter, not if something had broken the wiring like it had broken the pipes.

His tablet had a map of the facility's electrical wiring. He opened it to find it scattered with flashing red. Fuck. That was a lot of open circuits for one man to fix.

Lange peered over his arm and said, "That's useful as a map of its movements."

"Great. There's an 'it,'" Jake said.

"If we assume it came from the breach," Lange started. He touched the screen to trace a winding path through the map. "It's meandered through the electrical wiring and the pipes all up and down the left side of the facility. If I had to guess, it was last here."

He tapped the medical exam rooms at the top of the map, both of which were encircled with red, and asked, "Why stop there? Why hasn't it moved down the right side of the map?"

"An important question, but we'd better suit up before we figure out where the fuck it went," Jake said. "And I think we should cut the power before this gets any worse. That means we'll lose everything, including the gravity generator."

"The thermal management system will stop working," Lange said. "As will the machine."

"No comms, either," Emil said. "I'll find the others and make sure they know."

But first, he walked back to the greenhouse and touched the door so it slid open. "Carbon dioxide scrubbers," he said, gesturing at the plants. "I'll leave that open just in case."

"I need you to shut off the water, too. And that's a good reminder that every door in this place has a goddamn electronic lock," Jake said. "Better leave them all open. Whatever it is we're dealing with, it's in the walls anyway. Doors will only hinder us. Emil, if you gather everyone in Heath's lab, we'll find you after we flip the breaker."

Emil nodded and walked off. Jake and Lange went back to the dock to fetch their helmets out of the pod. The lights went on and off twice on their walk, and the third time the hallway stayed dark. Jake flipped the flashlight on his tablet and tried to ask Eliza to turn hers on, but she wasn't responding to his tablet anymore because the goddamn comms were down. Fuck.

He swallowed. "Eliza, lights?"

She obliged him right away.

Out of habit, he said, "Good girl."

"You don't talk to her in front of other people." Lange paused briefly before *her*, like he'd considered saying *it* and then changed his mind, which Jake wished didn't mean so much to him.

"I feel weird about it."

"But you do talk to her in front of me," Lange said.

"Lange, a *thing* came through the rip in space-time that is *still open* a short walk from where we're standing and now we have to walk around in the dark trying to find it before it does enough damage to permanently prevent us from closing the breach. Is *this* really what you want to talk about?"

"I have," Lange said at length, "no further comment."

Jake couldn't even see Lange without shining the flashlight in his face, but he knew Lange was smiling because he could feel *himself* smiling. Like Lange's humor was catching or something. Ridiculous. He should check the oxygen levels once he got to the breaker room. He might already be losing his mind. Neither of them had any reason to smile.

Despite his advice to Emil about leaving all the doors open, Jake closed the bulkhead to the dock once they'd suited up and he'd picked up his tools. The last thing they needed was for all their air to leak out.

He checked the map on his tablet again. It was probably out of date by now, but it was better than nothing. Fifteen open circuits to fix, plus the pipes in the greenhouse—and those were just the problems he knew about.

And the ones he knew how to fix.

When they found the thing that had come through the breach, Jake had no idea what they were going to do. Ask it politely to leave? Kill it? They didn't even know what it looked like.

"Let's flip the breaker," he said to Lange. "I know how to do that, at least."

The power panel and the gravity generator were located in a small room off the gym, which was just down the hall. A short walk. He sent Eliza ahead. She lit her own way, a little rolling beacon, but he swept the beam of his flashlight through the darkness beside and behind her.

The asteroid that housed Facility 17 was enormous. Most of it was still an untouched lump of metal. The portion that had been carved out for human use included not only the greenhouse, but a gym with a full-size basketball court. Jake and Lange entered the empty court behind Eliza.

Jake thought of once having been in his middle school gym long after the rest of the basketball team had gone home. His dad had forgotten to pick him up after a game. He'd had to wait by the exit, staring at his feet while his impatient coach pressed the push bar of the door, not opening it, but ready, like Jake's dad would show up any second. In the end, Jake and the coach had stood still so long that the motion-sensing lights had shut off.

Being forgotten was nothing new for Jake, and his time on the team hadn't lasted, but that moment—the small window framing the half-lit, empty parking lot, the vast darkness of the gym—had endured. He'd never cared for crowds, but it was far worse to be in a place that *should* have been crowded, should have been bounding with people and noise and lights, but wasn't.

At the half-court line, Eliza shuddered to a stop.

"Eliza?"

She beeped in recognition of her name, and her light had stayed on, so it couldn't be a battery problem. The beam of his flashlight wove through the darkness. There was nothing blocking her way.

"Why can't she move?" he asked Lange. No. Wait. Forcing himself to sound less panicked, he rephrased. "Can you move her?"

There was a long moment of silence. Lange was probably concentrating, which he always did with perfect stillness, no lip-biting or twitching involved.

"I could move her," Lange finally said. "But she weighs more than she should."

"The gravity generator's glitching," Jake said, relief at identifying the problem mixing with dread. He shone his flashlight at the door to the storage room where the huge machine was kept. Flipping the main breaker in that same room would cut the power to everything, the gravity generator included, and solve this problem. But they had to get there first. "It's all the way across the court. Do you think the whole room has heavy gravity? What do you think we're dealing with? One-point-five g? More?"

"I don't think it's enough to kill us immediately," Lange said.

"Your bedside manner sucks."

"I'll try to deliver my future conjecture in a more reassuring tone," Lange said. "I can't calculate the g-force by feel, but my best guess is something in the range you suggested. Two g, perhaps. More importantly, I can't manipulate something I can't see—not if I don't already know where it is. I don't think it would work for you to describe the room and the gravity generator to me. We have to cross the gym to turn it off."

"*I* will walk across the room," Jake said. "*You* will stay right here and not risk falling and breaking your damn legs."

"My coordination has improved considerably in the past few days." There was a tiny huff in the darkness, its sound caught and amplified by the microphone built into Lange's helmet. "But you're right. It would be a foolish risk."

Lange thought Jake was right and wasn't gonna be a stubborn asshole about it? Shit. The universe *was* all fucked up. Good thing Lange couldn't see the look on Jake's face. "Carrying twice your own weight would be a feat even if you were in the best shape of your life. I'm... well, it's not gonna be pretty."

"I am familiar with the concept of gravity."

"Yeah, I *know*," Jake said, wishing his helmet wasn't preventing him from covering his face with his hands. It turned out the only thing worse than accidentally explaining gravity to a famous physicist was trying to explain your feelings to that very same physicist. "I just—I'm watching out for you, not insulting you. You get that, right?"

"Yes."

"Okay, well, I'm going now," Jake said, caught off guard by Lange's earnest answer. God, what were they *doing*, talking about this when the world was falling apart.

Jake walked toward the spot where Eliza had gone still, his suit and his pack and the flashlight in his hand all weighing what they usually did. The magnetized soles of his boots tapped against the wood. He'd feel silly if they'd had that whole conversation for nothing and they could've just walked across the court.

As he passed the free throw line, something started to drag at him, pulling at his legs every time he lifted them, making his shoes thunk down heavier. By the time he'd made it to the center circle where Eliza was, he was panting. Cutting diagonally across the remainder of the court would get him to the door, but just like when he and Lange had navigated the distorted lab, the distance felt overwhelming.

His suit, the oxygen tank, the tools he was carrying, his fucking *body*—everything weighed too much. A hundred and ten extra kilos, maybe more. Even his blood was too heavy, and he could feel his heart frantically try to keep up his circulation. The dizziness lurking at the edges of his consciousness threatened to overwhelm him. He wanted to halt, to lie down, anything to get away from it, but if he did that, the gravity would just press him down into the floor. He'd be even more trapped.

There was nothing for it but to keep walking. Jake's legs resisted every lift and slammed down into every landing. Unaccustomed to this weight, his muscles no longer had the strength to control his movements, so the downward arc of each step nearly careened out of control. He wobbled, and his warning to Lange about falls and broken bones came back to him. That could happen to Jake, too. He tried to slow his already glacial pace.

"McCreery," Lange said, and the normal volume of his voice came as a shock. Jake had been walking for ages, but very little distance separated them. "Let me help."

"Don't come over here, that won't do any good."

"That is not what I intended to propose," Lange said.

"Oh." Jake panted. Even his brain was too heavy. He should have realized. "Telekinesis. Yeah, sure, why not. Do it. Throw me over there."

"I would prefer not to throw you," Lange said. "The likelihood that you will land poorly and break bones is too high, as you yourself pointed out. Also, I'm not certain I can lift you."

"You've done it in normal gravity. And you held the heat shield together. That was way heavier than me," Jake said, and then remembered Lange's bloody, sweaty face after they'd landed. "On second thought, scratch that."

"I wasn't worried about accidentally murdering the heat shield with telekinesis. *You* are not a ceramic panel."

"Yeah, I'm significantly easier to squish to death," Jake agreed. "What do you have in mind?"

"You'll have to keep walking. I will try to aid you where I can. This might not be... pretty, as you said."

"Hey, whatever gets us there," Jake said, a breathless laugh following the words.

Lange pointed his flashlight directly at Jake, just in case it wasn't clear that he meant to scrutinize every movement Jake made. Jesus.

Jake raised his knee to take a step and his leg jerked up

far faster and higher than he'd intended. It was easier than it should have been, but it wasn't a relief. Jake was already a little seasick, and being puppeteered via telekinesis made it worse. His foot came down to the ground more lightly, but no less abruptly, and then he raised his other leg. Maybe the motion was a little smoother the second time, but it was still weird as fuck.

It didn't feel like anything—or rather, it didn't feel like being touched. Lange was, presumably, pulling on Jake the same way he had been in the cabin kitchen, but the hyper-gravity made it hard to pay attention to any lesser sensation. Walking got a little easier but remained awkward, that was all.

"Thank fuck, we're almost there," Jake said out loud when they crossed the boundary line, and it was strange to think and say *we* when his was the only body in motion, but he absolutely could not think about the intimacy he had allowed Lange. He had a goal. Later, there'd be time to get philosophical. Or freaked out. Or horny. *Nope.*

There, that was the door.

The electronic door's circuit must still be working, because the door recognized his touch. It slid open at half-speed, all of its mechanisms grinding in protest at the extra weight. Jake was unspeakably grateful for its functioning.

He wasn't too exhausted to do a thorough check of the storage room with his flashlight before stepping inside. The gravity generator took up most of the space, a huge, square metal beast of a machine that came up to his waist.

Its once smooth surface was pitted with holes and streaked with rust.

He ran his flashlight over it again, unable to make sense of the sight. There was no discernible pattern to the damage. It looked like someone had poured corrosive acid over the top—except then he would have expected the liquid to run down the front of the machine in drips. Instead, the rough patches made irregular, loosely connected splotches.

Every exposed pipe and cable in the room was covered in them.

The room was empty, at least. He knelt down in front of the gravity generator—lowered himself with a groan, since as soon as he'd stepped into the room, Lange had stopped helping him—and entered the sequence of commands necessary to turn it off.

The change was instant. His lungs released. In the absence of hypergravity, the frenetic throb of his heart felt absurd. Jake would have floated off the floor if not for his magnetized boots.

Standing up too rapidly—fuck, he weighed *nothing*—and turning toward the breaker box on the wall nearly caused him to pass out. He switched off the power to the whole facility and then just stood there in the dark, one hand braced against the wall for reassurance, waiting for his pulse to slow.

"McCreery?"

Lange couldn't see him, but must have felt the change.

Still blinking away dizziness, Jake called, "I'm okay. You should come see this, though. Eliza, come here."

It was a relief when Eliza rolled into the room, unharmed. Lange followed her, the beam of his flashlight announcing his arrival. It had taken Jake an hour to cross the gym and they'd done it in seconds.

Lange halted not in front of the corroded generator but in front of Jake. He held his flashlight aloft and peered into Jake's face. "That drastic change in gravity put a great deal of stress on your body."

"Thanks, I'll take that into account next time."

Lange lowered the flashlight and continued to gaze at Jake. "Are you going to faint? If so, I can carry you."

Jake's cardiovascular system had been through enough in the past hour. He didn't need this—whatever it was, this useless fluttery feeling. And he shouldn't be feeling *anything* over Lange exhibiting basic human decency.

His voice low and raspy like something was stuck in his throat, Jake said, "Think you missed your moment, but I appreciate the offer. I actually called you in here to discuss *that*."

He swung his flashlight so it pointed at the rust-cankered generator.

"That's not good," Lange said.

"Uh huh," Jake said. He crouched down in front of the machine and opened the roll of tools he'd lugged all the way here. "I think we've gotta take it apart and see how far down the damage goes. For it to glitch like it did, something must be messed up inside. I need to see what it looks like."

"You have a hypothesis about what caused this," Lange said.

"Not much of one," Jake said. "But I'm guessing you have one, too."

"I do."

"Good. We'll compare notes. It's just another puzzle," Jake said. "Except for the part where if we don't solve it, we die and maybe all of reality goes with us."

For a long moment, there was only the tiny sound of Jake's screwdriver tapping and twisting screw heads.

Then, with his usual crisp detachment, Lange said, "Your bedside manner sucks."

12

DISTRACTION

Compared with McCreery, Solomon had exerted himself minimally, but his body was nevertheless exhibiting signs of stress: sweat, a rapid pulse, and a constriction in his chest that didn't correspond to any change in the environment. These were fear responses, he knew, but they were exaggerated. The damage to the gravity generator called for unease, not panic. Whatever had done that hadn't been present. As far as he could determine, Solomon was not now and had not recently been subject to a physical threat.

It was absurd that his body would yield to this overreaction simply because he'd momentarily lost sight of McCreery. The door had dragged itself open and McCreery had disappeared into the darkness and some prehistoric stratum of Solomon's brain had fired all its neurons in whatever pattern meant *he is going to die*. That had set all this nonsense in motion.

It was true that harm could have come to McCreery, either while he'd pushed himself through that zone of hypergravity or while he'd vanished into the storage room. But none had. He was fine now, walking at Solomon's side toward the lab where they'd meet the others. And *because* McCreery was fine, there was no reason that Sol should want to reach for him, to touch the small of his back or grip his shoulder, to make sure he was still there. Obviously he was.

Solomon extended his arm through the darkness behind McCreery's back, his fingers splayed open. He tried to imagine bridging the short distance between them, making contact, and couldn't. Slowly his hand curled in on itself. He withdrew.

This was a distraction. Solomon ought to be thinking of what he would report to the six remaining residents of Facility 17. They were standing in a loose circle in the lab, each holding a flashlight, and if not for the spacesuits and the modern laboratory, the scene might have resembled an occult ritual.

The second thing he noticed was that none of them were wearing helmets. They were all breathing the air.

"Lange, Jake, you made it back. Thanks for dealing with the power. You can take your helmets off, the air's free of contaminants. Better conserve the oxygen in case we really need it later," Singh said. Emil. That was what McCreery called him. Solomon should, too.

Dax nodded. "The six of us have had hours or possibly days of exposure and we're all in good health. The pipes and the wiring, not so much, but at least we can breathe."

Solomon removed his helmet but hung on to it, lest it float away. The lab benches, he noted, had been cleared of notebooks and test tubes and anything not bolted down.

The short, serious woman spoke next. Miriam. Her name was Miriam. He remembered that.

"Did you see it?" she asked.

In the bluish glow created by all the flashlights, Jake

looked pale. Paler than normal. Solomon curled his fingers into a fist at his side, willing himself to stop having these foolish reactions.

Jake was shaking his head. "We saw the damage it left behind in the gravity generator, but we didn't see anything, uh, alive."

"It damaged the gravity generator?" she asked. "This sounds more and more like sabotage."

"That's conjecture," Solomon said.

"Something destroys all our pipes and wiring and you think me saying 'sabotage' is *conjecture?*"

Her thick, dark brows arched high above her eyes. She'd put her arms on her hips, where there was a belt outside her spacesuit and a truncheon hanging by her thigh. Belatedly, Solomon remembered that Miriam's role on the team was as a security officer of sorts. She was thinking in terms of threats.

But so was he. And she was doing it wrong.

"It's not human," Solomon said. "Don't ascribe human motives to it."

"Things that aren't human can still hurt and kill us," she said. "I don't really care about why they're doing it. We need to discuss how we're going to kill this thing when we eventually run into it."

"We don't even know what it is," Solomon said. "What if it doesn't intend to harm us?"

"That's a hell of a leap to make," she said. "Have you looked around?"

"Hey, okay, let's not do this," Emil said. "I want to be clear on a few things before we continue this conversation. It seems like we all agree there is something alien in the facility with us. That residue we collected is likely biological in nature, although it doesn't resemble anything any of us have ever seen. It is of the utmost importance that we not transport whatever it is back to Earth, which means until we're more sure of what we're dealing with, nobody can leave—and nobody else should come here, not even via the Nowhere."

"Oh," Solomon said, his voice small. That was sensible, but it was bad news for his cats.

"Do you have something to say?" Emil asked.

"I was going to ask—" Solomon paused. His gaze fell on Kit, whose arms were crossed over his chest in his typical unfriendly posture. It was irrational to ask a person he'd nearly killed for a favor.

But the cats would go hungry. His heart seized.

"The cats," Solomon said, his throat half-closed.

"We left them on the surface," McCreery clarified. "We were hoping someone could check on them periodically."

"Sure," Kit said. "I'll message Laila or Aidan. They'll get someone to do it. No big deal."

Solomon gaped, almost too astonished to speak. "You'd do that?"

Kit rolled his eyes. "You know I'm the one who rescued your cats from the Nowhere, right? I'm not gonna leave them to starve. Those cats are, like, the single best thing about you."

That was undeniably true, but next to Solomon, McCreery stiffened, his spacesuit rustling. "Don't be—" he started, and Solomon laid a hand on his arm.

"Thank you," Solomon said to Kit, and then to everyone else, "That's all."

"Okay," Emil said. "Back to business. While we're all stuck here, be smart. Don't wander off on your own. Keep in regular touch with everybody. We'll sleep in shifts. Obviously with no power, some of our food is going to spoil, but there's only eight of us total, so we should have enough to get by. Once we're out of danger, getting the power back on will be a priority."

"We'll need power to run the machine," Solomon said, and Emil nodded at him, so he kept going. "Given the state of the gravity generator, and the likelihood that this entity arrived through the breach in my lab, our next step has to be examining the machine for damage. Closing the breach remains our first priority, and we can't do that without a functional machine."

Emil looked at Miriam, and she nodded her consent.

"We have to talk about the alien eventually," she said, her eyes on Solomon. "Intentionally or not, it *is* destroying the place we live."

"Ideally, it will return to its place of origin," Solomon said.

"And how do you plan to accomplish *that*?" Miriam asked. Her tone was harsh, though the question itself was perfectly fair.

"Okay," Emil interrupted. "You make a good point, but first things first, let's go look at the machine."

They crossed the hallway, Eliza at their heels. Their flashlight beams swept over the labyrinthine graffiti scrawled on the lab's walls and floor. Distortions glimmered in the air. The two curved parentheses of the machine still stood at the other end of the room. In the dark, at this distance, they looked the same. It might have been a hopeful sight—if the machine was still there, closing the breach would be possible—but Solomon could only feel dread.

The incessant whine of the breach, those two pitches a half-step apart, contributed to the feeling curdling in his stomach.

"I know you were the one who crossed this room last

time, and I know you can see the distortions, but I think you should let someone else do it today," Emil said.

Solomon recognized the gentleness in his tone and thought of McCreery saying *I'm not insulting you, I'm watching out for you.* McCreery, who was standing next to him, perhaps closer than was warranted. McCreery, who had subtly positioned himself between Solomon and the breach, as though his body could serve as one last defense against the dissolution of reality.

They were protecting him. But of course they would. They needed him to fix the problem he'd caused.

"If you help me navigate, we can send Eliza," Jake started.

"It's faster if I do it," Kit said.

Emil frowned at Kit, even though he'd asked for volunteers, and Kit was the only true runner among them. The task would be easiest and least risky for Kit. He could teleport. The Nowhere couldn't harm him. It was logical.

"Okay," Emil said after a pained silence. "Be careful."

Solomon might have scoffed at such an emotional reaction once, and he wished he still could. Instead he recognized himself in Emil's reluctance. When he'd been afraid in the basketball court, his fear had been *for* McCreery— and for himself, if he lost McCreery.

Solomon knew what a bad idea it was to get attached to anyone. People turned on you, or they left you, or they died. Suddenly, frequently, and inevitably. He'd confined himself to casual sex for good reason. It was a lapse in judgment for him to have allowed any non-sexual feelings for McCreery to develop. That way lay pain.

Kit had jumped to the other side of the room, taken some photos, and returned already. He offered the tablet to

Solomon, who tucked his helmet under one arm and swiped through the images of the machine.

The side not visible from where he was standing had long, ragged gashes in its metal, their edges dark with rust. The metal's surface, where it remained intact, had become lumpy. That was strange. The gravity generator hadn't looked like that.

"What is that?" Solomon asked, mostly to himself, not expecting an answer.

"I took another photo," Kit said. "It's weird-looking up close."

It was weird-looking enough in the first photo, but Solomon dutifully passed to the next. On closer inspection, what he had thought were lumps were dozens of tiny polyps, almost the same color as the steel but not quite. Their silvery flesh shimmered in the same way the distortions did. In the same way the mucus on the broken greenhouse pipes had.

Each polyp, once he zoomed in, was a tube with a tiny dark channel down its center. An orifice for food, perhaps. But what would it eat?

"Do you mind if I look?" McCreery asked quietly.

The sound of his voice brought the room rushing back to Solomon. He'd shut it all out while he was thinking, but here it was again: the murmur of his companions, the screech of the A flat and the G vying for dominance, and under it all, unflagging, the faint C.

Solomon held onto the tablet, but moved closer so McCreery could study the photo, too. McCreery remained blessedly silent, and Solomon sank back into contemplation.

The arrangement of the polyps on the metal had no discernible pattern. Their overall shape evoked a coral reef, something natural that had rooted and grown wherever it could. Up close, they reminded him of the pipes of a church organ.

"It's making the sound," he said, and then jerked his head up to see if any of the other people in the room understood him. They stared, waiting, so he repeated, "It's alive and it's making the sound."

"You mean the note you're hearing," McCreery said, first to catch on or first to believe him, and Solomon nodded. "You think this weird coral stuff is the alien."

"Yes."

"And the sound you're hearing is coming from it?"

"Yes," Solomon said again. "It's unclear how an organism like this would have damaged the greenhouse pipes or the wiring or the gravity generator. Perhaps it can move. Perhaps there's something else in the facility."

"The way the metal's corroded looks just like the gravity generator," McCreery said. "Which brings me to the only thing more important than figuring out what the alien can do—your machine is fucked."

———

DESPITE THE BAD NEWS, Emil had encouraged Jake and Lange to take the first rest. The weird little tubes growing on the machine didn't seem hellbent on killing anyone right that instant, and fixing the machine would require days, not hours.

It was midnight, Facility 17 time. Lange had been awake since long before they'd left the cabin, though Emil couldn't have known what an interrupted night they'd had.

Lange had shaken his head at the offer of rest, so Jake had seized the opportunity to speak his mind.

"I don't think I'm gonna be able to sleep right now," he'd

said. "I want to check the rooms where there are electrical faults. There might be more signs of the alien—or whatever. Lange can come with me."

"Have you considered that encountering the alien—or other aliens—might *not* put you at ease?" Emil had asked, and Jake had let slip something like a laugh. It wasn't funny, it was just true.

He needed to do this, regardless.

Eliza was recharging, so he and Lange walked to the medical exam room where the tablet's map showed an open circuit without her. It wasn't far, and it felt easy compared to the hypergravity, but his muscles ached. The need to check every part of the hallway for an alien presence stretched the distance into tedium.

Neither he nor Lange made any effort at conversation.

The exam room door was closed. Naturally, neither the electronic lock nor the opening mechanism was working.

Jake handed his flashlight to Lange, who didn't accept it. Oh, right. It hovered in place, lighting Jake's way while he unzipped the bag of tools he'd slung over one shoulder. He hunted through it, trying to keep everything strapped in its place so nothing floated away. He muttered, "For fuck's sake, it's a door. It works perfectly fine without electricity. Unless you ruin it because you're a rich asshole with no sense. I could kill Quint for this design."

"You didn't let *me* kill him," Lange said, and the accusation did make Jake laugh.

"I probably should've," he admitted, grunting as he worked a crowbar into the space between the door and its frame. "But you weren't in your right mind. I didn't want you to feel guilty later."

"I wouldn't have," Lange assured him. "Though you're

right that we should endeavor to commit only the most deliberate of murders."

Jake laughed again, half from the shock of it. It was uncomfortably close to home for a joke. He glanced over his shoulder.

"I regret hurting Kit," Lange said, suddenly serious. He met Jake's gaze. "And you. If I had—"

"But you didn't," Jake said. He turned back to the door and wedged the crowbar in until it scraped metal. "You don't have to apologize to me forever, you know. You didn't kill me or anyone else. And I know you regret all of it—attacking me and Kit, the accident, everything. And not all of that was your fault. Whatever there is to forgive you for, I do. I forgive you. You know that, right?"

"If you say so."

The latch broke. The dented door slid into its pocket, weightless and frictionless.

The room beyond was as unremarkable as ever: an exam chair, a counter with a sink, and a row of cabinets above. A box of tissues that had been on the counter was drifting in the air, probably moved by the room's ventilation rather than anything sinister. No sign of life. With the power off for the whole facility, this room's broken wiring was no longer obvious. Jake would have to take apart the walls to find the problem.

The ceiling tiles were all askew from the change in gravity, lifted by air currents and no longer resting in the grid that held them in place but drifting above it. He'd have to check up there, too.

"You feel anything? Hear anything?" Jake asked.

Lange shook his head.

They went in. On a second sweep of Jake's flashlight, one of the white ceiling tiles had a dark grey corner. He might have taken it for water damage, but there weren't any pipes up there.

"I'm gonna take a closer look at that," Jake said. He lifted his feet from the floor, releasing himself. He could have pulled himself toward the ceiling by using the cabinets as handholds, but he didn't have to. Lange lifted him higher. Jake let go of his flashlight, knowing not only that it wouldn't drop to the floor, but that Lange would position it somewhere useful for him.

"Thanks," Jake said. He took hold of one of the ceiling tiles and freed it from the grid, releasing a cloud of dust into the air that made him wish he was still wearing his helmet. He batted it away from his face.

The drop ceiling covered the facility's plumbing and electricity, which had been installed next to the bare surface of the asteroid. The rough metal glinted in the beam of his flashlight. He brought his gloved hand to the asteroid for no other reason than awe. He'd lived in space for twelve years and still the thought of it humbled him.

"McCreery," Lange said. "The dust."

Jake had paid no attention to the dust other than to get it out of his face, but in the flashlight beam, he could see it moving. In normal gravity, it would have scattered to the floor. In zero g, it ought to have hung suspended, moved only by the minor air currents in the facility.

It wasn't doing either of those things.

Instead the cloud had coalesced into a channel, and it was streaming toward the ceiling.

"Fuck," Jake said, removing another ceiling tile and leaving it hanging in the air. He grabbed the flashlight. "That's a leak."

Not a water leak. An *air* leak. One of the ragged indentations in the surface of the asteroid, all of which swallowed his flashlight beam into darkness—one of them was a hole to space.

"There are meters of asteroid between here and the vacuum," Lange said. "The presence of a channel that goes all the way through is extraordinary."

"Extraordinarily fucking bad."

Jake tried to keep his search thorough and organized, not moving the light too fast or too frantically. He just had to figure out where the leak was. If it was small, he could patch it. An air leak wasn't a death sentence. Any other day, he'd fix it without freaking out. All he needed was a deep breath—maybe not too deep. Methodically, he tracked the stream of dust in the air. The leak was close.

"The pipes, the wiring, the machines, the asteroid—" Lange started.

"I know," Jake said. Those holes in the gravity generator. The streaks of rust. He'd been planning to bring up his hypothesis earlier, but everything falling the fuck apart had distracted him. "Metal. It *eats* metal."

"Yes," Lange said. "I don't think the damage is sabotage. I think it's survival."

"Might still kill us, though."

"It is not ideal to be trapped on a large hunk of metal with something that consumes metal, no," Lange agreed.

There. That was where the air was going, a tiny crevice Jake would've mistaken for just one more rough spot in the rock face. Unlike a hole in a building on Earth, it didn't feel cold when he got close to it. There was no circulation of warm and cool air. Nothing emerged from the vacuum of space. If not for the dust, the leak would've been undetectable.

Thank fuck Lange had noticed it. Thinking about all the air they might have lost made him want to take a big gulp. His lungs felt empty, his heart too fast. Christ, he wanted to go home.

That wasn't a thought Jake had very often. Or ever.

If he had a home, this asteroid was it. He'd been living in various space stations and ships for twelve years. There was nothing for him on Earth. That wasn't home. But this little rock in the vastness of space, its systems crumbling one after the other, its air leaking into the void, its very existence threatened by the invisible gash in the lab—life didn't belong here. Fear and fatigue gnawed at his insides. He wanted to be somewhere else. What would it even mean to go home?

Jake glanced down at Lange. He cleared his throat. "Found the leak. Don't let this flashlight drift into my face, please."

When Lange held the flashlight still, Jake dug through his bag for a can of sealant. The hole was smaller than the diameter of his flashlight. It wouldn't be any trouble to patch. White foam hissed out of the spray can. It would harden into a seal in minutes. Jake could almost breathe again.

Something shot out of the hole.

"What the fuck?"

A jet of mercury-like liquid, painfully hot. Jake yelped as it burned his fingers. His whole body seized up. The thing reshaped itself into a wriggling, flat blob, gleaming like a puddle of gasoline. It rushed over the rock face and into the darkness.

"Jake!" Lange grabbed him by the ankle and yanked him toward the floor.

His fingers throbbed. Holy fuck.

An alien? A *different* alien?

Jake's mag boots clicked against the floor, grounding

him. When he'd seen that goo, he hadn't recognized it as... as an organism, if that's what it was. He'd thought the liquid was some byproduct, but the way it had charged him, the way it had heated on contact with his hand like it was defending itself—those things were responses to stimuli. It was alive.

Now Lange was floating above him, staring into the narrow, dark space between the ceiling tile and the rock face.

The blob reappeared, stretched thin. It wasn't gliding over the asteroid surface like it had been. It was being dragged.

Lange was dragging it.

"Lange, this is a bad idea," Jake said, but Lange ignored him and kept pulling the alien toward him.

Only half its mass was visible. Ceiling tiles hid the rest. It was big—far bigger than Jake had first thought. Lange didn't have full control of it.

It roiled. A handspan from Lange's face, the alien seethed and fought.

"Stop!" Jake shouted. That thing might touch Lange. It would burn his face. "Stop it! Stop right the fuck now! Let it go, Lange!"

With his uncontaminated hand, he grabbed Lange's calf and pulled him down. When Lange released his hold, the organism spilled back into itself and flowed into the darkness, vanishing.

The struggle had been silent, but the organism's absence made the room seem quieter. Jake's frantic pulse filled his ears.

"I almost had it," Lange said.

"It almost burned your face off, you mean. Fucking *Christ*, Lange. Are you out of your mind?"

"It hurt you." Lange was taller than usual, his face level with Jake's. He hadn't touched his boots to the ground yet. He was still staring up at the ceiling, ready to fly up there and try again.

"So you wanted to let it hurt you, too?" Jake asked. He wanted to shake Lange by the shoulders, but one of his gloves still had alien goo on it. With his clean hand, he pushed Lange down until his boot soles clicked against the floor. Probably he was gripping Lange's shoulder harder than necessary, but Lange had better fucking stay down here. "What exactly was your plan?"

Lange made a noise of frustration deep in his throat. "Not letting it get away."

"That was reckless. You—" Anger choked off the rest of his thoughts. He glared. Lange's dark brown eyes, lit up with fury, filled his field of vision.

Lange blew out a breath, hot against Jake's skin.

Jake kissed him.

They crashed together, too hard and fast. Fuck. Jake hadn't meant to, he was shit at this, Lange was pulling away —oh. Lange was adjusting the angle. Now he was kissing Jake.

Jake had never kissed anyone before one minute ago, but he'd been kissed. Or he thought he'd been kissed. Lange was proving him wrong. Jake had been the confused recipient of a couple of quick, teeth-clacking surprises that had left him wondering if *this* was really the experience everyone else wouldn't shut up about.

It wasn't.

With Lange, kissing was different. The answer rang through every living, breathing inch of his body. He pressed his mouth to Lange's, wanting the sensation and the taste not for their own sake but because they belonged to beautiful, brilliant, occasionally infuriating Solomon Lange.

Lange made it easy, angling his head so their noses didn't bump, parting his lips so Jake could slip his tongue into the velvet softness of his mouth. It was unhurried, and that was its own wonder—not just that kissing was good, but that he wanted to keep doing it, that he knew within an instant that he would want this again.

Patient but not passive, Lange pulled him closer by the hips. It was the gentlest of touches, one that would evaporate at the first hint of resistance, but it *was* a touch, not a telekinetic pull. Lange had wanted not only to shorten the distance between them, but to put his hands on Jake, to feel the shape of him. Jake went willingly. He hadn't anticipated the feedback loop: knowing that Lange wanted him made him want Lange more. He was fully hard by the time their bodies pressed together. He wished he could feel Lange.

The synthetic material of their suits crinkled between their bodies. Lange broke the kiss, pressed his forehead to Jake's, and said, "We have to patch the leak."

"Fuck." Reluctant to disentangle himself, Jake stayed still for one last moment. In the ensuing silence, he heard the hiss of the can of sealant. It startled a laugh out of him. "Are you fixing it? From here?"

"The other option involves you moving, which doesn't appeal to me."

Jake hummed in agreement. He tightened his arms around Lange and, with a boldness he hadn't known he possessed, kissed the side of his neck. His body brushed up against Lange's.

The hiss went silent. Lange exhaled. "I can't—you can't —I have to concentrate."

Jake laughed again. It was thrilling, having any kind of

power over Lange. He hadn't realized, when Lange had said *I find you distracting*, what pleasure there was in that.

Even though Jake wanted to be the sole focus of Lange's attention, he stilled. He wanted to live long enough to kiss Lange again.

He wanted a lot more than kissing.

[13]
THE SCIENTIFIC METHOD

IT WAS NOT POSSIBLE FOR SOLOMON TO THINK WHEN IN proximity to McCreery, which would probably get both of them—and everyone else—killed.

The sealant hardened in seconds, blocking the flow of air through the crevice. The leak was fixed.

It was only one problem among many. As much as Sol wanted to kiss McCreery again, they would need to exercise caution. He needed his faculties. Even now, something worried at the back of his mind. Not the air leak, or the pipes, or the darkness, or the broken gravity generator—

McCreery backed away and turned toward the cabinets. He tucked his flashlight into the crook of his right armpit and opened the doors with his left hand.

That didn't make sense. McCreery was right-handed.

"You're injured," Solomon said. The organism had flowed over McCreery's right glove. McCreery hadn't touched him with that hand when they were kissing.

Shit. This was serious. The kiss had distracted him. He took a few steps so he was next to McCreery again and breathed through the first vibrations of panic.

"I'm fine," McCreery said.

"You yelled when it touched you. Let me see," Solomon said.

McCreery offered his arm without a word. Solomon drew it close to his face and hovered McCreery's flashlight nearby. The gunmetal grey material of his glove was marked with an iridescent track over the knuckles. It was the same clear, viscous liquid that had been on the greenhouse pipes. Solomon tried to manipulate McCreery's fingers without touching the mucus. "Does it hurt?"

"You don't have to do that, I can move my fingers just fine," McCreery said. He wiggled them in demonstration. "I had worse burns working in the diner. We've got bigger things to worry about. Let's decontaminate my glove and then go tell the others what we saw."

McCreery sounded so sure. Solomon furrowed his brow. Safety first. "Your glove appears intact, but protocol requires that we examine your bare hand. We don't know what the organism is composed of. Something might have seeped through."

"Pretty sure it was just heat, Lange. Besides, if any of that stuff oozed through the glove, my skin won't present much of a barrier," McCreery said.

"Then let's hope it's not a contact poison," Solomon said, the dryness of his voice matching McCreery's, belying the distress that pierced him. It meant nothing that McCreery wasn't in pain. Something might have affected his nervous system. He could be dead in minutes.

They shouldn't have wasted time kissing, not if McCreery was going to die of some symptomless, painless, undetectable, incurable alien neurotoxin absorbed through his skin. Kissing hadn't felt like a waste of time, but— Now Solomon would have to live without McCreery, but *with* the knowledge of what it was like to kiss him, which would be neither symptomless nor painless. He'd rather go back to the Nowhere.

"I didn't expect *you* to be the one freaking out about a kiss," McCreery said. He'd already twisted his glove off and had, perhaps, been holding out his hand for examination for some time now.

Solomon had failed to take it. He blinked.

"I am not 'freaking out,'" Solomon said in a tone that didn't convey his point quite as well as it might have. "And if I were freaking out, it would be about your imminent death, and thus justified."

"Oh, it's imminent, huh?" McCreery held open his palm and then rotated his hand, which *appeared* uncontaminated. His blunt-nailed fingers showed no trace of the liquid that clung to his glove, though a red streak crossed his knuckles diagonally. The pale peach coloration of his skin appeared otherwise healthy and undisturbed. His movements were steady.

Solomon's thick gloves disguised the tremor in his own hands. He took McCreery by the wrist. Despite every concern and safety protocol, he wished he too was bare-handed, as if he could absorb McCreery's unruffled certainty through his skin. A contact antidote instead of a contact poison.

All evidence pointed toward McCreery being more or less uninjured, yet Solomon could not release his wrist. It was unbearable to care for someone, knowing they too were mortal.

"You called me Jake," McCreery said, causing Solomon to realize they'd both been silent for a long moment. "When you pulled me away from the alien, you called me Jake."

"I'm sure you're mistaken," Solomon said, clipped.

Lying was the last resort of the trapped, but he could not afford to be drawn any further into this. It was bad enough to have feelings in private. For someone else to pry back the screen and peek inside was too much.

"I know what I heard. But more importantly, are you okay?"

"Why wouldn't I be? The potentially lethal, unknown entity didn't touch *me*," Solomon said. He dropped Jake—McCreery's wrist. "We have work to do."

McCreery's calm expression slipped, his face tightening with worry for an instant. "I don't get it. You'll kiss me, but you don't want to call me Jake or talk about whether you're okay? What *do* you want?"

"There is a high probability that one or both of us will die in the immediate future," Solomon said. It was less terrifying to say that than anything pertaining to kisses, or wanting, or whatever havoc neurotransmitters were wreaking on his poor brain.

"If that's a fancy way of saying you changed your mind and you don't want to kiss me again, it's okay." His Adam's apple bobbed. "I mean, that's not what I want, but I get it."

"You want me to kiss you again?" Solomon hadn't meant to say that, at least not in such a hesitant, pathetic way. He was a good kisser. People usually wanted him to kiss them again.

But this was Jake.

"Well, yeah. I liked it. Did you not—"

Rather than endure the end of that absurd question, Solomon surged forward and kissed him, putting both hands on his precious, unbearable face. Jake was ready for him this time, parting his lips and letting Solomon slip right in. It was sweet, too sweet, and of course he liked it, he liked it entirely too much, he wanted to do it forever.

That was the flaw. Forever wasn't available.

When they broke apart to breathe, Jake said, "As much as I like this, which is a lot, we both need sleep. After we tell the others what we saw. But maybe we could sleep together?"

"As I recall, you objected strenuously when I asked for the same thing."

Jake turned a dull pink. "I, uh—I didn't phrase that right. I meant literal sleeping. Like what we did at the cabin. But if it's anything like the kissing, then maybe we should. Your control has gotten a lot better, so it would be safe if we did, I think."

Solomon had never slept with anyone who had tiptoed around the subject like that. Jake's nervousness was endearing, but enthusiasm would be better.

His silence caused Jake to keep talking. "Um, leaving all of that aside for a minute, I do actually think it's a good idea to be in the same room in case anything weird happens."

"Practical," Solomon agreed.

"I'm fine, but I'd rather not be alone. And maybe... you'd rather not be alone either?"

This question was a kindness, allowing Solomon to say "yes" in a way that had nothing to do with the future or his feelings. Still, not wanting to be alone was a step beyond the utilitarian "in case anything weird happens," and it took him a moment to find the courage to say, "I would prefer some company, yes."

"Thanks," Jake said, relieved and happy like Solomon was doing him a favor and not the other way around. "To be clear, you want to share a sleeping bag?"

Solomon forced away all thoughts of slippery slopes—of slippery *anything*—and said, "Yes."

The way Jake's eyes crinkled at the corners disarmed

him completely. "Oh. Good. Because I liked last night and I want to do it again."

If Jake continued to say earnest and hopeful things, Solomon's defenses would crumble. He might even admit how terrified he was.

"I might want to do more than literal sleeping together," Jake continued, and this time Solomon understood that his nervousness was not a lack of enthusiasm. Jake wouldn't bring up the subject a second time unless he wanted it. He was *shy*.

Sol wanted to kiss him senseless, strip him slowly, and lay him down, which was impossible because they were in microgravity and also because it would betray just how absurdly emotional he felt about this whole thing. Unprecedented. Nonsensical. He did not have time for this.

Besides, it was just sex.

"We could do that," Solomon said. He'd always been able to maintain a sex life uncontaminated by sentiment before. Surely he'd work out some new method. "We can sleep together. But it's a temporary arrangement *only*."

With far more cheer than was merited, Jake said, "Around here everything's a temporary arrangement."

That was precisely the problem.

———

JAKE COULDN'T FIGURE out what had happened between Lange kissing him and then getting all weird before begrudgingly agreeing that they could sleep together. It bothered him all the way through their brief meeting with Miriam and Chávez—the two team members on watch—about the strange blob they'd encountered.

He should probably have been more focused on the

meeting than on Lange, but he'd had his fill of dangers and space bullshit for the day. The only thing he could reliably hold in his brain was the dream that soon enough, he'd be unconscious. In bed. With Lange.

When they got to Jake's room, Jake tossed one sleeping bag to Lange and unrolled the other. They zipped them together and then tethered each of the double sleeping bag's four corners to hooks embedded in the walls. The cords would hold the sleeping bag in place so Jake and Lange didn't accidentally run into a wall while they slept.

It was useful as hell that Lange could hold their flashlights in place with no hands. Made working in the dark a lot easier.

Jake stripped off his suit, shoved it into the closet so it wouldn't drift off somewhere, and then floated up and slid himself into the sleeping bag. Lange joined him a second later, wearing the clothes he'd had on under his suit, which Jake knew was way more dressed than he usually slept. Lange switched off the flashlights and stored them in the closet.

They were side by side. At the contact, all the fatigue Jake had been carrying around suddenly lifted. Who had he been kidding about sleeping?

He rolled to his side.

"I know you said this was a temporary arrangement, but —" Jake cut himself off. Better to do it than to stumble through talking about doing it. He pulled Lange by the shoulder, slow and deliberate so Lange could get away if he wanted to. Jake might be bigger, but Lange had no reason to feel intimidated.

When their faces were aligned, Jake leaned in and kissed Lange. Without the adrenaline rush of survival driving him forward, the kiss he offered was careful and tentative, not because he didn't want to, but because he wanted this more than he could ever remember wanting anything. He didn't want Lange to back away, to tell him they couldn't, to say the other times had been a mistake.

Lange didn't. He moved closer—no, he moved *Jake* closer, dragged him in until he could wrap his arms around Jake and slide his warm hands under Jake's shirt. The embrace brought their hips together, and this time there were no spacesuits between them. The hard length of Lange's cock slotted next to his own, and Lange rocked against him.

A ragged breath broke free of Jake's lips. He only regretted it because Lange stopped kissing him.

"Tell me what you like," Lange said.

"Everything we're doing," Jake said. It felt impossible to think of anything he could like more than the feeling of Lange's hips rolling, Lange's cock catching against his.

"And? What else do you want?" Lange asked.

Lange was peeling Jake's shirt off, and Jake helped him. Tossing it out of the sleeping bag and letting it drift was a reprieve from answering the question. Jake pulled at Lange's shirt, but Lange put a hand on his wrist to still it.

"Jake," Lange said in that deep, authoritative voice of his, and fuck, but his name alone was enough to make pre-come pearl at the tip of Jake's cock. "Have you ever done this before?"

Ah, fuck. Goddamn geniuses and their deductions. "If I say no, are you going to stop?"

"Do you want me to stop?"

"God no," Jake said, grateful the lights were out since all signs pointed to him blushing the whole damn time. The only advantage of feeling this goddamn horny was that desperation made it easier to spit out the truth. "I've never done this before and I probably never will again. We might die tomorrow. *Please* keep going."

Lange made a sound between a hum and a laugh, and they were so close Jake could feel the lift of his ribcage when he breathed. "Am I to assume, then, that you don't know what you like?"

"We can figure it out," Jake said. "Make a hypothesis and test it already."

Lange laughed again. "Well. The scientific method it is, then."

He stripped off his own shirt and let it go. Then he drew Jake in and kissed him. With Lange's tongue in his mouth and their bare skin touching, this was closer than Jake had ever been to anyone. God, people were so warm. Lange. *Lange* was so warm.

In zero g, one of them couldn't lie on top of the other. They'd naturally drift apart. The confines of the sleeping bag kept them near each other—being together would have been near impossible without it, although as soon as he'd had the thought, Jake couldn't help engineering imaginary scenarios involving handholds on the wall and mag boots. Telekinesis, too. He didn't know very much about sexual positions, but he couldn't resist a mechanical problem.

The sleeping bag could keep them in the same vicinity, but it was their grip on each other providing that heat. That satin press of skin. That friction he wanted so much.

"Fuck, you feel good," Jake said, touching his forehead to Lange's, lining up their noses. Whatever shyness or nervousness he might have felt dissolved in a hot rush of desire. "I don't want to let go but I really, really want us to be naked. Can we make that happen?"

"You did choose a challenging set of circumstances," Lange said, and then a moment later, when his hands took hold of the waistband of Jake's underwear, "Don't mistake that for a complaint."

Lange tugged down the tight, stretchy material of Jake's shorts. Jake huffed out a laugh when he realized they were wearing essentially the same thing, a practical garment intended for use under spacesuits, and Lange paused.

"No, don't stop," Jake said. "Just didn't expect us to be wearing matching underwear, that's all."

"You had expectations? I think you should tell me what they were."

"Well, the zero-g thing didn't figure into them, that's for sure," Jake said. He hadn't expected to talk or laugh during this moment—he hadn't expected to laugh *today*—but he found himself smiling.

"That's new for me as well," Lange said solemnly. He peeled Jake's shorts down his legs until Jake could kick them off, and then Jake did the same for him. "So I suppose I've never done this before either."

"Mmm," Jake said because as soon as Lange embraced him, it was the only option available to his brain. Holy shit, they were both naked. Those were the smooth planes of Lange's slender torso, and the wiry curls of his sparse chest hair, and the sharp edges of his hipbones. That was Lange's cock he could feel, and it was hard. There was nothing else worth thinking about.

Jake kissed him for it, forcefully enough to knock his head back, and Lange responded hungrily, taking Jake's tongue deep into his mouth. His hands, no longer forgotten at his sides, roamed all over Jake's body, over his arms and his back and down to his ass. Lange kissed his neck, his collarbone, his chest. Not a centimeter between them, but Lange groped and squeezed him like all he wanted in the world was to be closer.

"Did you think about this?" Lange asked. "I thought about this."

"I know," Jake said, breathless even though all he done was hang on for dear life. "I heard you doing your thinking."

"You listened?"

"You left the door open," Jake said, defensive.

"Did you touch yourself?"

"Nope," Jake said. He hadn't wanted to then. Hard to imagine. "But I will now if you won't."

Lange laughed and reached between them to wrap a hand around Jake's cock. Jake shivered—God, it was electric, that touch—and said, "Fuck."

"*Do* you touch yourself?" Lange asked.

Maybe after all those science jokes, Jake should have predicted this curiosity. "Yeah."

"But you've never let anyone else do this," Lange said. Lange rubbed the pad of his thumb over the slit, slicking wetness over his palm and down Jake's shaft. His grip was loose, gentle, and so slow it should be illegal. But it made Jake's heart pound with want.

"I never wanted to before. This just sort of... happened," Jake said, his brain hopelessly fogged by the steady motion of Lange's hand. "Sorry—uh—guess that wasn't the nicest way I could've said that."

"Jake," Lange said, and fuck, but that first-name trick was as good as a touch. "When you're telling me I'm the only person who's ever made you feel sexual attraction, it doesn't matter to me how you phrase it."

"Oh," Jake said, and then made a choked-off exhalation as Lange shifted his grip so that it encompassed both of their cocks. Lange was so hard Jake could feel every ridge and vein. Hell, he could feel the hot thrum of Lange's pulse.

"Evidence," Lange murmured next to his ear, "that I want this as badly as you do."

Jake curved one hand around the back of his head and kissed him. Aiming for the same tone Lange had used, he said, "That's hot, but if you wanted this as badly as I do, you'd have jerked us off by now."

Lange hummed in response. He let go of his own cock and when Jake made a small sound of protest, he said, "I'm saving that for later."

Then Lange wrapped his hand around Jake and stroked him from tip to root and back again in one long, perfect, slippery movement, drawing a "yes" from Jake that was more breath than sound. When Lange stilled, Jake pumped his cock into the tight circle of Lange's fist.

"Good, just like that," Lange said.

At any other time in life, Jake would bristle at receiving instructions—praise—for something he already knew how to do, but *fuck*, if that wasn't the hottest thing Lange had ever said to him. He groaned.

"Show me how you like it. Let me feel you," Lange continued, his veneer of calm impervious to all the sounds Jake was making. A continuous stream of encouragements flowed out of him. "Good, that's right, that's perfect, you're perfect."

And just when Jake had approached the edge, Lange said, "Stop."

"What?"

"You heard me," Lange said, and then let go of Jake's cock and used both hands to brace himself against Jake's body. Using Jake as a ladder, he climbed down into the sleeping bag, wriggling awkwardly until he was crouched at Jake's feet.

And then he took Jake's whole length into his mouth.

"Fuck," Jake said, because nobody had ever done that before and if he died tomorrow, at least he didn't have to die without knowing how amazing this felt. And then, because he could never stop thinking like an engineer, not even when Lange had broken his brain, he added, half-laughing, "Good call, with no gravity it's gonna get messy."

Apparently he'd said the wrong thing, because Lange removed Jake's dick from his mouth. That was the opposite of what Jake wanted.

"That is not," Lange said, with a whole lot of offended dignity for somebody who'd stuffed himself down into the bottom of a sleeping bag, "why I am here."

And then Lange went to work.

The slick heat of his mouth was heaven. Jesus. The man was a genius in more ways than one. Probably the whole facility could hear the noise Jake made, but it was too late to care about that.

Jake had never considered before that a person's tongue could be dextrous, but he wouldn't forget it. Lange licked him and sucked him down like there was nothing he'd rather have in his mouth, and it was a struggle not to come immediately. Jake wanted this to last. He clamped down on his urge to thrust deeper into Lange's mouth and tried not to clench his hands too hard on Lange's bony shoulders. Tightness coiled in every part of his body. He'd never felt anything like this, a pleasure so intense that he wanted more and less at once, to drive deeper into it and to be released from it.

He wished he could see it, look down and see Lange's beautiful mouth on his body. Lange's eyes would be shut in concentration, or bliss, maybe. The idea that Lange might love this even half as much as Jake did, that Jake's cock in his mouth might make him so hard he ached, was too much.

Desire charged through him. Fuck, Jake wanted to make him feel just like this.

Lange slid his lips up and down the length of Jake's cock until Jake's self-control had frayed to almost nothing.

"Lange, I—"

Lange didn't stop. He opened his throat and closed his mouth and swallowed Jake's orgasm like the pleasure was his, too. Pulse after searing pulse shot out of Jake. When it ended, he pulled Lange back up, kissed him, and laid himself against Lange like they could pool together.

Lange's hard-on prodded him in the belly.

Jake grabbed it, wrapped his fingers around it and went a little stupid with how good it felt. Lange's skin was so soft, velvety everywhere it wasn't slick, but underneath he was rigid. Even in zero g, his cock was heavy in Jake's hand.

The movement came to him naturally. Familiar territory even if it wasn't his body. Even if he'd never done it before, jerking off wasn't complicated. He could glide his hand up and down and listen to Lange's breathing to know if he was getting it right. Strictly speaking, he didn't need instructions.

He wanted them.

"Will you tell me what to do?" Jake asked, his voice quiet like he was telling a secret. He was.

Lange kissed him, his tongue still carrying a trace of salt. "I imagined you all wrong," he said. "You're better in reality."

Jake was pretty sure that wasn't a comment on his skill at handjobs. It was thrilling and intimidating, this comparison to Lange's imagination. Lange probably knew about stuff that wouldn't occur to Jake in his wildest dreams—but whatever Lange asked him for, he'd figure it out. "What did your fantasy version of me do?"

"You were a lot more exasperated," Lange said. "And bossy."

Jake choked off a laugh. "Thought you were gonna name an act. But if that's what you want—"

"I want everything," Lange said, and then, in demonstration, he pressed the pad of his thumb into Jake's lower lip, which he found unerringly in the dark, and said, "I want you to suck my cock. Can you do that for me?"

Jake nodded, and when Lange removed his hand, said, "God, yes. Anything. Everything."

He braced himself against Lange, bent his knees, and squirmed down into the sleeping bag. It was even more awkward for Jake, since Lange had the advantage of being smaller, but he didn't care. In the dark, he traced his hands over the shape of Lange's hipbones, the tops of his thighs, the triangular patch of hair.

"Wrap one hand around the shaft," Lange said. "Get it wet first. I don't care how."

Oh. Oh fuck. He'd asked for instructions and he was gonna get *instructions*. It probably said something hopelessly nerdy about him that this was what he wanted, the detailed guide, the full walk-through—he'd never given a shit about porn but he absolutely would have looked at a diagram of this—but he couldn't afford to dwell on that, there were steps to be completed in the process. Jake would memorize it backwards and forwards, he'd take it apart and put it back together, he'd learn everything there was to know about making Lange come.

Lange was dripping already, so it was easy to swipe his palm through that and stroke Lange as requested. He couldn't wait to taste it, so he lowered his mouth to Lange's skin and kissed him right on the head. The taste wasn't as strong as he expected. Not bad either way. Lange sucked in a breath, so

Jake kept going. He moved his hand aside and kissed his way down the shaft and back up, sloppy and enthusiastic.

One of Lange's hands splayed over the crown of his skull, not pushing him in any direction but just rubbing the short fuzz of his hair, gripping him lightly, like Lange needed something to hold on to. "Good, that's good," he said. "Take the head into your mouth, all the way until your lips meet your hand."

Lange felt way bigger inside Jake's mouth than in his hand. He loved it. Jake's mouth was so full he couldn't imagine moving his tongue as skillfully as Lange had, but even his clumsy attempt produced a gasp from Lange. Worth it.

"Astute," Lange said, breathless, and it was a little bit absurd—Jake would have laughed if his mouth wasn't full—but so hot. It was absurd for Jake to get hard again, too, but he could feel himself swell. Lange liked this. He thought Jake was good at it. Jake wanted him to say so again, maybe with a different, even fancier vocabulary word.

Damn right he was astute.

He licked the slit and Lange moaned. Fuck, Jake wanted more of that, too.

Lange's next words were a little less composed in tone and timing, but the man clung to his complete sentences. "Move your hand and your mouth in concert."

It was easy with everything so slick already. Jake set up a rhythm, steady but not too fast, and felt Lange's fingers rub the back of his head.

"You love this," Lange marveled. "You love it when I talk to you, too. Are you hard again already? I bet you are. I wish I could see you. I bet you look beautiful down there, sucking my cock."

Christ. Jake *was* hard again. His balls drew in tight. Lange was going to come in his mouth. Jake wanted that, wanted to feel it and taste it.

Lange's words were coming a little faster, his breath a little shallower, and finally a stream of barely coherent praise tumbled out.

"Yes, just like that, *fuck*, perfect, keep going."

Jake did keep going, never letting up. His hand was soaked now, every stroke slippery and loud, but not as loud as Lange, who'd switched from sentences to sounds. Jake sped up.

"Jake, please."

That knocked them both for a loop. Jake's name was still a rarity, and he didn't think he'd *ever* heard Lange say please. He slipped his free hand between Lange's thighs and fondled his balls. He wanted to make Lange come, but he didn't want this to be over. There was more he hadn't touched yet. But he didn't slow down.

Lange thrust into his mouth. His orgasm splashed against Jake's tongue. Jake swallowed it down, listening to Lange breathe. When it subsided and Lange was quiet again, Jake's heart was pounding. He slid Lange's cock out of his mouth, wiped the back of his hand across his face, and dropped a kiss on Lange's hipbone.

"Come here," Lange said, and Jake's knees protested as he straightened his legs at last.

Then Lange was kissing him, reaching between them to stroke Jake off again.

"You don't have to, you already—"

Lange silenced him with a kiss and kept his hand moving. His touch was gentle, but remarkably effective. Jake would be embarrassed about how desperate he felt, but

Lange had moved from kissing his mouth to kissing his neck, and now he was murmuring in Jake's ear.

"You were so good at that. I love how much you want this. I want you to come for me again. You can. I know you can."

Lange was proven correct. Jake cried out and coated his hand.

"Good," Lange said and gave him a long, luxurious kiss on the mouth.

"Fuck," Jake said when they were done, satisfaction mingling with exhaustion.

Lange hummed in response. Jake didn't want to think about where Lange had wiped his hand, because then he'd have to think about how limited their options were for rinsing off with no running water in the facility, and then he'd have to think about everything else. So he wrapped his arms around Lange, closed his eyes, and didn't think at all.

"Goodnight, Jake." Lange settled against him and went to sleep.

Jake drifted off and woke in the darkness some time later to Lange kissing his neck again. He mumbled, "What?"

"It's early, we don't have to get up yet," Lange said.

"Mm. Okay." His body had woken up before his brain, but he liked the feeling of Lange's hands on him. "You wanna do it again?"

"We should," Lange said very seriously. "Experimental results are worthless if they can't be reproduced."

14

MAGIC TOUCH

With Jake trailing sleepily behind him, Solomon brought his guitar to the lab. The beam of his flashlight landed on Clara Chávez, who'd been on watch last night. She was standing with one arm lifted to grab a wall hand-hold, wearing the same gunmetal grey spacesuit as both of them and tipping a tapered zero-g cup of coffee toward her mouth. Because of the lack of gravity, her short brown hair lifted off her head. The flashlight beam made her look like a saint in a painting—maybe after death. Fatigue shadowed her eyes.

"Chávez? You didn't sleep?" Jake asked.

Solomon made a careful, private note that everyone addressed her by her last name. It seemed to be her preference.

"I traded the last half of my shift with Lenny so I could nap—whatever, that doesn't matter. I wanted to talk to you," she said, pinning Solomon with her gaze.

Solomon blinked. Historically, the only people who said that were co-authoring papers with him, but Chávez wasn't a physicist. "You did?"

"Yeah. That stuff you said yesterday about how the alien's making a sound, I can't stop thinking about it. Is that a guitar?"

"Yes." Solomon took the instrument out of its case. He stopped the case against the floor to keep it in place, then took the guitar in both hands.

"Oh good, that's so great," she said.

Solomon studied her, searching for indications of sarcasm, and found none. Perhaps her enthusiasm was genuine.

Her whole face lit with a smile. "It's gonna help so much. You can play me what you're hearing, and then we can try communicating with it. Oh, fuck, is it wrong to be so excited about this? I know this whole situation is... bad. But I wouldn't miss this for anything."

"That's what we're doing? Talking to the thing?" Jake asked, rubbing a hand over his eyes. He'd nearly fallen asleep during breakfast. Yesterday had been exhausting for both of them, but it was Jake who'd walked through the hypergravity. And then Solomon had kept him awake long into the night *and* woken him up with a handjob this morning.

Solomon couldn't regret the sex, no matter how foolish it had been. He did feel a touch guilty when Jake yawned, though. Ordering him to go back to bed to get a few more hours of sleep hadn't worked. Jake had laughed and said, "Yeah, not happening."

And now they were here in the lab.

"Jake, man, are you okay? Do you want some coffee? Not to be rude, but you look like you need it," Chávez said.

Jake snorted. "Thanks. I feel about four hundred years old, so I'm not sure coffee's gonna help."

Watching them interact, Solomon was reminded of how

Jake had been much closer to the rest of the team than he ever had, even if Jake had always held himself a little apart. They'd all still liked him. He was easy to like.

"Coffee is the *only* thing that will help," Chávez said gravely.

Jake shook his head at her, then crossed his arms over his broad chest. "Your concern is appreciated, but I'll live, Chávez."

Sol had been so very wrong to think, as he had at the cabin, that sex with Jake would make him *less* distracting. The mistake was, at least, an honest one. All the sex Solomon remembered had functioned exactly like that. He'd had a physiological need, he'd seen to it, and then he'd gone back to what really mattered—work.

He'd never spent the night entangled with any of those people. He'd never wanted to.

Worn out and scruffy, wearing a spacesuit that shouldn't have been to anyone's aesthetic advantage, Jake still looked like a person Sol wanted to strip naked and fuck.

Worse, he looked like a person Sol wanted to give a long, warm hug.

Lust was familiar, but the second feeling was not. He didn't know how to categorize the urge, which perplexed him, but did nothing to diminish the desire itself.

Jake and Chávez were chatting without him. She swayed toward him, her mag boots keeping her rooted. They smiled at each other and it stabbed right through him —not because it represented something romantic or private or special, but because it didn't. Other people were friendly with each other all the time.

It was meaningless, and yet it meant everything.

Like a man who'd been slowly freezing to death, Solomon had gone numb to his own loneliness, unable to feel it until the temperature suddenly changed. He'd craved solitude, not total isolation, and somewhere in his adult life, one had given way to the other.

Jake made eye contact with him. It was a kindness to be checked on, one Solomon had never recognized before. He'd always resented being the object of people's concern.

Jake didn't look concerned. His expression was soft. Fond, maybe. Whatever it was, it was fleeting, gone when he glanced at Chávez and said, "You wanna talk about why you were waiting in here? Do your thing, I can tell you want to."

Solomon couldn't remember what Chávez's "thing" was, and he braced himself to find out.

"I wanted to ask you about the sound," Chávez said.

"I doubt I can provide you with a satisfactory explanation," Solomon warned her.

"No, that's fine, that's not my question. Or that is my question, but in like, a less accusatory way. I believe you! I swear I'm not here to tell you you're wrong. I just wanna talk about this because it is *amazing*. Anyway. It seems like we have two options here. Option one: the thing you're hearing is a sound in the way that we all understand sound, but it's outside the range of normal human hearing, so none of the rest of us can hear."

"No," Solomon said.

His blunt dismissal didn't slow Chávez down. "Okay then, that brings me to option two: the thing you're hearing is *not* a sound, not in the way we typically understand it, but your brain doesn't have any other way of processing it. So you're hearing it."

"Yes," Solomon said, impressed that she'd arrived at the same conclusion he had. "It's only a small distinction from your first idea, but it's an important one. This 'sound' is outside human perception in a more fundamental way than simply being a frequency that's too high or too low to hear."

"Right! Oh my God this is *so cool*," she said. All signs of fatigue were gone from her face. She made an excited gesture with her empty cup and paced back and forth. Her boots clicked as she did. "The human body has a limited number of senses, but our brains—your brain especially, maybe—are more adaptable, and after you spent all that time in the Nowhere, you came out with extra senses. And telekinesis, obviously, which maybe is connected, but right now let's just focus on your new not-hearing sense, which is like, your brain having reprogrammed your ears for some new purpose."

She beamed at him, and Solomon discovered that he could make that same expression. He liked Clara Chávez very much. It was as strange and novel an experience as hearing the breach and the alien.

"Is this your 'thing'?" Solomon asked. "Cognition?"

"Oh, uh, not really? If you're asking what I studied, the answer is a lot of things, mostly anthropology. Not the bones kind, though, the culture kind." She bit her lip, perhaps in recognition that the old Solomon would have been rude about that. He'd made her doubt herself. When Solomon said nothing scornful, she shrugged one shoulder and tilted her head to the side and said, sheepish, "I'm actually here to make friends?"

Solomon couldn't tell if he was meant to find that funny. When the silence lasted a moment too long, he said, "That falls far outside of my expertise."

She rewarded him with a laugh. The nervous energy went out of her, and she stopped moving quite so much—though she didn't stand still. "I know. You told me not to bother trying to be friends with you. I guess you don't remember that."

"I don't, but I think it's best forgotten. I'm sorry I said it."

Jake, Solomon noticed, had his mouth half-open. As soon as he caught Solomon looking, he closed it.

"So you know about language," Solomon continued, addressing Chávez.

"That's too narrow a term," she said, more confident now. "It suggests something far more systematic than what we'll be able to achieve. We don't even know if the alien *can* communicate. Maybe it's sentient, maybe not."

"And you want to make friends with it either way?" he asked, amused. She hadn't been joking, he'd realized. Whatever her academic expertise was, it was only part of what made her suited to this role of interspecies diplomat.

"Making friends is better than making enemies," she said. "Even Miriam agreed with me on that, and *enemies* is her area of expertise. Will you play me what you're hearing?"

He nodded and picked up the guitar. "The loudest pitches are A flat and G. I suspect they emanate from the breach." He demonstrated one, then the other, their sound overlapping.

Both Jake and Chávez considered the sounds. Chávez said, "I kind of like the two pitches together. It's a little uncomfortable, but... shiny? Hard to describe."

"I can also hear a C," Solomon continued, playing it for them. "It's not as loud, and my best guess is that it comes from the organism. With all three together, it sounds like this."

"When we were over there," Jake said, tilting his head toward the machine, "you were humming."

"E flat," Solomon said, demonstrating the pitch. "The chord is A flat major seventh."

It filled the space around them, rich and resonant and shivering just a little. The interval of the breach was still at the heart of the sound, but it could be layered into something beautiful.

"Wow," Chávez said.

She was so earnest that Solomon couldn't look at her. The admiration on Jake's face was also excessive. Solomon hadn't even done anything. It was a chord, not a concerto.

"So that was your impulse?" Chávez asked. "You heard those three notes and you added one more to make that chord?"

Solomon nodded.

"Do you think maybe—" she started, and then stopped when Jake spoke.

"It seems like you two are good here, and I have wiring to fix, so I really should go," he said. "Maybe in a few hours, you all won't have to be doing this by flashlight."

Solomon almost protested. But everything Jake had said was logical, so he realized as soon as he opened his mouth that his only objection was that he didn't *want* Jake to go. He wanted to glance to the side every now and then and catch Jake smiling at him.

Abashed, Solomon only said, "Okay." He wasn't even sure why Jake had come with him to the lab.

"See you later," Chávez said, and then shimmied her shoulders, unable to contain herself, and said to Solomon, "Let's talk about why the organism might be making that sound."

"Speculate wildly, you mean," Solomon said.

"You know it." Undeterred, she grinned at him and

leaned conspiratorially close. "Come on, Lange, I know you want to."

Jake was lingering in the doorway like he might need to step back into the room and intervene. He'd stayed to mediate, Solomon realized. He'd been worried that Chávez and Solomon wouldn't get along—and Chávez was superhumanly warm and outgoing, so it wasn't her behavior Jake feared.

"The game," she said, counting off rules on her fingers, "is to start out with the most generous possible interpretation. Assume good intentions. Explain the alien."

He could do that. Determined to ease Jake's worries, Solomon looked Chávez in the eye and said everything he'd been mulling over all at once, despite a natural inclination to keep the ideas to himself until they'd solidified further.

"The first question is 'why has nothing else come through?' We've seen a very small amount of human traffic cross the breach—infinitesimal if we take the whole multiverse into account. Very few living things have access to the Nowhere, but that doesn't account for the quiet. One." He held up his index finger. "The breach is repellent to anything or anyone that can sense it."

"Kit hates it, Lenny hates it," she agreed. "You think it makes a weird noise."

"Therefore anything that comes through the breach is either unaffected by its repellent nature—or drawn to it. We know this organism isn't unaffected. It's producing a pitch in the same non-sound way that the breach is, suggesting that it can 'hear' the breach just as I can. Also, it's growing on the remnants of the machine, right next to the breach, and since we suspect it can move, that represents a choice. Two." Solomon lifted a second finger. "The organism didn't simply come *through* the breach, it came *to* the breach. For the organism, the breach is not a form of transit, it's a destination."

"It's not here by accident," she said, barely breathing.

It was exhilarating, telling someone he hardly knew all the ideas he'd been tending in secret. This much sharing should have made him uncomfortable, but from the rapt way Chávez was nodding, he didn't get the impression she was passing judgment. Normally, this much attention—positive or negative—would have made him say something mean just to get the other person to leave, but the urge didn't arise.

Jake was still in the doorway, listening.

Solomon kept going. "The breach makes two continuous pitches, only a half-step apart. Perhaps when there was no rent in the fabric of reality, the Nowhere produced a single pitch. As I said, the organism is sensitive to the nature of the Nowhere. It can hear the breach—not just the sound, but the pitches. The pitch it's producing is meant to harmonize."

He took a deep breath and held up a third finger. "It's trying to fix the breach."

"Marry me," Chávez said, and Solomon heard Jake snort as he finally turned and walked down the hallway, leaving the two of them to play.

———

JAKE HAD SENT Eliza back to his workspace last night, and he found himself absurdly relieved she hadn't been in Lange's room while they'd been having sex. She came rolling into the greenhouse now.

Thanks to the blinds over the windows, it was as red as ever in the space. With the valves shut off and the irrigation system not functioning, it was quiet, without even an occasional drip from the broken pipes to interrupt the silence. Whatever liquid remained inside the pipes was still there, sticking to the surface and to itself. A problem for later.

"We're looking for broken wiring," Jake told Eliza. She couldn't understand that as a command, but it was nice to talk to someone. He sent her back up to the hole in the ceiling to investigate.

Eliza was too big to move through the walls. If he reworked one of the smaller robots, he could send it along the cables. Maybe he could even program it to splice the wiring back together. Messing around with the robot would take time, but it might ultimately save him a lot of work.

"Jake? You in there?"

Startled out of his reverie, Jake looked over his shoulder. "Hey, Dax."

Dax walked into the greenhouse and craned their neck to observe Eliza on the ceiling. Their red hair, gravity-defying even in normal conditions, was in spectacular shape.

"Shouldn't you be in the lab with Lange and Chávez where they're tossing around the big ideas?" Jake asked.

"Ugh, I just woke up, it's too early for big ideas," Dax said. "Give me some pliers. Me and Eliza, we'll be your assistants. Wait. Did you say Lange and Chávez? Is she in there talking to him about *feelings*?" At Jake's look, they waved a hand in the air. "You know what I mean. Communication. Conflict resolution. Not physics."

"Whatever they're talking about, it's definitely not physics," Jake agreed.

"And he hasn't ruthlessly stripped her of all her self-worth?"

"No, actually, they get along great," Jake said, strangely

proud. It wasn't *his* accomplishment.

"Holy shit, Chávez has the magic touch," Dax said. Their gaze slid toward Jake. "Or you do."

"Uh," Jake said. It would be nice if his body would calm the fuck down and not flush pink at the slightest hint that he had touched Lange. "Wanna build a robot?"

"Hell yes," Dax said. "Lead the way."

That was how he and Dax ended up in his workspace, reprogramming his smallest robot to detect broken wiring. Dax was easy to work with. Super smart, very focused, and not chatty, which Jake appreciated.

Dax had lifted a panel from the wall and set it aside, revealing a multicolored bundle of cables. Jake stuck in the probe, a flat, flexible polymer form no bigger than his palm. It clipped to the cables by way of three short, curved legs on either side, making it look a little like a robotic beetle. It would crawl down the bundle of cables until it found a break, at which point they'd open the wall or the ceiling and splice the wires back together. A more sophisticated robot would have done the repairs itself, but in the interest of time, Jake had decided to rely on the machinery he already had—his brain and his hands.

The little robot beeped as it burrowed into the wall and they followed its progress down the hall and into the darkened, silent kitchen, where it found the first chewed-up wiring.

"Should've made two of these," Jake said, removing the wall panel and pulling out the two broken cable ends. "Then we could've split up and fixed twice as many."

"We're still technically supposed to stick together," Dax said. "Didn't you and Lange encounter some kind of alien ooze last night? Aren't you worried it's seeping through the walls right now?"

"I don't think that thing wanted to touch me any more than I wanted to touch it," Jake said.

"I'm entirely reassured," Dax said dryly.

"It heated up on contact," Jake said. "Didn't really burn me since I was wearing gloves. I think it was a defense mechanism."

"Like it was growling a warning at you."

"Something like that, yeah. It was also kind of... shy, I guess? Looking back, I don't think it was charging at me—I think it wanted to get away from me. It disappeared fast. We wouldn't even really have gotten a look at it if Lange hadn't pulled it out of the shadows."

"He fought the alien?"

"Sort of. It resisted his telekinesis, that's for sure." Jake shook his head, remembering. He and Lange hadn't discussed that moment, and he couldn't make sense of it. "I still don't know what he was thinking. I guess maybe he was imagining that he could get a hold of the thing and dump it back into the breach, even though that would've been almost impossible. We both know from experience how hard it is to get close to the breach."

"Maybe he *wasn't* thinking," Dax said.

"Doesn't sound like him."

"He doesn't sound much like himself lately," Dax observed.

Their tone was neutral, but Jake felt like maybe there was a bundle of live wires buried behind it, so he didn't touch that. He finished splicing the conductors together and set the little beetle probe moving through the wall again. The two of them followed its beeping out of the kitchen and into the hallway.

There was damage in the greenhouse, which wasn't a surprise. They'd probably end up retracing the path Jake and Lange had taken yesterday when they'd found the hypergravity. For now, Jake lifted a panel in the greenhouse wall out of its track and set it on the floor.

"You wanna wait just a second to make sure the wall is empty?" Dax asked.

Jake shrugged, but he stepped back from the wall. "I'm not that worried about it. You should have heard Lange and Chávez bouncing ideas off each other this morning."

"Yeah?"

Jake summarized, as best he could, the argument that the alien was not hostile, but might actually intend to fix the breach.

"But that's the coral-like stuff growing on what remains of the machine," Dax said. "The thing that might be slipping through the wall is different, right?"

"I think maybe the ooze is related to the coral-looking stuff in the lab," Jake said. "They're the same color, and if you zoom in on the photo, it looks like the coral is coated in something clear and gooey. I know that's not rock-solid evidence or anything."

"We have to start somewhere. So you think it can solidify itself? Or... deliquesce?"

"Gross," Jake said, and was silent for a moment while he fiddled with the wire. "But yeah, that's what I think. It can transform itself. Caterpillar, butterfly."

"And back again, maybe," Dax said. "It's pretty cool. So do you think we're dealing with two aliens? Or maybe it's all the same organism. Coral's like that—a colony."

"Couldn't say," Jake said. He'd finished the splice, so he replaced the robot onto the bundled cables. "I doubt we'll ever find out."

Dax nodded. The two of them and Eliza left the greenhouse, following the robot in the wall. They stopped again in the hallway for another fix.

"Can I ask you something personal?" Dax said. "I'm sorry, I hate to pry and you don't have to answer, it's just so I'm clear on what's happening. Am I making things up or are you and Lange—" there was a pause so long Jake thought Dax had just quit mid-sentence "—together?"

"It's temporary," Jake said. "Casual. Whatever. He practically made me sign a waiver to that effect."

"Yeah, that sounds *very* casual."

Jake was glad he couldn't see the look on Dax's face. Their tone said enough. "Look, I don't know any more than you do, and I can't talk about this and splice conductors at the same time."

"I'm pretty sure you could fix wiring in a coma, but I'm also happy to stop talking about Lange. Sorry for bringing it up."

"It's fine, don't worry about it. Honestly I'd like to know the answer, too." Fuck, he did wish that. He also wished he hadn't said it out loud. Fewer accidental confessions, more electrical work.

"Speaking of things we might never know, with the machine not functioning, our ability to measure the breach is hampered," Dax said. "I'm not sure how we'll know if the alien is affecting it—other than the obvious, undesirable method of getting too close for comfort."

"Lange can see it. He'll know. And I bet we can pull some remnant of the machine back together, at least enough to measure what's happening," Jake said, glancing over his shoulder. "Failing that, your trick with the tennis balls was pretty effective."

"It may come to that," Dax said, but at least they were smiling.

15

POSSIBLE FUTURE OUTCOMES

Solomon had ceased to notice the darkness and the flashlights by the time the power came back on, but Chávez whooped.

"Oh God, that's a relief," she said. "Not that I don't believe in what we're doing here—establishing that the alien is not hellbent on murdering us—but it's a lot easier to believe when the lights are on, you know?"

"No," said Solomon.

Chávez laughed. She did that often, and he hadn't tired of it. Her laugh was a nice sound, joyful rather than malicious, like she found his company delightful even when he was brusque or strange. Her continuous enthusiasm for their experiments had an effervescent, slightly intoxicating effect on him. He hadn't thought there was anyone in the world he could tolerate for hours, other than his family and Jake, but she was proving him wrong.

And her laugh was a welcome contrast to the few notes he'd been playing on the guitar over and over. The result of their experiments was that if Solomon played a C, the organism would gradually shift to producing an E flat, which maintained the sound of the chord.

If Chávez played the guitar, the organism responded similarly—if Solomon could hear it. With his ears blocked, he could still perceive the breach and the alien, but not the guitar. If Solomon couldn't hear the guitar, there was no change in the organism's behavior. The same was true if Chávez sang the note rather than playing it. (She'd been embarrassed about that set of tests. Solomon's attempts at gentle encouragement had been so dismal that she'd eventually snorted and said, "I can't be nearly as bad at singing as you are at *this*." He was grateful she didn't seem to be holding a grudge.)

They had done the tests over and over. The instrument didn't matter. Solomon could affect the alien's behavior simply by *thinking* of a pitch. The organism responded not to sound, but to him.

He had no idea how to apply this knowledge. In any other circumstance, with any other person beside him, he would have been pacing the room in frustration. Instead, Chávez wandered in circles around him, almost like a fluttering bird except for the tap of her mag boots, while Solomon stood, stewing.

She interrupted his thoughts to say, "Can I ask you something?"

"You've been asking me things all day," Solomon said.

"No, I know, but... it's delicate."

He rolled his eyes. "Yes, Jake and I had sex."

She laughed. "I know *that*. I want to know what brought you here. To Quint Services Facility 17."

"This place doesn't belong to Quint Services anymore."

"But it did when we signed up to work here," she said. She waved a hand. "I know the whole thing turned out to be corrupt and dangerous and awful, and I'm not looking for you to justify yourself. I signed up too. I'm asking because I came for this. Talking to aliens. I mean, the money was good and I got along with all the people Emil picked for the team and I definitely didn't mind the idea of gaining superpowers or exploring the unknown, but the real draw was *this*, right here in this room. We communicated with an alien, Lange. No matter how rudimentary it was, I have wanted to do this my whole life."

"I felt the same about opening up the Nowhere," Lange said. "It didn't go as planned."

"Will you continue that research after we repair the breach?"

"You're very confident in our success."

"If we fuck it up, we die, so there's no need to plan for an after," she said. "If we live, *I* am absolutely going to keep looking for ways to talk to aliens."

"You're passionate about this."

"Yeah. How could I not be?"

"But it doesn't consume you," he continued, and she nodded. "My research on the Nowhere was the only thing in my life. You're not like that."

She considered him for a moment, her brown eyes narrowing. "I don't think you are, either."

"I am," he insisted. "Or I used to be. I didn't care about having friends or a partner or children. I didn't care about money or prestige or power—not for their own sake, at least. Just the research. Only ever the research. It, uh, caused a number of fights with my colleagues."

"Why?"

"Why did my colleagues resent me?"

"No, why didn't you let yourself have a life?" she asked. "I'm sorry your coworkers were shitty, though."

"You're assuming the fault lies with them."

She gave him a crooked, sad smile. "It's not that hard to be your friend, Lange."

"It used to be."

"Well," she said brightly, stretching her arms above her head. "I don't know how long we've been messing around in here, but it was long enough that Jake fixed *all* the wiring. Let's take a walk to the kitchen."

He nodded, put his guitar in its case, and left it in the lab as they exited.

Chávez said, "You think Jake'll fix the gravity, too?"

"A gravity generator is a complex machine," Solomon said. She made a face—she knew that already. He'd just spent hours working with her and she'd been both informed and perceptive. He cleared his throat and continued, "I'm sorry, what I meant to say was that ours was severely damaged and we may not have all the necessary replacement parts. If we do, it won't be a problem. And even if we don't—if anyone could engineer a solution, it would be Jake."

"You think highly of him," she said.

"It's not what I think, it's what I observe."

"Sure," she said, smiling at him. "Science."

"You shouldn't doubt me," he said. "I'm right."

"I'm not doubting you or your observations. I've made some of my own, that's all. You admire him."

"He's admirable," Solomon said shortly.

"Well, yeah, of course he is. He's smart and kind and a damn good person to have on your team"—by *team*, she might have meant the crew of people remaining at the facility, or she might have meant the silly made-up sport they used to play in the gym every Sunday afternoon, a ridiculous social ritual Solomon had never participated in—"but I don't think you often feel that way about other people, do you?"

"Is there a point to this?" Solomon demanded, unsettled. They barely knew each other and she'd seen so much of him. She'd zeroed in on the thing that made him most uncomfortable: what he felt for Jake was different from any set of feelings he'd ever had for another person.

"Okay," she said, raising her hands in surrender. "We don't have to talk about it."

"Correct."

"But you know not talking about it doesn't make it go away. It's *science*." She tapped her temple. "True whether or not you want it to be."

He rolled his eyes.

"Also," she said, her whole face alight with mischief, "it's cute whether or not you want it to be."

She walked into the kitchen ahead of him, her boots clicking loudly against the floor. Solomon followed, perplexed. He ought to be scowling, but he couldn't make his facial muscles obey him. He didn't like that his troublesome feelings were so easily divined by others, but nobody had implied that he was cute since childhood. People usually described him as *brilliant* and *strange* and *intimidating*. They'd mutter *asshole* if they thought he couldn't hear—or sometimes they said it to his face. *Cute* did not fit into that set. He was unsure what to make of it.

It was bright inside the kitchen—and crowded. The whole team was there, standing shoulder to shoulder, raising their bagged beverages like they were clinking beer bottles together. By now, he knew all their names: Emil, Kit, Lenny, Chávez, Miriam, Dax, and Jake. This was an accomplishment that no one else would remark on, but he was secretly proud of himself. He'd remembered them, and he'd learned things about them, and some of them even tolerated him. Jake did a lot more than tolerate him, but Jake was an outlier.

Solomon supposed they were celebrating the return of the electricity, but as he'd never joined them for dinner before, perhaps they were always this cheerful.

Without gravity, and with all the food in individually foil-wrapped handheld servings, the long metal table bolted to the floor was unnecessary, but everyone gathered around it out of habit. Chávez had chosen to stand next to Lenny, and she called to Lange so loudly that no one could miss it, "Get in here."

And then Dax, next to Jake, moved aside to make space for him. Solomon stood next to Jake, curious and jittery like there was a current running through him. Everyone in the kitchen acknowledged his presence with a nod or a greeting like they'd always done this together. Like he could have joined them at any time during the lonely, angry months he'd lived here, and they would have made room. He hadn't believed that then. He wasn't sure he believed it now.

"Hey." Jake nudged Solomon with his shoulder. "You okay?"

Solomon considered his answer. This type of social interaction—everyone squashed together, all talking over each other—didn't suit him. He'd never feel at ease here. Still, it was moving to be invited, and that made the atmosphere almost tolerable. Standing next to Jake, close enough to touch, ought to be a pleasure regardless of where they were. Perhaps he could narrow his focus to that sensation and only that sensation. It could carry him through.

"I can do ten minutes of this," Solomon said.

"Okay."

Solomon had braced for mild disappointment, or

bargaining, or mockery—well, Jake was unlikely to mock him, but someone else might. Or maybe there wouldn't be mockery, but they'd all be hurt that after extending an invitation at last, Solomon had snubbed them by leaving after ten minutes. Solomon tapped his fingers against his thigh in rhythm.

He closed his eyes. It was loud in the kitchen, almost loud enough that he couldn't hear the breach, though no true sound could drown that out. Not even the loud and laughing back-and-forth conversation as the crew traded flavors of emergency ration bars. *Surely* it had been ten minutes by now.

Jake's voice cut through it all, low and close to his ear. "Hey, you know you don't *have* to, right? Ten minutes is great if that's what you want to do. But if this is too much, I get it."

"They're your friends," Solomon said. It was only a fragment of the argument he wanted to make, but the whole thing felt too complicated to articulate right now. They were Jake's friends and they'd asked Solomon to join and he didn't want to upset them by rejecting their invitation. If you wrecked the first one, there was never a second. That always hurt. The only way to avoid the whole fiasco was to be the type of person who never got invited to anything, which Solomon had perfected before Jake came along.

Damn it.

He could be here for another few minutes. He wasn't enjoying himself, but dinner wasn't going to ruin him. No, ruin would come later, when these people no longer needed him to solve a problem. He couldn't allow himself to like them. Either he'd fail and they'd die, or he'd succeed and they wouldn't want to put up with him any longer.

Even Jake.

It wasn't a personal failing on Jake's part. It was a law of the universe. The entropically favored state of a relationship was *broken*. Just as there were more ways for a pair of dice to roll a seven than to roll a two, there were more ways for a relationship to end than for one to remain whole. All relationships ended. People died or they left.

One more minute of standing here was one more minute of deluding himself. Solomon extracted himself from the crowd and quit the room.

He strode right back to the lab, shifting the balance of sound from real and chaotic to unreal and constant. There was no peace here, and he didn't understand this noise, but at least neither did anyone else.

He only had time to pace the width of the room once before Jake appeared in the doorway.

His lips pressed together with worry. "Can I come in?"

"Why are you here?" Solomon asked. He could make Jake go away. He could make Jake angry. He knew how. It wouldn't be difficult—except with Jake's eyebrows creased like that, Solomon found that it would, in fact, be difficult. Instead of an insult, he managed only a curt question. "I was rude. Aren't you angry with me?"

"No?"

Scaring someone off used to be so simple. All the time he'd spent with Jake had caused him to develop reflexive remorse. Solomon exhaled through his nostrils. "I suppose you might as well come in."

Jake advanced cautiously, coming to stand within arm's reach of Solomon, but not reaching out an arm. "Are you okay?"

"I don't like large groups of people," Solomon said, which was true, but inaccurate. It was one reason he'd left the kitchen, but it wasn't the only reason or even the most important. As much as he valued accuracy, he couldn't bring himself to say the others, though he could feel the fear beating against his ribcage.

"I know. That's why I told you that you didn't have to stay," Jake said.

It was absurd how *ideal* he was, how understanding. It was absurd how much Sol wanted to believe in him. If only Jake would be disappointed in him for leaving, or angry, then Solomon could drive him away easily.

Solomon reiterated, with more force, "I don't like large groups of people and I'm never going to change."

"Okay."

Solomon shook his head and began again. "We're too different. I'm good at being alone—I used to be good at being alone—"

"Lange. Did it ever occur to you that maybe I knew you weren't having a good time in there because *I* wasn't having a good time?"

"No," Solomon said, so stunned that this brief true statement comprised his only available answer. Jake was *good* at people.

Jake's shy, slightly embarrassed smile should be classified as a weapon. It had cut Solomon off at the knees. "Well, I don't like large groups of people either."

"Oh."

"I like all those people a lot," Jake said. "Individually."

"But you put up with them as a group quite often," Solomon said, and then added in further protest, "And you play sports."

"Sports have rules, that's different. As for dinner and all that, I tolerate it, I guess. Doesn't mean you have to," Jake said, infuriatingly reasonable. "You know I don't want you to be somebody else, right?"

Here, at last, was the hard crux of the matter, something to hold onto, a problem Jake could not simply shrug off or melt away with his smile.

"Yes, you do," Solomon said, his conviction carrying him several paces away from Jake. He turned back so they were face to face, but with new distance making a gulf between them. "You want me to be your boyfriend. And I can't."

"Whoa, okay. Slow down. I don't recall saying that, so maybe walk me through your logic here."

Solomon took to pacing again, stopping every so often to count on his fingers. "You don't have sex with people you don't have feelings for, you said that already. We had sex and it was good, so you must want more, and if we keep having sex, you'll want a relationship. There are three possible future outcomes: one, we both die in the very near future, thus ending the relationship. Two, one of us dies, thus ending the relationship. Three, improbably, we both live through the immediate future and once the looming threat of death is gone, you come to your senses and realize I'm more trouble than I'm worth, and then you leave me, thus ending the relationship."

Solomon had crossed the room four or five times and Jake was still standing there, a fixed point, his mouth drawn to one side, unimpressed by Solomon's reasoning.

Jake said, "So you don't want to do anything that might make you feel good in the present because there's a chance you'll feel bad in the future?"

"Yes," Solomon snapped. "And it's not 'a chance.' It's a certainty."

"Wouldn't go that far," Jake said, remarkably unagitated. "How come *you* leaving *me* isn't one of the options?"

"It's not probable."

"It feels pretty goddamn probable," Jake said. "Since that's what you're trying to do right now."

At last, in that *goddamn*, a reaction. Only a small one, and that disappointed Solomon in a way he couldn't articulate. Did he want a fight? No, of course not. He was right and he wanted Jake to agree with him. Solomon said, "I am preventing a disaster."

"Uh huh," Jake said. He crossed his arms. "You're jumping to a lot of conclusions."

"I'm being rational."

Jake laughed. "You're being dumb as hell and kind of a dick. You think I'm not scared shitless too? Come on."

"Why would *you* be afraid?"

Jake uncrossed his arms, walked over to where Solomon was standing, draped one arm across his shoulders and used the other to make an expansive gesture that encompassed the rest of the lab.

"Right," Solomon said. Chávez had been wrong; the lights being on didn't reduce how threatening it felt. Now he could see the maze of black tracks on the floor and the walls, marking places of great danger. The static of each distortion rippled in the air.

"Are you so afraid of a future where we both survive that you have to stop what's between us before it even starts?" Jake asked.

"Jake," Solomon said with urgency.

"Yeah?"

"The distortions have changed. They don't align with the marks you made anymore." Solomon went breathless with excitement. It was the first time he'd looked at the shimmering sweep of the room with anything but dread. "I think they're smaller."

"So it's working, whatever you and Chávez were doing?

You communicated with the alien and now it's fixing things?"

"I don't know. Can you get Eliza? Let's redraw the map."

Jake went to fetch Eliza from her charging station in his workspace and Solomon went to the storage closet to get paint. Blue this time to contrast with the black that Jake and Eliza had used before.

The next ninety minutes were dedicated to outlining what Solomon could see. Of the twenty-three distortions marked on the floor and on the original paper map they'd made together, which Jake had carefully labeled A through W, nineteen had shrunk. Eliza drew new lines to circle their ragged shapes. The remaining four distortions had disappeared, so they switched to white paint and covered up those markings.

"Can the laptop still give accurate readings about the size of the breach?" Jake asked, tipping his head back toward the table. He was leaning over Eliza to detach the used paintbrush from her arm. "Or has the condition of the machine disrupted those?"

Solomon shook his head. "It's not working, but you're right that we need that data. We could assemble a new sensor."

"Tomorrow," Jake said, yawning.

Their glances collided and then bounced apart at the thought of their shared sleeping bag. Solomon braced to resume the argument they'd set aside.

With the paintbrush he was still holding, Jake gestured at the wet paint Eliza had tracked all over the floor. "All of this, it's amazing. Kind of like Chávez said this morning— it's not that I would ever have wanted any of this to happen, especially not what happened to you. But an *alien*, Lange."

"Is that why you moved to space?" Solomon asked, relieved that Jake, too, wanted to talk about the lab instead of the bedroom. "To encounter aliens?"

Jake shook his head and laughed a little. "Nope."

"But you were young when you left the surface," Solomon guessed. Jake had said so little about his life; guesses were all Solomon had.

"Gotta be eighteen to join up," Jake said. "I was on my own before that, though. The life I'd led by then—the shitty little towns I'd lived in, the shitty little jobs I'd worked—I don't think I could really imagine good things for myself. I didn't come to space to see wonders, I came to get as far away as I could."

"You've stayed for years."

"Twelve years," Jake said. "I never imagined I would. Not because I wanted to go back to Earth. I just always assumed the future was for other people. Except here I am. Thirty years old and witnessing an alien."

Jake smiled, the slight curve of his mouth like one long, smooth bow stroke over a string somewhere inside Sol, drawing out an answering smile. It was irresistible.

"I'm glad you're here," Solomon said, and it was an understatement by orders of magnitude—*I'm so glad you're here that the mere thought of you ever* not *being here sends me into paroxysms of terror*—but he could only bring himself to add, "It is, as you said, amazing."

"I'm glad you're here, too," Jake said. "You're one of the wonders, you know."

"What?" Solomon had been called a prodigy or a genius plenty of times, but it always carried with it some implicit excuse for the rest of him, and he'd come to resent it. Arguably, "wonder" fell into the same category—something inexplicable, an aberration. He searched himself for resentment and found only warmth.

"I didn't expect you," Jake said, as if that explained everything, as if he wasn't leaving Sol to squirm in the aftermath of this compliment, as if his words hadn't drawn forth some tremulous note of hope. "Hard to expect any of this. Did you know any of this was gonna happen? The organism, the distortions?"

Still awestruck, Solomon answered, "No."

"Would you have guessed that it was possible?"

Jake offered his free hand to Solomon, who took it.

"No, I don't think I could have guessed the existence of such an organism—not until I saw it. That said, if you had proposed the idea to me, I wouldn't have categorized it as impossible. In an infinite multiverse, even a one-in-a-trillion chance is a certainty."

Jake didn't let go of his hand. He pulled Solomon closer. Too late, Solomon realized what Jake had coaxed him into admitting.

"It's hard to say for sure what's possible or impossible," Jake agreed. He leaned in and pressed a kiss to the corner of Solomon's mouth. "You can move things with your mind, but you can't see the future. Come to bed."

[16]

HOLD ON

JAKE ARRIVED IN THEIR ROOM CARRYING A LARGE BLACK
tool bag, which Solomon found suspicious, alarming, and
entirely too exciting. Jake manually slid the door shut
behind himself, checking to make sure they had privacy
without being trapped.

Solomon, to his own consternation, arrived carrying a
bottle of lube. So much for his determination to end things.
Jake had smiled at him and said one nice thing—no, several
nice things and one astounding thing—and here Sol was.
Wanting Jake made him feel alive.

He'd retrieved the lube from the room where Jake had
stored all his belongings during the period when Solomon
had been throwing objects around uncontrollably. Having
to go get the bottle was a strange reminder of how much
things had changed.

He rubbed his thumb over the tiny ridge in the plastic
bottle cap, watching as Jake rummaged in his tool bag,
quietly competent. He was fully clothed and perhaps
working on something unrelated to sex, and still the sight set

something thrumming under Solomon's skin. Only his need to see what Jake was doing kept him still. He wanted to strip him, to revel in his nakedness, to put his hands everywhere, to sink his teeth into Jake's flesh, to slam into him and fuck him hard—no matter that the lack of gravity made that last one exceedingly difficult. They needed the sleeping bag, or else there'd be a lot of useless thrusting and sliding away from each other.

Jake pulled something metal out of the bag. It looked like a flat rectangle, larger than his hand. He raised it above his head and brought it close to the metal panel of the wall. It connected with a thunk. When Jake let go, Solomon saw what his grip had obscured.

A magnetized handhold.

Solomon caught his breath. Of course there were plenty of such objects at Facility 17, in addition to the variety of safety equipment built into the walls. If you relied on a machine to generate gravity, you had to be prepared for that machine to fail.

The other uses of this equipment had not occurred to him.

"This is why you're the engineer," Solomon said. "You're brilliant."

It was very easy and *very* satisfying to make Jake duck his head and avert his eyes from a compliment.

"Thanks. Thought of this last night."

"If you were able to think last night, that's a grave insult to my skills," Solomon said.

"No, it's, um—I wanted to see you. So I was thinking of ways we could get out of the sleeping bag. If one of us holds this, between that and the mag boots—"

Solomon kissed him. Jake let it happen, parted his lips and let Solomon sweep right in, settling his arms around

Solomon's shoulders. Solomon grabbed him around the waist and pulled him close, wishing that they were already naked.

"Will you do it?" Solomon asked. "Will you hold on and stay right there and let me touch you? I want it to be you."

"Yeah." The flutter of Jake's pulse was visible high in his throat. "Yeah, if that's what you want."

"Did you want it to be me?" Solomon asked, struck with curiosity. The thought that Jake might have imagined him all spread out and immobilized against the wall sent an unexpected thrill through him. He'd save that for later.

"I think I just—wanted," Jake said, his breath hitching as Solomon swept a thumb over his cheek. "You or me or—anything. I want to see you. I didn't get to see you."

Right. Engineering expertise aside, Jake had a sexual history of precisely one night, and it consisted of Solomon groping him and sucking him off in a sleeping bag in the dark. It had been an excellent blowjob—they all were—but still, anything they did in full light would be new.

Jake's pupils had dilated as Solomon had continued to touch his face, a fingertip brushing Jake's eyelashes. They were darker than his hair and surprisingly luxuriant.

"You are so pretty," Solomon said. He didn't mean to. It wasn't the sort of thing he said to people he fucked. Or at least, he was reasonably sure he hadn't said things like that before, in his other life. Sweet, slightly stupefied things. Sincere things.

So it was a shock when Jake huffed and said, "You should maybe get your eyes checked, Lange."

"You are so pretty," Solomon said again, affronted that Jake would question his judgment. "And I suppose, under the circumstances, you could call me Solomon. Or Sol."

Jake grinned at him. "What circumstances are those, exactly?"

"Hush."

"Is it only when I'm yelling your name or—" Jake's voice cut out as Solomon worked his fingers under the panel of fabric that covered his zipper, found the tab, pulled it down, and sucked a fierce kiss into the skin at the base of his neck.

Modern intravehicular suits were less bulky than their predecessors, and they had the advantage of coming off all in one piece. Jake obligingly stepped out of his, stripped off his underwear, and stepped back into his boots.

He was on Solomon in no time, kissing him and unzipping his suit. Jake got the zipper all the way down to Solomon's waist before Solomon pushed him back against the wall. Jake's bare skin was hot against his hands, his body solid and welcoming where Solomon collided with him. He was hard already. Solomon should've let Jake strip him, then they'd be skin to skin, but they'd made a plan. He hated to deviate from a plan.

"You agreed to hold on," Solomon said.

"You're gonna get naked and not let me touch you?"

"There will be plenty of touching." Solomon leaned in and kissed him deeply, nipping his bottom lip. "Put your arms above your head and both hands on the handhold. Let me look at you."

Jake obeyed without question despite the faint bloom of pink in his face and his neck.

Solomon stepped back to enjoy the view. Jake was a sight worth studying. With his arms lifted and his feet in boots, he looked more exposed than he would have lying unclothed in a bed. There was nothing casual or accidental about this posture, and Solomon didn't intend to be casual or accidental in his appreciation. Jake's thick, uncut cock jutted out above his thighs and under the soft curve of his belly. His chest hair, concentrated over his pecs, was a shade browner than what grew out of his head. His nipples had tightened to small, rosy points.

Solomon couldn't hear Jake breathing, but the rapid rise and fall of his chest was visible with the rest of his body so still. Whether it was nerves or excitement or a potent combination of both affecting Jake, Solomon couldn't say. The thought that Jake had never let anyone else study him like this made Sol's own breath come shallower.

He stepped forward and kissed Jake again. There was nothing to stop him. Jake was just there, waiting. His mouth was as sweet as it had been a moment ago, more so now that Solomon knew how willing he was.

Solomon snaked a hand between their bodies and wrapped it around Jake's cock, velvet-smooth to the touch. Jake exhaled sharply, but his hands didn't move.

"Perfect, just like that. You're so good at this already. I'll make it good for you, I promise." Solomon shrugged out of the sleeves of his suit, stripped the whole thing off along with his underwear, and put his boots back on, just in case he needed to stick to the floor.

A series of practical choices, not a performance, but from the wide-eyed way Jake looked at him, it might as well have been. Solomon couldn't recall ever having felt so naked. In his previous life, he'd had the naturally unselfconscious bearing of someone whose partners had always admired him, but what he'd mistaken for unassailable confidence in himself was inextricable from his disregard for their opinions. He'd known he was beautiful. It hadn't mattered whether anyone else thought so—until now.

It was cruel that he should find himself longing for Jake's approval when there was so much less to approve of.

The grace he'd once prided himself on was long gone. A catalogue of flaws spiralled through his thoughts, every complaint he'd accumulated since his return to life, and he wondered if Jake could see all those things. It was awful to stand naked in front of another person and not know if you were enough.

Jake's gaze slid down his body, slow and hot.

Oh.

"Fuck, you're gorgeous. You gonna touch me or what?"

There was an advantage to caring what other people thought of you: it meant a great deal more when they licked their lips like they'd never seen anything better.

Solomon smiled and went to him. He wanted to press so close, so deep into Jake that nothing could pass between them. To fuck him, yes, but also to stay right there, touching from hips to chest, with his face buried in Jake's neck and Jake's pulse louder than the sound of the universe.

It had been a mistake to ask Jake to grip the handhold. He could be holding Sol instead. The regret Solomon felt was almost enough to stop the game, but no, not before they'd gotten an orgasm out of it.

Solomon lifted his head, dragged a series of open-mouthed kisses up Jake's neck, nipped at his earlobe, retraced his steps, and went lower, caressing with lips and tongue, letting his teeth graze Jake's skin. Jake whimpered. He squirmed a little, too, especially when Solomon ground against him, rubbing his cock against Jake's thigh. Solomon could tell he wanted to respond in kind, and Jake made the most beautiful, frustrated little sound about it. Between the mag boots and the handhold that made him stretch his arms over his head, he could barely move.

Unless he let go. A simple thing, entirely within his

power, and one he would not do. Because Solomon had asked.

"You are so good," Solomon told him, maybe more earnestly than he'd ever said anything in his life. He moved back up to kiss Jake on the mouth. "And so pretty."

"Yeah, but are you ever gonna *do* something about it?" Jake asked.

Solomon laughed and kissed him again. "So you admit I'm right."

"I'll admit anything you want if you'll touch me already."

"I am touching you." Solomon's fingertips met the short fuzz of his hair and the smooth shell of his ear. He ran his hands down Jake's sides then slid them back to squeeze his ass, sinking his fingers in.

Jake groaned. "Sol."

Oh. That was—that was good. His lips curled in a smile. "What did you have in mind? Do you want me to suck you off?"

"I mean, I don't *not* want that," Jake said. Fuck, it was delicious to watch him work his way up to talking about it. The contraction and release of his muscles, the way his teeth briefly sank into his lower lip. "And if we did that again, I think I could do a better job this time around."

"It was already perfect," Solomon said, drawing a finger along the stubbled underside of Jake's jaw. It hadn't mattered that it was a little hesitant—no, it *had* mattered. He'd had a shattering orgasm last night simply from knowing that it was Jake touching him. And there was nothing more characteristic than Jake wanting to figure something out so he could do it better. Solomon hadn't even asked him for anything; Jake had offered.

It was so sweet that it made something in his chest ache.

That kind of generosity—no, Solomon couldn't think about that, about how rare and precious this felt, about how even if he lived, he'd probably never have this again.

Solomon brought his focus back to Jake's face. Those reddened, bitten lips. He said, "I notice you're assuming whatever we do will be reciprocal."

"Is that not how this works?" Jake's brows drew together.

"Reciprocity is an excellent idea," Solomon assured him. "We can put it into action right now."

He stepped out of his boots, held onto Jake's hips again, and kicked off the floor. Maneuvering himself into position —upside-down, his mouth level with Jake's cock—was easy, though he had to take some care not to knee Jake in the face.

"Whoa."

"Is this okay?" Solomon asked. He wasn't concerned for himself. Upside-down was a malleable concept without gravity, just as *wall* and *floor* were interchangeable.

"Yeah. Yes. Absolutely. You weren't kidding about reciprocity. You sure we can make this work?" Jake asked. "You'd be better stabilized if I held onto you with one hand. I don't want you to float away."

"Keep your hands on the handhold. Use your mouth."

Jake muttered "oh" very quietly and Solomon could *hear* him blushing. He craned his neck. It was comically awkward for a moment, and they both laughed, but then Jake got his mouth around Solomon's dick, and it was hot and tight and perfect.

"Fuck," Solomon said, exhaling. And then he wet his lips and reciprocated, as promised.

He couldn't exercise much finesse like this, distracted and halfway to bliss, but it didn't matter. He loved it anyway—the slippery, salty fullness in his mouth, the loud, hot slide of Jake's lips against his skin, the intensity of feeling that they were trading back and forth. It was these things, the smells and tastes and textures that would have been the same here or in his bed in the cabin, that made him wildest.

Jake made little noises, panting and gasping around Solomon's dick, every time Solomon took him particularly deep. Stuttering and irregular, desperate, pleased, they were better than music. Sol never wanted to hear anything else.

He had both hands gripping Jake's massive thighs, all the tension in his body focused into the tips of his fingers so he could relax his throat all the way open. The skill had come back to him quickly—or maybe it was easy to do this for Jake. He trusted Jake. He wanted Jake inside him, just as he wanted to be inside Jake, to thrust until the heat of Jake's mouth enveloped him to the root. Their interlocking closeness was heaven. It ought to last forever.

It couldn't—he could already feel the end barreling down on him—but there was sweetness in that, too. He craved the ending just as much as he craved the repetition, that slick, slow circling in and out. He wanted to do this again and again, to do other things, to do everything, to repeat this feeling in all possible variations, always with Jake.

When it came, he couldn't say what had happened first, the spill of his own orgasm or the swallowing down of Jake's. A simultaneous burst of sensation, of filling and emptying, left his heart pounding and his body slack.

He wiped a hand across his lips.

"Jesus," Jake said, his breath frayed around the edges.

Solomon hummed his agreement and carefully extracted himself. He pushed one foot off the wall to flip himself over and landed with his back to Jake. His bare foot touched the cool floor just long enough for him to turn around and face Jake, and then he drifted upward by a few centimeters.

Surveying his work made him smile. Flushed and mussed, Jake looked even better than he had. And he was still holding on, as instructed, which was its own little rush.

"You can let go," Solomon said, and Jake's arms came around him instantly—almost magnetically. With his own arms trapped against his sides, there was little for Solomon to do except rest his hands on Jake's hips. Gravity or no gravity, he wasn't going anywhere.

"That was good," Jake said, his voice soft next to Solomon's ear.

"It was." Sol pressed himself into Jake just for the pleasure of it, nestling his face against Jake's shoulder.

He felt Jake shift minutely.

"Did you, uh, bring a bottle of lube in here? There's one just kinda floating."

"Oh," Solomon said. He'd forgotten that. "I thought we might want it, but—"

"For what?"

"Is that a serious question?" Solomon raised his head. Jake might not have experience, but surely he had basic knowledge.

"No, I know it's for anal sex," Jake said, and Solomon was both proud of him for getting through the whole sentence and charmed by his little pause in the middle of it. "I mean what specifically did you, Solomon Lange, want it for."

"To fuck you," Solomon said bluntly, and had the satisfaction of watching Jake's lips part and release no sound. "But only if you wanted."

"Is that offer still open? I could go another round."

"Yes." Solomon might need a minute, but he could be ready by the time Jake was. He couldn't miss this. There might never be another chance. "Put your hands back on the handhold and spread your legs."

Solomon slicked up his fingers, slid them in, and had the pleasure of watching Jake's dick swell back to fullness as he worked. It was leaking by the time he was satisfied with his thoroughness—and so was his own. No matter that he'd just come, he felt wild again, need burning inside him. He held it in check so he could kneel down and slip the mag boots off Jake's feet and put his own pair back on.

"Sol?"

"I'm going to lift your legs," Solomon said, surprised to hear anything other than a grunt exit his own throat. "Okay?"

"Yeah."

Solomon picked Jake up, holding him so his legs were folded, his calves draped over Solomon's arms. It was an unusual position, and an exceptionally helpless one for Jake. Solomon ignored his own wants for a moment so he could say, as gently as possible, "Still good?"

"Very. You have a thing for picking me up, you know."

In zero g, and with telekinesis, Solomon didn't actually need his hands to hold Jake still. So it was easy to reach between them, stroke one finger lightly up his glistening cock, and say, "You have a thing for it, too."

Jake huffed. "Maybe I do."

They were quiet after that, both watching as Solomon braced himself, fitted his cock against Jake, and then slid carefully into the tight channel of Jake's body. It shocked sound out of both of them, two wordless grunts, and then Jake said, "Fuck. Kiss me."

Solomon obeyed, plunging his tongue between Jake's

lips as he thrust deeper. With Jake panting and pleading into his mouth, there was no question of slowing down. Solomon gave himself up to desire. Jake felt too good around him, slippery and tight, and he could think of nothing. There was only his need, honed down to a single motion. In and out, in and out, he drove his hips and clung to Jake, licking sweetness from the inside of his mouth and salt from his skin, until his balls drew in tight and he couldn't hold off any longer. He shoved his hand between their bodies to grasp Jake's dick. Jake came in his hand, a flood of hot liquid over his fingers, and Solomon lost it, crying out at the rush of bliss. He came in a few fierce, uncontrolled thrusts.

They freed themselves carefully, Solomon letting Jake stretch his arms and legs, and then leaned against each other, sticky and breathing hard.

"Holy fuck," Jake said. "That was incredible."

"Mmm," Solomon agreed. "Next time you're doing all the work."

"So there's a next time, then? Will it be you holding on, since I already proved that I'm not going anywhere?"

Jake's tone was teasing, but Solomon still lifted his head to meet his eyes. All the languor left his body. Their earlier argument, which was less an argument and more an airing of all his fears, roared back to life. His life was strung taut between nearly losing himself in the Nowhere and whatever terrible accident came next. Falling in love—because that's what this was, no matter how much he denied it—meant setting himself up for another loss.

Solomon said, "You can't promise that. It's not within your control."

"You're right. I can't promise not to die," Jake said easily. "But for now, I'm here if you want me to be here, Sol."

"I do want it," Solomon said, the confession sliding out

of him like the point of a knife that had gone into his back and pierced right through his heart. Painful. Inadequate. There was so much more lodged inside him. "But what I want is worth very little."

"No," Jake said, a fond smile creeping into his expression. "It's worth a lot."

A DRUNKEN GEOMETRY QUIZ

JAKE LEFT THE ROOM THE NEXT MORNING BUOYED BY having woken up with Sol, who did indeed want *something* from or with him. It was okay that Sol's confession hadn't been more specific. He'd been through some shit and they weren't exactly in the clear.

Besides, Jake didn't have any idea what he wanted, either. He'd never been in a relationship before. Maybe that should scare him, but enjoying someone's company and having great sex seemed like a pretty solid foundation. He really, really hoped they figured out how to fix the breach without massively damaging reality or each other, because he wanted to know what the future held after that.

He smiled at Sol over breakfast. Jake had assumed that Sol wouldn't be a morning person. Genius scientists had all their brilliant revelations in the middle of the night, either lying awake in bed or staring into the blue glow of a screen in their lab, and in the morning they scowled and grunted until they'd been supplied with enough coffee. Something like that. But Sol's grouchiness wasn't confined to any particular hour of the day—not that the hours of the day meant much here in lunar orbit—and this morning, Sol was content to smile back. That was gratifying.

"I'm gonna work on fixing the gravity generator today," Jake said.

Dax and Lenny walked into the kitchen, preventing him from adding that he'd like to feel Sol's weight on top of him in bed.

Jake continued, "No sense in fixing the plumbing until the generator's done, since we can't run any of the taps with the gravity off."

"You're a godsend, Jake," Lenny said. "You know that, right?"

"Gravity *and* a shower," Dax said with palpable yearning. "It's true what they say, that you don't know what you've got 'til it's gone."

"Weightlessness has its charms," Sol said, his expression perfectly neutral and appropriate, but his eyes on Jake.

"Uh," Jake said, wishing Sol weren't fixing him with that look, wishing the thought of last night didn't make his dick swell. Christ, he shouldn't be enjoying this. Fuck, fuck, fuck. What were they talking about? Repairs to the generator. "Just... trying to be useful."

"Of course," Sol said, like he wasn't the multiverse's worst little shit. "You're always solving problems. I appreciate that about you."

The only thing worse than sexual innuendo was earnest praise, and Jake couldn't tell which that was—fuck, what if it was *both*—so he stared blankly at the sink to give his brain a second to buffer.

"We cleaned up the mess in the greenhouse yesterday," Lenny said, oblivious to whatever was between them. "I'll probably play lab assistant for Emil today, not that we're gonna discover anything from those samples we took."

"If you're looking for work, there are more things that need fixing," Jake said. Lenny had been an aerospace engineer before he'd come to work for Quint Services and made his home at Facility 17, and he and Jake had taken apart many machines together. "I could use a second set of hands with the generator—should be a simple fix, I have all the parts—and Lange needs help building another sensor in his lab. Our new method of measuring the distortions is, uh, pretty primitive."

"It's simple and effective," Sol countered, his stare equally as intense as when he'd been speaking in innuendo.

"You took measurements?" Dax asked, their ginger brows drawing together. They'd been essential to all of Sol's work at Facility 17, so they were understandably perplexed by news of progress that had happened without their presence.

"Not really," Jake said. "We were in there last night after dinner and Lange noticed that the distortions had shrunk, so we repainted the floor to reflect the new arrangement. Didn't get close enough to the breach itself to tell what's going on there."

"Well," Dax said. "I look forward to throwing a tennis ball in. Science at its finest."

"You say that as if I didn't spend hours yesterday playing guitar at it," Sol said, and when he offered a wry smile to Dax, their face froze in shock.

"Symphony in WTF minor," they said, once they'd recovered.

"I'll make you second author, just for coming up with the title," Sol promised.

"Do symphonies have second authors?" Dax asked, their eyes crinkling at the corners. "Anyway, I'll meet you in the lab in just a sec, I'm gonna go clean up a bit."

"I should do the same," Sol said, and then they both left.

"Don't get me wrong, I do wanna help you," Lenny said once he and Jake were alone. "But I also wanna see the lab. Your masterpiece."

"It's not exactly museum-worthy. But sure," Jake said. He and Lenny cleared the air of empty drink pouches and protein-bar wrappers from breakfast. Jake's plans to fix the generator and the pipes felt mundane compared to the day Sol was about to have, in which he would attempt to communicate with an alien through music and then perhaps together they'd repair a rift in the universe. But people lived in this facility, and they needed to eat and wash. He could make that happen. He could be useful.

And if he fixed the generator, then maybe later he could sit in bed, pull Sol into his lap, and feel the weight against his thighs.

Next time you're doing all the work.

Jake set that thought aside and led Lenny out of the kitchen and toward Sol's lab, wondering what Lenny would make of it. Jake had been honest—the paint lines criss-crossing the floor didn't look like anything he'd ever seen framed and hanging on a wall, but he didn't exactly frequent art museums. When he and Sol and Eliza had finished painting last night, the floor had looked like a nonsensical diagram, just a scattering of polygonal forms laid over each other. Walking down the hall, he amused himself with possible comparisons: a drunken geometry quiz, a chessboard he wasn't advanced enough to play, a series of road signs for alien traffic.

The hallway seemed longer than usual.

Jake stopped. Nothing in his surroundings looked differ-ent. Ahead, he could see the brown paper covering the windows to Sol's lab, and the grey door that had been purposefully left ajar so as not to trap anyone in the room while the electricity was unreliable. The lights were on, and he was grateful he'd spent the time to make them that way, so the empty corridor in front of him was bright white and non-threatening.

Or at least, it would have been non-threatening if he didn't have the distinct impression that something was fucked.

"Lenny," Jake yelled.

No answer. Shit.

Cautiously, Jake turned around, hoping to catch sight of Lenny behind him. He kept his feet exactly where they were and moved as little as possible, recalling Sol shouting "not that far to the left" at him when they'd navigated the maze in his lab together.

Lenny wasn't there. Worse, the kitchen wasn't there. The hallway behind him looked exactly like the hallway in front of him, including the door to Sol's lab. It was empty and bright white and very, very threatening.

He'd walked into a distortion. Last night they'd charted what they thought was shrinkage and disappearance among the ones in Sol's lab, but maybe none of the distortions had disappeared. Maybe they'd just moved.

Sol was the only one who could see them, and Sol hadn't been here to tell Jake not to walk down this hallway.

Jake hadn't thought it would be like this. When Emil had walked through the breach, into the Nowhere, and out the other side, he'd gone to some alien planet. Jake had assumed that the distortions in Sol's lab would work like that—step into one, you'd end up in the Nowhere, or maybe on the other side of it if you were lucky. The void was, after all, a membrane that touched all of space. That was how runners could use it to get anywhere.

Jake felt stupid, having done the fucked-up physics equivalent of falling into a hole, but in his defense, he couldn't see the damn thing. Sol had never really described his perception, and before this, Jake had idly imagined the distortions as windows hanging in the air, as if he might glance down a hallway at Facility 17 and suddenly find himself looking at a moonlit ocean or the surface of some unknown planet. But it had all just looked like hallway.

A new landscape would almost have been reassuring. The sameness of his surroundings made him doubt his own perceptions. Creepy as shit.

Nothing was actively trying to kill him. That was good. He could just wait here. Lenny had probably already gone to tell the others about his disappearance, and in just a second, Kit would come get him out.

Still, it was worth examining his surroundings one more time to see if he'd missed some detail. Maybe there was a way to rescue himself. He turned back around, expecting the funhouse-mirror setup from a second ago—infinite, identical hallway in every direction.

Mere meters from where he stood, the walls and floor begin to melt and stretch, their edges collapsing into each other. The white-coated metal panels that made up the walls of Facility 17 vanished, revealing no sign of the wiring he'd spent all of yesterday fixing, or the rough surface of the asteroid. There was nothing but a pool of featureless white, oozing closer, shrinking the space around him.

Well. That wasn't good.

He searched his spacesuit pockets and came up with a screw. He'd stuck a handful in there, since the ones in the grav generator were all corroded and he'd meant to replace them today. Experimentally, he tossed one into the whiteness. It was instantly swallowed.

Jake turned and ran the other way, hoping the hallway would hold out.

———

CATCHING sight of Lenny in the bathroom mirror sent a foamy mouthful of toothpaste down Solomon's throat. He coughed, wiped his mouth, and blurted, "What's wrong?"

It was clear from Lenny's expression and the way he hovered in the door that this was the appropriate opening question.

Before Lenny could get a word out, Solomon added another. "Where's Jake?"

A waste of time to ask. His heart was pounding with the answer he already knew. The wreckage of his disastrous experiment had cost him yet again.

"Show me," Solomon said, shoving his hygiene kit back into its bag, and Lenny nodded and led him to the hallway between the kitchen and his lab. Dax followed.

The new distortion—or perhaps not new, but newly migrated to this spot—snaked through the middle of the corridor. From this angle, the glimmer took the form of an integral symbol, a stretched-out S wavering between the walls. It was wide enough that it would be almost impossible to walk around—and Solomon could *see* it. No one else would stand a chance.

Jake had walked into that.

Solomon didn't realize he'd taken a step toward it until he felt Lenny's hand clamp around his shoulder.

Lenny was a large man, bigger than Jake even, and he wasn't afraid to make that clear with the strength of his grip. It was at odds with his easy demeanor. "No. Not letting you run headlong into a mysterious hole in reality. We're not doing that today."

"Jake's in there," Solomon said, and it was the most evident and the most urgent thing he'd ever said in his life. He could think of nothing else.

Jake. Trapped. His fault.

"He *was* in there," Lenny corrected. "Look, I'm not a physicist, but I did have access to the Nowhere for a little while, so I know you can't always count on space to work like you think it will. It's a whole thing. You wrote a book on it? At least I think that's what your book's about. Anyway, I'm gonna vote that you don't hurl yourself in there."

"I *am* a physicist and I agree," Dax said. "Let's retreat to somewhere space *isn't* making a mockery of everything we perceive."

The soles of Solomon's shoes were attached to the floor with something stronger than magnets, and even in zero g, his body was an immovable weight. He peered into the distortion, aching for a glimpse, for anything, some flash behind the smoky ripple in the air.

It had happened. He'd feared some terrible accident would end his relationship with Jake—yes, *relationship*, having sex with someone you cared for was a relationship, to call it by any other name was foolish—and here it was. Fearing the worst had left him no more prepared for it than he would have been otherwise. Indeed, it had left him *less* prepared.

He had imagined, naively, that he could make this moment easier. He had known it was coming. If he felt less for Jake, he would hurt less when Jake was gone. What was a feeling but some cocktail of hormones, a few synapses firing? It only had meaning if he gave it meaning. Unacknowledged, it was a bodily reaction, no more important than a rash or a runny nose. It would pass. Silence would allow him to exert control over himself, over the situation, over the inevitable suffering. Fear of pain had kept him silent; his silence had not protected him.

Jake was gone, and Solomon had never told him even a fraction of how he felt.

It hurt like hell. There was something freeing in that. He was hurt and afraid and he was right to be both of those things. Solomon was not more than the sum of his parts. He was all synapses, all adrenaline, a body awash in feelings, and he would not have traded away one single drop of sweat to lessen his own reaction. He didn't want distance or control. This was the body that Jake had touched and kissed and adored, and it *was* Solomon. He was here and alive with his heart pounding in fear. It was awful. It was necessary. Inside his skin was a delicate, complex branching of nerves, every last one lit up with emotion, all the way up his spine and into his brain, and he was going to use absolutely all of it to get Jake out.

The first step of a plan had already come to him.

Solomon opened his mouth and discovered that though it was a complicated operation to vibrate his vocal folds and shape sounds with his tongue, it was easy to say, "I can't do this alone. I need your help."

———

THE WHOLE TEAM—MINUS Jake—gathered in the common room, after Solomon had meticulously checked the remainder of the facility for invisible interdimensional hazards.

Outside his lab, there was only the one. It was one too many.

He surveyed the six people in the room. They were leaning on each other (Chávez, Lenny), standing at the ready (Emil, Miriam), industriously pumping water into the coffee maker in the absence of plumbing or gravity (Dax), or somehow affecting a careless, slouched posture even while weightless (Kit).

It should not shock him that they wanted to help. It was well established that they all liked Jake. But there was something in their faces, something in the way Chávez had touched his shoulder on her way into the room—Solomon couldn't think about it, not if he wanted his throat open and his eyes dry.

He was terrified, and yet there was calm in it. He poured all of his focus into the plan.

"The simplest option, and thus the first one we should try, is for Kit to retrace Jake's steps," Solomon began, his voice steadier than he'd thought.

"Yeah, sure," Kit said and was gone before Solomon could finish.

The space Kit had vacated quivered with his absence, the wall too bare, the floor too grey. Despite an entire career specializing in the physics of the Nowhere, Solomon had not spent a great deal of time with runners. There were so few of them in the world, and they tended to stay well away from anything resembling scientific research. Still, he suspected that even for people who'd spent their whole lives around runners, it was difficult to accustom oneself to their sudden vanishings. His heart had jumped at Kit's disappearance, seized with a potent combination of shock and hope. Maybe Kit would come back with Jake.

He didn't.

Kit reappeared alone and shrugged in apology, displaying his empty palms, the gesture revealing a pair of outrageously frivolous black lace fingerless gloves at the end of his spacesuit sleeves. "Sorry. I went to the hallway, but there's nothing there."

"What do you mean there's nothing there?" Solomon asked.

"No distortion, no Jake," Kit said. "I walked all over in regular space and nothing happened, and then I checked the Nowhere just to be sure, but he wasn't there, either."

If the distortion that had swallowed Jake had already disappeared, that boded ill for finding him. "So the distortions are unstable," Solomon said. He'd known that already, given that one had moved into the hallway.

Kit said, "The Nowhere's unpredictable, especially around the breach and all these distortions. I know it's only been minutes since Jake walked in, but he could be anywhere. It took me *days* to find and catch your cats."

"You could try again later. Or ask Laila for help," Chávez said to Kit, because for her, asking for help was an everyday occurrence. So was optimism.

"Sure," Kit said. "I could ask every runner I know for help. But the Nowhere is... if you're not using it for instant travel, it's different. It's hard to explain. Imagine an ocean. That's how hard it is to search. When Lange was trapped, I only ever knew where he was because he kept slamming into me."

This was not an accusation, but an observation, and accordingly, Solomon did not flinch. He didn't move at all.

"We're cool now, you already said sorry, it's fine," Kit said, flicking a black-gloved hand in the air. He addressed Chávez and the rest of the room. "I'm not saying I won't look again, or that I won't ask for help. I'm saying it might not work even if I do."

"I hate to interrupt with more bad news, but all of this

assumes that Jake is *in* the Nowhere, trapped like you were," Emil said, nodding at Solomon. "Can we be sure that's the case? Isn't it possible that he might have gone *through?*"

There was so much in those few sentences worth despairing over—*trapped like you were*—that for a moment, Solomon could only nod, his throat closed. "Yes. It's possible Jake passed through the Nowhere and is now on some other planet, or in some other reality, or already dead."

Most of the people in the room recoiled, but Solomon didn't see any point in euphemism. Death was a highly likely outcome. The best way to survive the experience was not to have it.

They were past that point.

"If that is the case, obviously our chances of rescuing him are so infinitesimal as not to be worth considering," Solomon said.

Before assembling everyone into this room, he'd been grateful for the intensity of his feelings. The force would carry him through. Now that he was presenting his ideas to six other adults, he wished his face felt less like a dam holding back a flood. *Cry later*, he told himself, *think now*.

"We know very little about what happens when non-runners encounter the breach or its attendant spatial distortions. One thing we do know is that the Nowhere, in its usual condition, ejects non-runners. If Kit were to let go of a passenger mid-jump, they wouldn't be trapped, as I was. They would simply reappear in normal, folded space— usually exactly where they had been. Evidently, this has not happened to Jake."

"So maybe he's not in the Nowhere," Kit said, catching on.

Solomon nodded. "I think the distortions might constitute their own, separate phenomenon. They may be pockets of space, unconnected to the Nowhere."

"Well, it's easier to search those than the infinite rest of the multiverse, right?" Lenny asked.

"I can probably get into them," Kit said.

"Perhaps you can," Solomon agreed. "But there were 19 at last count—no, there were 20, we miscounted. I suppose there are 19 now, if the one in the hallway is gone. Either way, that is more jumps than you can safely make in a day. We should narrow down our options first."

If Jake were dead, their options might already have narrowed to nothing. But it wasn't death that worried Solomon the most. Jake might be alive, but crushed or stretched by the volatile space around him. Sol sucked in a breath, the memory of his own torture in the Nowhere piercing his senses.

He had to get Jake out now.

As grateful as Solomon was for the team's support, he was also relieved to find himself in the lab with only Chávez, whose company he liked very much, and Kit, whose company still mystified him, but whose ability could be crucial to rescuing Jake. Lenny and Emil had gone to work on the gravity generator. Dax, as the only other person with a sense of how Lange's machine worked, had been tasked with building a new sensor to measure the breach, and they'd taken Miriam with them to help. The two of them had wisely decamped to another room for this purpose, leaving Solomon to compare the original hand-drawn map of the distortions with the lines that he and Jake and Eliza had painted on the floor.

Eliza had not followed Jake wherever he'd gone. She'd been in the hallway outside. She was at Lange's heels now, as though she'd latched onto him in Jake's absence.

Jake had annotated his original map of the room, assigning each distortion a letter. Solomon froze at the sight of Jake's handwriting, block capitals that had nothing in common with his own impatient scrawl. Jake's crossword puzzles had looked just like that. Solomon had watched Jake enter the answers when they'd done them together in the cabin, but he could picture the one they'd done together in the pod, the one where Solomon hadn't seen the page and Jake had complimented his ability to hold the whole shape in his mind's eye.

Useless. None of that would save Jake's life.

There were 23 distortions at first count, so Jake had lettered them A through W. Last night when they'd repainted the lab, they'd thought H, K, M, and P had disappeared. From the original placement, Solomon suspected that it was distortion M that had drifted into the hallway and caught Jake. And now it was gone just like H, K, and P. Solomon hadn't seen them in his check of the facility, and he'd been as thorough as possible. And yesterday he and Chávez had convinced themselves that maybe the alien was working to repair things, which might mean the distortions *were* vanishing.

But what would happen if one vanished with Jake inside?

"Looks like a fucked-up jigsaw puzzle," Kit said, observing the painted lines.

Solomon was trying to think, and he didn't appreciate being interrupted with inanities, but before he could say so, Chávez spoke.

"Really, just a regular jigsaw puzzle before you put it together," Chávez said. "Sucks that we can't move the pieces around."

"To make what, exactly? Another breach?" Kit asked.

Chávez shrugged. "I dunno, I'm just here for moral support. The physics is all Lange."

"Yeah, I don't get that part, either," Kit said. "I learned to play by ear."

Chávez laughed and said, "You know, the way Jake lettered them on that page, it kind of reminds me of signs in a subway station. Except we don't know where any of them go."

"I would have said 'all signs point to the Nowhere,' but I guess maybe they don't," Kit said.

"Wait," Solomon said, something about this conversation nagging at him. "Stop talking. Say that again."

"Contradictory instructions, my friend," Chávez teased. "But sure. Um, we talked about jigsaw puzzles, moving pieces around, and, uh, subway station signage?"

Solomon turned all of that over in his mind. There was *something* there. He put his head in his hands. He needed more time to think this through, and there was none.

Distortion M had moved as a result of what the organism had done yesterday. What *he* and the organism had done yesterday.

What else can you move? Jake had asked him that when they'd been down on the surface. They'd experimented with solid objects. Solomon had also moved liquids. When they'd discovered the air leak, he'd briefly stopped the flow of air just to see if he could. He'd been too limited in his thinking. Yesterday, working with the organism, he had changed the shape of space itself.

"We *did* move the puzzle pieces around," Solomon said. "And maybe they do fit together. What if the distortions are connected? They don't lead to the Nowhere, but they might lead to each other. Bring me all the tennis balls you can find. And some permanent markers."

Kit nodded, and then he and Chávez left.

Hurtling toward the Earth's surface in the pod with the cracked heat shield, all Solomon had known was that he had to hang on. This was exactly the same. He'd had an idea and he would see it through.

With no one else in the lab, the sounds of the breach and the organism pierced his brain. Every time he thought himself accustomed to it, the strangeness of it struck him anew. This sound that wasn't sound, this hearing that wasn't hearing—it was connected to how things moved.

I learned to play by ear, Kit had said. The phrase fit Solomon's new ability even better.

All of that wanted more reflection, but Kit and Chávez had come back not only with supplies, but with Dax and Miriam, who were carrying a laptop and a new sensor, respectively. The device was lopsided and had all its wires showing, so it looked significantly more homemade than its sleek chrome predecessor, but Solomon had no doubt it worked.

"Heard you were gonna toss some tennis balls into Volatile Discrete Spatial Distortions and I wanted in," Dax said.

"The Dax Strickland technique," Solomon said.

"Is that a joke? I can't tell with you anymore," Dax said.

Solomon couldn't bring himself to smile, not when Jake was still in danger, but he did feel a certain appreciation for Dax. Maybe even affection. So instead he said, "You're smarter than I was at 23. And a lot less prickly. And probably the best scientific collaborator I've ever had—of any age."

"I think this might be worse than when all you did was occasionally grunt criticism at me," Dax said, their face scrunched up in distaste, but pink all the way up to their ginger hairline.

Chávez laughed at both of them, then reached into the basket of tennis balls in her arm and threw one at Solomon. who caught it, grabbed a marker, and wrote "A" on it.

Solomon looked at the four people who'd gathered in the lab to help him. "Can one of you take notes?"

"I can try. What are we doing exactly?" Miriam asked.

"Making a map," Solomon said. "Jake's original map is still on the table. Can you copy it?"

"Sure," she said.

While she worked, Solomon maneuvered the tennis ball in a curving path through the room until it disappeared into the distortion that Jake had labeled "A."

It didn't reappear, but that didn't trouble him. "The ball we sent into distortion A didn't come back. Mark an X."

Miriam dutifully noted that on her copied map. Dax, Chávez, and Kit caught onto Solomon's plan quickly, though they served more as moral support than actual help. None of them could see the distortions, and Solomon could manipulate the tennis balls in any direction he wanted. Help or no help, their presence comforted him. He did not have time to investigate that.

Distortions B and C returned nothing, but the ball he sent into distortion D floated out of distortion J a moment later. It blinked out of view for a few seconds and then reappeared in a seemingly unrelated location, its path defying all the usual understanding of how an object ought to move. There were *tunnels* between the distortions. Chávez's subway analogy wasn't so far off.

"Yes! Write that down," Solomon said. "There's a tunnel between D and J. Draw a line between them."

"Not that I object to this," Miriam said, "but I wouldn't mind knowing *why* we're doing it."

Solomon said, "Jake walked into distortion M, which

has since vanished. Jake is not in normal space—the hallway —and Kit didn't see him in the Nowhere on his first check, so the collapse of distortion M didn't spit him out in either of those places. But some of these pockets of distorted space are connected to each other, so there is a chance we will find Jake in another one."

"Oh," Miriam said, her brunette head bent studiously over the map she had copied. She did not ask any questions about what might have happened if Jake had *not* exited distortion M before it collapsed and vanished, which Solomon supposed was a small kindness.

The five of them were quiet. The work went quickly, which was good because it left less time to dwell on how infrequently they discovered connections. Distortions E and F were connected, but they were right next to each other, and neither was close to where Jake had disappeared. Distortion I also connected to both E and F, but that was no use to him.

Distortions H and K were two of the vanished ones. Solomon tried vainly not to hope for anything as the alphabet approached M, but he inhaled sharply when distortion L was a dead end.

When it came time to throw something into distortion N and the air was bare of any sign of a glimmer, his whole body stopped moving—muscles, heart, lungs, everything. On any other day, reality returning to its normal parameters would be a comfort. He'd spent all of yesterday trying to achieve exactly that.

Today, Jake was gone. They'd found almost nothing useful and the pockets of distorted space were collapsing right in front of him.

Solomon forced himself to say, very steadily, "Strike distortion N from the map."

Chávez came up to him, nudged his shoulder with her own, and said, "We still have almost half the alphabet left. And even if we get to the end without finding him, Kit can look again. It's not over."

Solomon took a deep breath, searched the lab for that telltale glimmer in the air, and felt his stomach drop. "Strike distortion O from the map."

Distortions H and P had vanished yesterday. The whole cluster around distortion M had collapsed.

"You don't know," Chávez told him, and he thought she might be reassuring herself, too. "You don't know which ones are connected. It might not matter that these are close together."

Q, S, and V were connected, while R and T were dead ends. Only U and W remained. Solomon had almost stopped breathing. There were no thoughts in his head, only the action of his hand dragging the marker in a long semi-circle over the curved felt.

The tennis ball he threw into distortion U disappeared.

"Mark distortion U as a dead end," he said, his voice flat.

Chávez reached for his hand and squeezed.

He shook her off to grab one last tennis ball. The point of the marker made a vaguely letter-like zigzag on it. It didn't matter how well he labeled the last one. Nothing would come of it.

Solomon hovered the ball into the air, but didn't direct it anywhere.

A tennis ball sailed out of distortion W, clanged against the wall, and drifted into the air. Solomon held it still before it could float into another distortion and disappear.

"What was that?" Dax asked. They walked forward as

if to retrieve it, and Solomon barred their passage with his arm. "Tennis balls don't sound like that."

"I know," Solomon said. "*Please* don't walk any closer."

Solomon pulled the ball nearer. He could tell it was too heavy, but he didn't understand why until it met his hand.

It was the one from distortion U. Opposite the letter, there was a screw stabbed into the green felt.

As good as a signature. A couple of tear globules rose into the air before Solomon could speak. "He's alive."

"Oh, thank God," Chávez said, and there was a collective sigh of relief.

Lenny and Emil entered the lab then, and Lenny said, "Heads up, everyone, we fixed the generator and we're gonna ramp up to normal gravity starting now. Should take about fifteen minutes. Why are you looking at me like that?"

"We found Jake," Chávez said. She grinned at him. "Lange found Jake. And nice work on the generator."

"Where is he?" Lenny asked, and Chávez pointed to the general area, which must look to her like a random empty space near the lab wall.

Jake had walked into distortion M in the hallway, and now he was trapped in a pocket of space on the opposite side of the lab. It was fascinating to consider how he might have arrived there, what unseen tunnels and whorls of space linked the two, but Solomon could only think of how to get Jake out.

Emil said, "That's great that you found him. How do we save him? Is it safe for Kit to retrieve him?"

"The distortions have been collapsing," Solomon said, which alarmed Emil. "So I think it's preferable for me to pull Jake out, rather than sending Kit in."

"Can you do that?" Emil asked with a slight, doubtful pause before the word *do*.

"Yes," Solomon said, thinking again of the cracked heat shield. Of lifting Jake by accident on the morning they'd done all those experiments outside the cabin. Of helping Jake walk through the heavy gravity in the gym. He'd successfully manipulated heavier, more massive things than Jake, and despite how delicate and complex the human body was, he'd managed not to hurt Jake in the gym.

Solomon thought about picking up one last tennis ball and writing something on it, an instruction or a reassurance, but he didn't. He couldn't think of anything brief enough to fit, and he shouldn't waste time. Jake knew what Solomon's telekinesis felt like. He wouldn't resist.

Solomon walked forward, grateful that distortions U and W were accessible from the untouched, safe part of the lab, so he didn't have to crawl through what remained of the maze. He could simply stop at the edge where the air rippled and stare into it.

Staring revealed nothing, as expected. He couldn't see inside. Distortion W had the footprint of a scalene triangle, but it was only one side that concerned him now. The side extended all the way to the ceiling, tall enough that Jake would be able to pass through it while standing, but the ragged bottom edge hovered just above Solomon's head, about two meters from the floor. The drop wouldn't matter in zero g, but it might be jarring in normal gravity—and it was impossible to say how things were oriented inside the distortion. "Up" and "down" were arbitrary in Facility 17 when the gravity was off; where Jake was, they might be meaningless.

The lack of sight was the real obstacle, but he hadn't needed sight to hold the heat shield together. He'd sensed where it was. Certainly, he had understood the shape and structure of the pod better than he understood the partially invisible distortions, but he wasn't without reference points. He could see where the distortions intersected with regular space, and better than that, he knew where the tennis ball had entered and exited.

Jake had thrown that tennis ball. Solomon thought of him fishing a screw out of his pocket and puncturing the felt with determination. He was resourceful. Thoughtful. He didn't fidget or pace. Only when he had a solution in hand would he act. It had been brief, the span of time between the tennis ball leaving Solomon's hand and finding Jake's. Jake had worked quickly.

And he was *close*.

Not close enough to touch or to see, but Solomon could sense him. His thoughts caught on the shape of him, of that body he hadn't had nearly enough time to explore, and the feel of him, not just the solid warmth, but the steadiness, the curiosity, the patience.

This was nothing like holding onto the heat shield. There was no headache, no clenched jaw, no nosebleed. Solomon had pulled on Jake in the cabin kitchen without trying. It was easy to let it happen again, to stop resisting, to fall back into his natural state. Of course he wanted to pull Jake closer. That was what he wanted all the time.

The shimmer in the air darkened, a violet-grey silhouette wavered under its surface, and Jake emerged.

Jake was upright and whole, and the sight of him left Solomon too frantic to discern more. Solomon no longer felt like he was pulling on Jake, but like a tether between them had snapped taut. He stepped closer.

Someone grabbed him from behind to keep him from danger. That startled Solomon into yanking Jake downward. They collided, Solomon stumbled, and the newly normal gravity dragged them down.

Jake was on top of him, his full weight pinning Solomon to the floor, breathing hard, smelling like sweat and ozone. Knocked flat on his back on the lab floor, all Sol could think was that there was nowhere else he'd rather be.

[19]

COMMUNICATION

J ake blacked out for a second. His brain refused to process the transition back into the real world from the awful melting, shrinking, not-a-place place where he'd been trapped. Just a brief, total shutdown of function. No sight, no sound.

After all the panicked sprinting he'd been doing, trying not to get stuck in a disappearing space, fainting was a huge relief.

When he blinked awake, Sol was underneath him. They were lying on the floor. Jake's vision swam. He must have fallen on top of Sol. Nothing to be done about it. He closed his eyes again and laid his head on Sol's shoulder. His body felt liquid and unresponsive, like the oozy quicksilver thing they'd seen in the exam room, except he had no plans to flow anywhere. Life as a puddle sounded fine. Someone else could scrape him up off the floor.

Sol stroked a hand through his hair and down his back, then wrapped both arms around him, reminding Jake that he did, in fact, have a solid corporeal form, one that was likely crushing Sol.

Somebody had fixed the gravity generator, then. Shit, he was back in Facility 17 with all its problems.

"Uh," he said. He should get up. He fumbled for the words, which felt as distant as the action. How did getting up work? It probably involved arms. His were busy trembling.

Sol kissed his temple. "You're okay."

"Uh," Jake said again. The relief of his escape wore off, leaving fatigue in his bones and buzzing in his nerves. Sol's arms were tight around him, at least. That was good. Sol smelled like sweat and skin and soap and Jake buried his nose in Sol's neck. It was so real and comforting, he almost burst into tears.

"Okay," Sol repeated, soothing. "You're okay."

Slowly, Jake collected himself and sat up. It was a complicated, exhausting process. Standing was beyond him. Being upright did allow him to glance around the lab, which contained a lot more people than he'd previously noticed. The walls seemed to be staying place. It was hard to grasp that it wouldn't all warp and disappear in a second.

None of the people in the room looked any different. It was the same day. Jake had been gone for a matter of hours, but it felt much longer.

Sol stood and offered Jake a hand.

Jake considered ignoring it and just staying on the floor. Sol bent down, took his hand, and pulled him to his feet. Standing was easier than it should have been. Sol had lifted him.

Jake wobbled on his feet, but didn't fall. His eyes met Sol's, and then Sol laid a hand on his cheek.

"You should rest."

Jake had no argument with that. Sol's eyes were huge with worry. Lying down sounded alright, but the idea of walking out of the lab—into the very same hallway that had nearly killed him—*nope*. The possibility scared him to full alertness and he shook his head vehemently.

"You don't want to?" Sol asked.

"Yeah, I'm good. I'll, uh, stick around."

His pause felt obvious, even ridiculous, to him. Jake had no idea what any of them intended to do next, or even what time it was. All he knew was that he couldn't go anywhere alone. The thought made him want to throw up.

Sol was watching him.

Please, please don't tell me to go to bed.

"I think," Sol said after a pause where he interlaced his fingers with Jake's, "that given how volatile the distortions have become, it is not safe for any of us as long as they still exist. So I move that we stay in this room and work to close them right now."

"How do we do that?" Emil asked.

"With the alien's help," Chávez said.

Sol must have nodded at her or something to get her to explain. Jake had missed it because Sol had started walking, tugging him along. She was still talking, but Jake didn't follow. The few, slow steps made him a little seasick, and he kept having to check that the walls and the floor were still where he'd thought they'd be.

There was still a single table in the room, one Sol had pulled in days ago, the first day Jake had painted the floor. It had a laptop and some papers on it—the map Jake had made, a copy with colorful lines all over it, a few blank sheets—and two of Facility 17's standard grey rolling chairs behind it. Dax was sitting in one and they pulled out the other and gestured for Jake to sit down.

Oh. Sol and Dax were *managing* him. Normally Jake would object, but as long as they weren't going to make him leave, nothing else mattered. If they knew how tired and freaked out he really was, they'd try to send him somewhere with a real bed, and he couldn't do that. Couldn't walk down the hallway. Couldn't be alone. Couldn't close his eyes.

They didn't know that yet and he didn't plan to let them. So—desk chair. In the same room as everyone else, with a clear view of the walls that were not melting. Acceptable.

Better than acceptable. He really, really wanted to sit down.

Sol's hands settled on his shoulders and didn't move. That was good. Jake was strongly in favor of nothing moving ever again.

He'd missed a huge chunk of the conversation, but nobody seemed to require his input. If they'd asked him anything, he'd failed to answer. Someone had scooped out the inside of his head and filled it with cotton. He didn't feel present enough to sit up straight, let alone contribute an idea.

Jake had carefully avoided looking too hard at the other side of the lab, the part of the room with the breach and all the discrete distortions he couldn't see. All those lines he'd had Eliza paint on the floor that hadn't helped him at all.

With Sol touching him, the near part of the room didn't feel so daunting. Dax had stood up and they were plugging a homemade-looking device—a new sensor to measure the breach, he thought—into the laptop, adjusting it, talking quietly to Miriam as she read aloud whatever was on the screen.

Lenny and Chávez were sitting on the floor. Chávez had Sol's guitar in her lap and was plucking at it and explaining something. Emil had picked up the paper maps from the table and was standing a short distance away examining them with Kit. They were all working as a team. No insults or arguments or anything. Jake had seen it before, but never with Sol participating.

Sol offered him a metal water bottle, the top already unscrewed. It might as well have been an alien artifact. Where had it come from? Sol had been standing behind him the whole time.

"It's water," Sol said, something unfamiliar in his voice. "Do you think you could drink some?"

Jake accepted it and took a sip, more for Sol than for himself. It was sweet and cold in his throat. He took another sip.

"Good. Could you eat?" Sol asked him softly. He trailed a hand down Jake's arm as he crouched down. "Soon we're all going to need dinner, but I could get you something now."

Jake shook his head. "Maybe later."

"And you're sure you don't want to lie down?"

Jake was sure he did. With Sol giving him a searching look, he managed to say, "I don't want to go anywhere."

Sol squeezed his knee. "You don't have to. I can go get—"

"No, don't."

"I can see the distortions, so there is very little risk for me."

Jake didn't say anything.

"I'll stay, then." Sol rose from his crouch and put his hands back on Jake's shoulders. "I can't promise not to let anything happen to you. Something already did. But we *will* solve this problem. Do you believe that?"

"Yeah," Jake said. He wanted to explain that he could know something in his mind—a fact like *Sol knows how to close the distortions* or *I got out*—and the knowledge couldn't stop the twitchy sense that maybe the room was shrinking and he needed to run. But he was too out of it to string all those words together.

"I wish you could see what I see. The room looks different. Our latest paint job is out of date. Several of the distortions have closed."

"I know." *Closed* was such a soothing, civilized word. *Slammed shut* was more like it. *Imploded*, maybe. He confined his unfocused gaze to the table, his lap, anything but the other side of the room.

"Jake." One of Sol's hands slid down Jake's chest to press against his heart. "I'm sorry."

"Not your fault." Jake put his hand over Sol's and craned his neck to look up at him. "And don't argue with me, I'm too tired for that."

"Can I not express a wish that you hadn't suffered?"

"Sure, if that's what you meant."

Sol grimaced, but it was gone from his face as quickly as it had come. "You don't need anything else?"

"I need to feel like the walls aren't about to close in," Jake said and shuddered.

"I will do my best." When Sol spoke again, it was disarmingly earnest. "I'm glad you're here."

"I'm glad I'm here, too," Jake said. His chest went tight. He couldn't begin to explain the terror and the relief of it all. "I'm glad *you're* here. But don't let me keep you. Go fix space."

Sol didn't move. Didn't say anything, either. He was humming softly to himself, not a song, just one droning sound. It didn't mean anything to Jake, but he picked it up, pressing his lips together and letting his hum blend with Sol's. It was meditative. Something to concentrate on.

Sol remained behind Jake, hands resting lightly on his shoulders, for long enough that Jake gave in to the temptation to follow his gaze and figure out what he was so intent on.

He gasped and jerked back against the chair when he saw it. Sol tightened his grip, and that was the only thing that kept Jake from bolting out of the chair.

The lab should have been a familiar view: white walls, dull grey flooring, a tangle of painted lines, and the two curved parentheses of the machine, now rusty everywhere it wasn't ridged with clusters of the coral-like organism. Jake could see all of that, but there was a film over it, like a rumpled sheet of plastic wrap catching the light. Here and there, it glowed like a tablet screen at night, cool and flickering.

None of it was still.

This was what Sol could see. These were the distortions. Three-dimensional shapes—at least, according to his brain, that's how many dimensions they had—carved into the air and left hollows, or stretched it out until it was bulbous and twisted. Narrow corridors of normal space ran between them, though sometimes the distortions snaked together or blended into each other.

He'd crawled through the room and carried Sol, taking it on faith that all of this was there. Today he'd fallen in and been pulled back out. And now he could see it.

Christ, it was weird.

Their oil-in-water motion unsettled him, and he was already seasick, but if he could grit his teeth and ignore that... they were almost beautiful. A fucked-up, deadly aurora.

In the distant left corner of the room, one winked out of existence. No more shimmer.

Above him, Sol stopped humming and spoke. "Strike distortion A from the map."

There was a scramble in front of Jake and a rustle of pages, but he couldn't take his eyes off the rest of the room. That was what it had looked like from the outside—whatever *that* meant—when that spreading whiteness had almost swallowed him alive. From normal space, the erasure was quick and noiseless, but just as final.

Or at least, it was noiseless as far as Jake could tell. Maybe Sol could hear something. He'd been humming. He could hear the alien and the breach, and Jake hadn't detected either.

"Got it," Miriam said. Her pencil scratched the paper.

Sol hummed again. Another flicker cut out, this one in two places at once. It hadn't *looked* connected, but it had been.

Sol said, "Strike distortions B and G from the map."

"Sol, are you—" Jake stopped when Sol minutely tightened his grip again, a wordless plea not to interrupt his concentration. More humming.

It was answer enough. Of course he was the one doing it. He was closing the distortions with telekinesis.

The room was silent except for Sol humming, working his way through the alphabet, and the tiny scrape of Miriam's pencil. Jake had lettered that map himself, and there had originally been 23, but he knew from experience that some were already gone. And B and G had disappeared in tandem.

Both were marked as dead ends on the map. The early tests had missed their connection, since neither shape had returned a tennis ball.

God, they could so easily have missed him while he was trapped.

Jake took a deep breath, matched Sol's steady, droning hum, and returned his attention to the map and the room.

Sol had named B and G without looking at the map. It was like the crossword—he'd fit the whole of it into his head.

That shouldn't have been the thing to make Jake catch his breath, not in this multidimensional hamster cage of a room, not when Sol was reshaping space with his thoughts, but it was. Maybe because that skill was almost within his reach, he could be impressed by it. Everything else was impossible to imagine.

Across the room, something emerged. It was a slow movement, totally different from the swaying pulse of the distortions. A quicksilver puddle pooled at the base of one half of the machine.

The alien was liquefying itself, like he'd suspected it could. The coral-like solid forms growing on the remains of the machine washed down in waves until the puddle was unmistakably far, far larger than the base of the machine. It stretched toward the right wall of the room and began to ooze across the floor.

Jake opened his mouth. "Um—you all see that, right?"

"Yes," Miriam said, clipped but soft. She'd been the one most worried about the alien as a threat. She was standing with one hand braced against the table and the map she'd been annotating. Her other hand held a pencil like a weapon.

The alien flowed until it hit the wall, and then it stopped moving. It wasn't any closer to them. It hadn't gone far from the machine, either. What was the point?

It solidified, going rigid and then forming dozens of little tubes along the bottom of the wall. The process was quick, but not as quick as the disappearance of several distortions from the air.

"Strike distortions E, F, and I from the map," Sol said.

The cluster of three that vanished was between Sol and the organism.

"Holy shit," Jake said, and Miriam turned sharply to look at him. "Look at the map, and look at where the organism is. It moved over there on purpose, in response to what Sol is doing. It's like... it's like they need to pull on opposite ends of the distortion, or something. The alien moved to be in position."

"You can see the distortions?" Miriam asked.

"Yeah. Since I got out."

"Can you hear what Lange hears? You were humming," Chávez said, and Jake shook his head.

The alien liquified itself again and slid back toward the center of the room.

"If you're right, then you should be able to guess which one they're working on, based on where the alien goes," Miriam said. "Point to it."

Jake glanced from the alien to the map in her hands, and put his finger to D and J, which were connected, according to her notes.

A second later, both closed.

"Strike distortions D and J from the map," Sol said. Maybe Jake was imagining it, but he sounded a little smug.

"Well, damn," Miriam said. "You were right."

"They're communicating," Chávez said, like it was the best thing she'd ever seen in her life—and she couldn't even see the best parts of it. "More than that, they're working together."

The alien glided across the floor according to some inaudible instruction from Sol, and together, they cleared the room of another distortion, and another. The air flashed and calmed as they worked.

Sol leaned on him more heavily as his energy flagged. His voice grew strained, so Jake took to announcing which distortions had closed.

And then, at last, Miriam had crossed out every shape on the map. The alien slid back to the machine and solidified. The room was almost restored.

Only the breach remained.

Jake could see it now if he cared to look. The gash that stretched between the two halves of the machine had none of the appealing shimmer of the smaller distortions. It was a warped, impossible, colorless shape—or sometimes black, from the corner of his eye. Staring right at it made bile rise in his throat, so he decided not to.

But if Sol and the alien could repair the distortions, they could seal the breach. He hoped.

Sol sagged against him. Jake grasped his hands and stood carefully so they could support each other. He felt much better than he had. The work had distracted him, and now that the distortions were gone, his fear had quieted. He no longer needed to check over his shoulder to see if the wall was where it had been, at least for right now. The tight band around his lungs had loosened. He hadn't expected the reprieve so quickly.

Sol had given him that gift.

Jake kissed him. Laced with salt, the kiss tasted like relief and gratitude. They clung to each other, solid and real.

[20]
FAITH

It was a novelty to sit down on Sol's bed instead of crawling into the suspended sleeping bag. Jake was tired, but he didn't lay back to make space for Sol. Instead, Jake caught him around the waist. Sol wasn't weightless anymore, but he put up no resistance, letting Jake pull him into his lap. Sol settled there, straddling him, as heavy and real as Jake could ever have wished for. Jake wrapped his arms around him and squashed their bodies together. Sol's skin was hot and smooth. His spine arched and the hard angles of his shoulder blades shifted under Jake's arms, but he didn't try to escape the embrace. They both smelled faintly of the rinseless shampoo and soap they'd used in the absence of a working shower. He could feel the pulse in Sol's neck and the beat of his heart and lower, the hard length of his cock nestled between them.

Jake was hard, too, his dick stretching the fabric of the shorts he hadn't had the foresight to strip off. He hadn't known he was going to do that, reach out and grab Sol like that, until his arm had already been extended. They hadn't talked about this. By rights, they should both be asleep.

Jake wasn't sure sleep was in the cards for him tonight, and he really didn't want to contemplate that, so he kissed Sol's cheek and then gently bit his earlobe.

"We were both told to rest," Sol said, amused.

"If you pick *now* to start doing what you're told, I swear I'll—"

"You'll what?" Sol asked.

Jake exhaled a laugh, unable to bring himself to say anything, just in case Sol really did want to sleep. "Lie awake with this hard-on, I guess."

"You wouldn't even furtively jerk off? Disappointing."

"I—what? Fuck." Jake buried his face against Sol's neck. He was thirty goddamn years old and had lived through a lot of shit, but Sol could make him flush with shame and arousal like flipping a switch. Probably because now if Sol *did* want to go to sleep, then Jake would lie in bed next to him contemplating how quietly he could stroke himself.

Sol tsked and shook his head gravely. Then, his eyes bright, he reached between them to cup Jake through his underwear. "I don't intend to let this go to waste. Tell me what you want."

"To not think about anything but this. You. Us." Jake ran his hands over the muscled plane of Sol's back and all the way down to the curve of his ass.

"How do you feel about fucking me?"

Sol had the answer throbbing in his hand. Jake said, slightly breathless even though he hadn't moved, "Yeah—I mean, good, I feel good. I want to."

The way he'd felt when Sol had fucked him, that fullness, that blackout rush of sensation—he'd never come so hard in his life. Just the thought that he could make Sol feel a fraction that good made his cock swell.

It would probably be a fraction, though.

"I... might not be as good at it as you are," Jake said.

"I wouldn't have asked if I didn't want you to," Sol said, as though that swept aside all of Jake's self-doubt.

And maybe it did. Sol knew this was his first time. He'd probably adjusted his expectations accordingly.

Sol unfolded himself—God, his long legs, the muscles of his thighs, the slight upward curve to his cock, the way it bobbed as he moved—from Jake's lap and crawled onto the bed. He lay on his back with his knees spread, and by the time Jake had peeled off his shorts, Sol had a bottle of lube in one hand and two fingers in his own ass.

Jake's mouth went dry at the sight of Sol's clever, slender fingers working in and out of his body. His own hands curled with envy. "Can I do that for you?"

Sol handed him the bottle. "Be generous with it."

The lube was cool against his fingers, and he rubbed them together to warm it. He touched a fingertip to the tight little whorl and drew a careful and curious circle. Sol had done that to him, and he'd liked it.

"In," Sol demanded.

Well, it didn't get much more direct than that. Jake went slowly. It had been strange, feeling Sol push into him yesterday. Good-strange, but still. He didn't want to fuck this up. His fingers suddenly felt ridiculously thick.

Jake glanced between the tip of his finger disappearing into Sol's body and the much, much larger erection leaking between his thighs. The calculation gave him pause.

"Jake. You are not going to hurt me. I want this. Put your finger all the way in and find out how much."

Jake slid his finger forward, past the tight ring of muscle. It was hot—literally warm, heat radiating from all sides, and

Jake should have known that, of course people were hot inside, but knowing was different from feeling. The inside of Sol's body welcomed him.

Jake's mouth had fallen open and he wasn't quite breathing, so he must look absurd, but Sol had his eyes closed and his head thrown back. He hummed with pleasure as Jake eased in and out. Sol had been using two fingers on himself, so Jake added a second.

"That's so good," Sol told him, "so good."

Fuck. Jake had to reach down and squeeze himself. He kept his other hand working steadily. Could Sol come just from this, from his fingers? Sol's untouched cock lay rigid against his stomach, a thin thread of precome dripping from the tip.

Sol wrapped a hand around Jake's wrist, stopping him, as though he'd read Jake's mind. "Fuck me."

"Yeah," Jake said, his mouth dry and all other thoughts evaporated. He slid his fingers out with care. "Okay. Yeah. Like this, with you on your back?"

Sol rolled to his side. "Lie behind me."

"Spoon you, you mean?"

"Just do it."

That was easy enough, and with only some minor adjustments and a few short, borderline curt instructions from Sol, they got themselves aligned. Jake entered him, smooth and slow, and had never felt anything so blissfully perfect in his whole damn life.

"Fuck," he said, hoping that conveyed everything, and Sol sighed happily in response.

This wasn't like when Sol had fucked him, and not just because they'd switched. That had been adventurous, experimental, more about force and depth and angles. It had been goddamn glorious, but they were doing something different now.

This time was about wrapping an arm around Sol and kissing the back of his neck. It was about closeness. Sol wanted to be held. No matter that he didn't want to admit it or talk about it, or that he couldn't give gentle, encouraging directions to make it happen, the fact that he wanted it—enough to *ask* for it—made Jake melt. He opted not to embarrass Sol by saying anything and instead pulled Sol back against his chest.

They settled into a rhythm, languorous and unhurried. Everything unspoken was there, in the slide of their intertwined bodies and the clutch of their intertwined hands. In every breath, Jake could smell the mingled, earthy scent of them and taste the salt on Sol's skin. He could feel Sol everywhere. It was impossible to be anywhere but here.

When he reached down to stroke Sol's cock, hard and slick with longing, he did that gently, too. There was so much pent up between them that even a light touch was enough to set Sol off. A tremor took him and he shuddered against Jake, his hips snapping erratically. His orgasm spurted into Jake's hand and overflowed. His body clenched tight around Jake's, squeezing again and again, and Jake couldn't have stopped himself from coming even if he'd wanted to. Pleasure slammed into him and kept going, dragging a few last thrusts from him long after the sensation should have subsided. It left him motionless and happy. He kissed the back of Sol's neck again.

They slid apart, cleaned up, and came back to bed. They lay face to face. It wasn't until the lights were off in the room that Sol spoke.

"I didn't want that to happen to you," Sol said. His voice was rough.

"I know," Jake said. He braced to say *it's not your fault.* Given every other conversation with Sol, he'd need to.

Instead, Sol said, speaking barely above a whisper, "I didn't want it to happen to me, either."

Jake pulled him closer. How shitty that there was no equation you could write or machine you could build that would stop bad things from happening. No matter how smart you were, or how careful, or how kind, or how deserving of kindness, still life might make you suffer. The multiverse was vast and incomprehensible, but Jake knew that.

He knew one or two other things, too.

"I was scared," Jake said. "But not as scared as I could have been. I knew you would look for me."

"You could not have known that I would find you."

"Yeah." Jake didn't like to think of other versions of events. He tightened his arms around Sol and dropped a kiss on his temple. "But if we limit ourselves to *things a human being could know—*"

"I don't appreciate your tone—"

"I know you're really fucking stubborn," Jake said, interrupting him. "And I *knew* you would look. It made me feel better, and I'm sorry you didn't have that when you were trapped. I wish I'd been looking for you then. You should know that if anything happens to you now, I will turn the whole damn multiverse upside-down and shake it."

"That is—" Sol seemed to reconsider his words. "Thank you."

Jake had been hoping for something else, something more, but he'd hedged his own bets, so "thank you" was the best he could expect.

Sol released a breath. "I need to tell you something."

Good. Jake hadn't expected Sol to go for it, but if they were going to confess shit flat out, that would be so much easier than dancing around it.

"I don't know how to do it," Sol said. "I don't know how to make it work."

Fuck.

"Your faith in me—it's too much," Sol continued. "I can't repair the breach. I've thought through it so many times now and I'm not enough—"

"Oh," Jake said, louder than he meant to. "Thank fuck. I thought you were kicking me out."

"You're *relieved* that I'm talking about the breach?"

It was too dark to see Sol's expression, but Jake could picture the skepticism. He couldn't contain his slightly panicked laugh. "Yeah, actually. Thought you were working your way up to 'I don't know how to be in a relationship' or something. Worrying about the disintegrating fabric of reality is our everyday life at this point."

"Jake," Sol said, softly enough that it was cause for alarm. "I *don't* know how to be in a relationship. But it doesn't matter because I can't fix the breach."

"We can figure it out," Jake said. "On both counts."

"When you were gone, I wished I had told you," Sol said. "The set of feelings I have for you—the joy and comfort I derive from your presence, but also the fear when you're in danger—I think they might most succinctly be described as 'love.' I want you to know that, even if this is all we get."

"Wow." Jake kissed him, because he wasn't gonna say anything half that good, and it slid from sweet to fierce in seconds. When they broke apart, he said, "In case it's not clear, I love you, too. And I'm not ready to give up on our chances of fixing the breach—but I think the first step is for both of us to get some sleep."

Sol rolled to his back. Probably he had his eyes wide open so he could brood in the dark. Jake touched his shoulder, nudged him until he was on his side, and then gathered him close. It was good to have someone to hold.

[21]
EAT THE MOON

THE COPPER TUBING WAS HEAVIER IN SOLOMON'S HAND than expected, but it had nothing to do with gravity. Solomon hadn't had much cause to hold lengths of pipe— literal ones, anyway.

"Why did you give this to me?" he asked Jake.

"Because we're fixing the leak so we can turn the water back on. Give it to Eliza, she'll get it where it needs to go."

Jake was tapping at an electronic blueprint of the facility on his tablet. Solomon bent to set the copper tubing in the clawlike grip at the end of one of Eliza's arms. Two of her other hands latched around short, wide copper tubes, and the last had its grip altered to two flat pincers, but Solomon couldn't say what for. Eliza rolled away Jake's feet and up the interior wall of the greenhouse, toward the water-damaged hole in the ceiling.

"You want a shower, don't you?" Jake asked, his attention still alternating between Eliza and the tablet.

"It's not the most pressing of my obligations."

Solomon should be back in his lab, staring at the breach until an answer came, but instead Jake had asked him to come here. So he had. Even though reality was falling apart. As they'd walked together, Jake had handed him the pipe as though Solomon knew what to do with it, and Solomon had accepted it, because it came from Jake.

His priorities were as disordered as his mind.

Jake interrupted his thoughts by pressing the tablet into his hands. Solomon held the tablet horizontally, with one hand on either side, and his thumbs hovered over two columns of icons likely meant to control Eliza's arms.

He could see nothing unusual, no reason for Jake to have given him the tablet. The center of the screen was video from the camera affixed to Eliza, and it was showing the wreckage left by the organism. Jake and Eliza had broken off the corroded portion of the water line days ago, and now there was a long empty space without pipe.

"Okay, start with the coupling in her first arm on the left," Jake said.

"What?"

"I told you, *we're* fixing the plumbing. That includes you."

"I am quite sure you can do this more efficiently without me," Solomon said, but he didn't object when Jake came around behind him, then picked up his hand and made him touch the controls.

One of Eliza's arms jerked. Solomon had never seen her move like that, whether Jake was speaking to her or using the tablet, so it must be his fault. He made a smaller, gentler motion, and she extended her arm slowly toward the end of the pipe. Fitting the coupling over it required delicacy. It took him several tries, and when he had it in place at last, he whispered, "Yes."

"Satisfying, right? Now you slide the new pipe into the

coupling, and then we'll put the other coupling on," Jake said.

This, too, demanded concentration and a light touch. Solomon fiddled with the tablet controls until Eliza finished fitting the new pipe into its couplings, and then he said, "Tell me why we're doing this."

"You said you couldn't fix the breach, so we're fixing something else," Jake said, and then, a moment later, "Good, that looks great, now we just have to crimp it."

"How is this helping?" Solomon asked.

"The crimp? We have to make a seal between the new pipe and the old pipe if we don't want it to leak. It's easy, Eliza has the tool on one of her arms already. That'll finish this part, but there's a few other leaks that need patching along the line."

"Stop deliberately misunderstanding me," Solomon said sharply. "It won't matter if we have running water if something else comes through the breach. Or if it gets any bigger —the distortions could come back, or—"

"Okay," Jake said. He stepped away so they could speak face to face. "We need to fix it. Just thought it might help to work on something easily fixable instead of brooding in your lab. Besides, the breach is basically a leak, right? It's a hole in reality. I know, I know, it works in ways I don't understand, goes up, down, sideways, forward, backward and in heels, but—"

"You think we could patch it," Solomon said. Luckily it was Eliza who was handling all the pieces of this project, and she was harder to startle, so nothing clanged to the floor.

"Just brainstorming," Jake said.

"No, it makes sense," Solomon said. "I was able to repair the smaller distortions with the organism's help—to pull them flat

—but the breach is simply too big for that method to work. The organism has been trying for days. The breach can't be stitched back together, or crimped to make a seal—at least, I can't do that, and I don't think the organism is powerful enough. But maybe with more matter, the hole could be patched."

While Solomon was speaking, Jake lifted the tablet out of his hands. His fingers flew across the screen, far defter with the controls.

Solomon continued, "The question is *what* matter. Where would we get something with enough mass?"

"How big are we talking?" Jake asked. "Would one of the pods be enough? We could shove one in there. We could shove *all* of them in there, if that would do the trick."

"No," Solomon said. "I know the breach looks like it stretches from one side of the machine to the other—"

"But it's bigger than that," Jake finished. "Yeah. Okay. Well, what about this place?"

"Facility 17?"

"Yeah, the asteroid," Jake said. "Is it enough?"

"It might be. But it would be destroyed. This whole project would be over."

"The whole project is already over," Jake said. "Heath and Winslow are in prison, Quint's dead, there's just a few of us left here who were unwilling to leave the breach unguarded—and I guess we don't really have anywhere else to go. But that's a solvable problem."

"And the eventual goal of exploring the multiverse?"

Jake shrugged. "It'll be there if people want to explore it. No need for a fixed departure point. This place is just a lump of space metal. And it's a lump of space metal designed and formerly owned by an evil trillionaire. I won't miss it, and I don't think anybody else will."

"If 'people' want to explore the multiverse?" Solomon pressed, momentarily sidetracked. "Not you?"

"I... wouldn't mind going back down to the surface for a while," Jake said. He cleared his throat. "I don't really have people there, or a place to live, but I'll figure it out. I'm tired of space."

"I'm tired of space, too," Solomon said. Saying it aloud was exciting. So was the way Jake had averted his gaze. Maybe they could get out of this mess. "Eliminating this place from reality sounds cathartic."

Jake laughed. "Okay, so how do we do it?"

"I'm not quite sure. When the alien and I repaired the discrete distortions, we were pulling them flat from different points. If you imagine a crumpled piece of paper, you'd have to flatten it by pulling in opposite directions. Pulling from one spot can't change the shape. It just moves the paper."

"You think you and the alien aren't enough?"

"I don't know," Solomon said. "If we tried this, we'd only get one shot. It would be a delicate, time-consuming process. If we destroyed the asteroid without closing the breach, I don't know what we'd try after that. And there's a risk of making things worse."

"If we destroy the asteroid and it doesn't seal the breach, then we'll have no asteroid, plus a giant, invisible anomaly in space, waiting to eat the moon or whatever," Jake said.

Solomon wished he could laugh at that.

"God, this stuff still fucks with me so much. The breach is *inside* the asteroid, but you're proposing that we put the asteroid *inside* the breach?" Jake wrapped one hand around a fist and then reversed their positions to illustrate this question, a hopelessly inadequate hand gesture that Solomon shouldn't have found charming.

"Think of it as turning the asteroid inside-out, if it helps," Solomon said.

"Which you're gonna do with your mind," Jake added.

"That is how I do most things."

"What you're doing with the alien, is it like what the machine was doing? Making some kind of dimensional harmonic resonance?"

"Yes."

"So if you had another machine—or several more machines—would it help? You could place them wherever you needed to, uh, pull the crumpled piece of paper flat? They'd help you and the alien reverse what happened on the night of the accident."

"You're offering to build these machines," Solomon said.

"If we have the materials, then sure. You tell me what to do and I'll do it. But what's inside your machine that allows it to affect dimensions humans can't perceive? I hope it's not that stuff Quint was injecting into runners to ground them —the dimensional prions? We don't have any more of those."

"It's not a prion, merely a catalyst," Solomon said. "And I have plenty, but we'll have to go out to get it."

"Wait, you mean *out*-out?" Jake tilted his head toward the greenhouse windows, toward the vastness of space.

"I was rightly suspicious that Heath and Winslow were stealing my research," Solomon said. "I took precautions."

"Shit," Jake said. "No wonder you didn't wanna be friends with us. You knew Heath and Winslow were up to something shady and you didn't know who was collaborating with them."

"Yes. Though it has also been my policy to keep my colleagues at a distance even in workplaces where nobody was stealing anything or conducting any flagrantly unethical experiments. As gratifying as it is to be understood, we don't have time to get into that."

"This catalyst, is it something Eliza could get?"

"Yes, it's stored in a small antigrav field on the exterior of the asteroid, tucked out of sight of surveillance," Solomon said. "I can direct her to it, now that you've shown me how."

Jake focused on the tablet. A moment later, Eliza had crimped both ends of the pipe, finishing the project. She rolled back down the wall to join them.

"There was no need to fix the pipe, given that we're going to destroy the entire facility," Solomon said. "But nicely done."

"Thanks for helping."

They admired the shiny new length of copper tubing set into place above them, and Solomon reached for Jake's hand.

A sound came like someone had slammed their forearm down on a piano, far too many pitches at once, and Solomon whipped his head around, seeking the source, until he realized it wasn't a sound. It was his other sense, the one that perceived the alien and the breach.

He dragged Jake closer, something prickling at his senses.

The room shuddered. The pipes groaned and, with a shriek, sheared apart. One of the new couplings bent. The copper tube they'd just added quivered and dropped down at an angle.

A trivial problem—or a warning of more to come.

"What the fuck. You think the organism is snacking on our pipes again?" Jake frowned, studying him. "You heard something."

"I did." Solomon cast a careful appraisal over the greenhouse. A thin but deadly lacework of fractures seamed the windows. They needed helmets and oxygen tanks, but the air supply wasn't his only worry. "Does it look smaller in here?"

"Fuck," Jake said. "The alien is doing what we talked about, isn't it? It's turning the asteroid inside out."

"With us still inside," Solomon agreed.

———

Solomon refused to be separated again, so after they sent a message to the others to meet them in the lab, he didn't drop Jake's hand the whole way there, except when they stopped to retrieve helmets and oxygen tanks, and even then, he didn't look away for longer than he had to. When they arrived, he clamped his fingers so tight that Jake yelped.

Or maybe it was the walls that scared him.

Solomon didn't make a noise when he saw them. That would require breathing.

Yesterday, the organism had been living on what remained of the machine in its more rigid, coral-like form. It had liquefied part of itself in order to move and help him repair the distortions, and as an amorphous blob, it had been perhaps a meter in diameter.

Today all four walls of the lab—even the one beyond the machine—were blotted and splotched with iridescent grey tubes. The organism had not doubled or tripled, but increased in size by ten or twenty.

"It gains energy from repairing space," Solomon said. What they'd done yesterday had allowed the organism to grow. "Chávez will be excited to learn that."

"*That's* what you're thinking about?" Jake asked. "I was

thinking it seems smaller in here, although maybe it's just the walls being covered in creepy shit."

"The organism is not creepy," Solomon admonished. "It is trying to help. Though it has moved our timeline up rather abruptly."

"You still need me to build robots? There's a lot more alien here than there was."

"There is," Solomon said, uncertain. He had to raise his voice to be heard. "I worry it's moving too fast. The tremor we felt was violent, and that could cause more harm. Having instruments would allow me to exert a steadying influence."

The others arrived then, all wearing helmets and oxygen tanks, the stampede of their boots quiet in comparison to the sound Solomon was awaiting.

"What's happening? How do we stop it?" Emil asked. He pivoted, taking in the growth on the walls. "Holy shit."

"The question isn't how we stop it, but how we control it to ensure that it successfully repairs the breach. Either way, it's going to destroy the asteroid."

Solomon waited for an objection, but none came.

"Okay," Emil said. "We'll have to make sure we evacuate on time, then. What do you need?"

"You all can help me," Jake said, and briefly explained their plan to amplify Solomon's ability by distributing a number of small machines around the breach.

Solomon was grateful he spoke up. The ever-present whine in the lab had grown louder, its dissonance now unpredictable, and he kept waiting for another crash. It was hard to concentrate.

"I could use a few pairs of extra hands," Jake finished.

"Of course we'll help," Miriam said to Jake, and then

she turned to Solomon and asked, "But what about the alien?"

"What about it?" Solomon replied.

"Will it be okay?"

Solomon was having trouble following. He stared at her. "Aren't you the one who wanted to kill it?"

"Yes, when I thought it was trying to kill us," Miriam said impatiently. "Now I want to know if it's destroying itself, or, for that matter, if you are."

"I'm not," Solomon said, and he hoped it was true.

"And you know I'm as pro-ooze as they come," Chávez said. "But it is technically an invasive species. It should probably be returned to its own, uh, ecosystem. We gotta make sure it gets home safely."

"That's what I'm trying to do for you," Solomon said. He was shouting again, but the din—like someone had dumped a piano into a blender—was unbearable.

Jake squeezed his gloved hand. "You do your thing. I'll yell at them for you."

It was a relief to let the conversation drop from his mind, although Solomon retained enough awareness to note that Jake did not, in fact, do any yelling. Instead he gave a calm, firm explanation that the alien had transported itself here through the Nowhere and could likely transport itself back, meaning its chances of survival were much higher than those of anyone else in the facility. The others seemed to agree, thankfully.

Solomon breathed deeply and tried to pick apart the sounds he was hearing. When he'd worked with the organism yesterday, they'd been in tune. He hadn't needed the guitar. Thinking of a pitch had sufficed to put himself in harmony with the creature and the space surrounding them.

If he could find the right pitch, or the right chord, he could slow—or smooth—the next tremor.

That hellish, all-the-piano-keys-at-once sound again. Solomon winced. The room shifted, rumbling in protest just as the greenhouse had. Jake and Solomon grabbed each other for stability. The floor dragged them closer to the breach.

When it was over, they exchanged silent, wide-eyed looks and filed out of the door as quickly as possible, all headed for Jake's workshop.

———

JAKE HAD a high fucking dexterity score, but he'd never had to build a robot during an interdimensional earthquake before. Every forty minutes or so, Sol, who could hear the warning sounds, would calmly say, "Brace." And then Jake would freeze, his hand hovering above the robot in his lap, and every tool on the wall and jar of hardware on his workbench would rattle.

The whole team had packed into his workshop, which was crowded on a normal day—one where nobody visited and the walls weren't literally closing in. They were all watching him assemble a prototype under Sol and Dax's direction. Mostly Dax's direction, actually, since in the beginning Sol had been busy directing Eliza to retrieve his secret stash of catalyst from the surface of the asteroid.

And after that Dax and Sol had bent their heads to murmur over a multicolored simulation of some squiggly, impossible shape on Dax's laptop while gesturing at different parts of the screen. Jake guessed they were talking about where to put the machines. The only part of the conversation he'd understood was when Dax had said, after

Sol's last, most emphatic poke at the screen, "No. That's a mistake. Let's run it again."

Sol had said, very gently, "You did it right, Dax. You always do."

Jake didn't like the sound of that, and he didn't like the long silence that followed it, either. But worry didn't blossom into panic until Sol patted Dax on the shoulder and said, "It would be a shame to lose all the data we've collected here. Let's pack up the labs."

The two of them picked their way through the crowded workshop, spoke in the hallway for a moment, and then Sol came back in and Chávez left to go help Dax.

Jake had a million questions—or maybe just *what the fuck*—but he also had a job with a looming deadline, so he kept his mouth shut and went back to work.

Even assured that the vials of clear, colorless liquid weren't dimensional prions and couldn't hurt him, Jake handled them with dread. It was strange to work on something he didn't understand. These machines required no treads, no wheels, no magnets for hovering or sticking to the walls. They had hardly any moving parts. No software, either. Sol would manipulate them with his mind.

The prototype in Jake's lap had little in common with the machine Sol and Dax had designed. There were no sleek curved panels this time. He'd bolted a few metal plates together into a cube with no top, so the inner workings were still exposed. Transparent tubing carrying the liquid catalyst snaked through thin metal strings running taut from one side to the other. It looked like a weird musical instrument.

It was, sort of.

Placed strategically around and inside the breach, the instruments would give Sol better range and control of his ability, in theory. Then he'd be able to keep up with the organism.

Or rather, to slow it down.

With the prototype finished, Jake switched his focus to overseeing the construction of three others, which mostly meant digging through his accumulated junk for parts to reuse and then tossing them to whoever needed them. The room had cleared out a little—after Dax and Chávez had left, Lenny and Miriam had gone to do pre-flight checks on all the pods.

Another quake struck before the last of the machines was finished, and the four of them remaining in the workshop bent toward the floor and covered the backs of their necks. The glass in the window behind him splintered. The power flickered and went out. Tools clanged against the groaning walls, but nothing fell.

Jake was relieved until he turned and a beam of light from his suit fell across the unfamiliar, lumpen objects strewn across his workbench. In the crunch, the hardware and loose parts that had been scattered there had fused together. A vertical seam of contracted space ran up the wall, marked by wrenches and pliers that had melded with each other.

He shuddered. Thank fuck he hadn't reached for Sol that time.

It only took one glance around the room to be sure that everyone else had seen it, too.

"Everyone out right now," he said.

Dax was the only colleague Solomon had ever worked with who could truly keep up, and when they were alone in the hallway together, Solomon said so.

"I know I was difficult to work with, and I'm sorry. It was a sort of armor I adopted after years of—"

"People not respecting you and trying to take your work," Dax said. "Plus, for all you knew, I was exactly as much of a piece of shit as the other scientists who worked for Quint. That's a damn good reason to be rude."

"Yes," Solomon said, marveling at being so easily understood. "I regret that we weren't friends—I see now that we could have been. I trust your work as much as I trust mine, and you should know that. Whatever happens here today, the choice I'm making is my own, and you're not responsible for it. And regardless, everything that's in that lab—our lab —is yours."

Behind the glass visor of their helmet, Dax blinked back furious tears, then said, "Fuck you, I hate this," and clamped him in a hug.

Solomon lifted his arms to return the gesture. He and Dax had never talked about anything other than the physics of unfolded space, so it was easy to forget that Dax was twenty-three years old. Twelve years and one lifetime younger than him.

"You're going to have an incredible career," Solomon told them, patting them on the back and letting go. "You already do. Get to the pod on time."

Then Solomon went back into the workshop while Dax and Chávez left to salvage what they could from the labs. He watched Jake and the others finish assembling the instruments and waited for the next spatial contraction.

It crashed down right on time. A painfully chaotic shriek and boom that only he could hear exploded an instant before the movement, and then the world burst into real, gut-churning sound.

The contraction's effects were more easily visible than the others—and more disturbing, buckling the walls and leaving objects materially entangled like they'd been melted and reformed. Solomon was grateful. That meant everyone would hurry.

Jake, Emil, and Kit left the workshop with him. They rushed down the hallway in the direction of the dock, which was the only sensible direction to go. The pods were the only safe escape route.

Solomon watched them, standing in the hallway with all four instruments hovering in the air around him.

"Sol," Jake called. "We have to go."

"I know," he said. "I'm staying. I need to see this through."

All three of them shouted in surprise.

Jake ran back and grabbed him by the wrist. "No. We

made the instruments. You don't have to be here. You can do this from far away. From the passenger seat of the pod."

"Each instrument has to be positioned precisely," Solomon said. "Including me. Dax and I did the math. We can't risk screwing this up, Jake. I have to stay."

"No," Jake said. "We'll find another way. You can't stay here, you'll die."

It would be grisly to stay in folded space and get compacted into an unrecognizable tangle of flesh, which was why Solomon wouldn't be doing that. To have any hope of remaining intact long enough to see this through, there was only one place he could go. He'd known it even before he'd seen Dax's simulation, but it was hard to think about, let alone say out loud.

Solomon said, "I'm not staying here, exactly."

The betrayal on Jake's face was a punch to the gut. "You're going back into the breach."

"I don't want to," Solomon said, his voice thick with tears. He removed his wrist from Jake's grip. "I swear I don't. But it's the only way to be sure. I'm sorry, Jake. You have to go. I need you to take three of the instruments down to the dock with you. Dax has the coordinates. They'll tell you where to go. You have to hurry. Another contraction is coming, I can hear it."

"Fuck that, I'm not leaving you."

"I don't want you here," Solomon said and shoved him back.

It was only a small push, but it was enough to put Solomon out of arm's reach. From their previous struggle, he knew that if Jake grabbed him, he'd lose.

Jake planted his feet and glared.

Solomon took a step back, widening the distance between them, angling himself toward the hallway that would lead him to the breach. He caught sight of Emil, several meters behind Jake, frozen with concern.

Kit wasn't with him. When Solomon turned to leave, Kit was blocking his way, still quite small even fully suited up.

"So," Kit said, raising his hands with their palms up. "I didn't want to interrupt, but... what if I go with you? Jump you out at the last second? Nobody has to die?"

"I can't ask you to do that. There's still an overwhelmingly high chance of death. Having two of us stay most likely means both of us will die."

"You're not asking, I'm offering," Kit said.

"You'd... do that? Were you not listening?"

"Ugh. How many times do we have to go over this? We seriously don't have time. This is the best solution." Kit raised his voice and yelled down the hall, "Emil and Jake, get the fuck out of here. Meet me at Zin's, okay?"

"Kit," Emil said, distressed. He didn't make any other protest.

"I love you," Kit called. He waved one gloved hand, jarringly casual. "See you later if I'm not dead."

Sol wished he could kiss Jake one last time, but the dwindling air supply meant taking off their helmets was a bad idea. He closed the distance he'd put between them and squeezed Jake's hand.

"Don't do it," Jake said. "Get in the pod with me and we'll fly somewhere really far away. Forget this place, Sol. I'd rather have you than the universe."

"There won't *be* anywhere really far away if I don't fix this," Solomon said. "I'm sorry, Jake. I love you. I want you to be safe and happy. Please get out of here."

Jake hugged him fiercely, choked out "I love you," took

three of the cubes he'd built in his arms, and then—thank-fully—departed. Eliza rolled after him.

———

SOLOMON COULD FEEL the devices long after he lost sight of Jake. Ever since Jake had routed the thin tube of catalyst fluid through them, they'd hummed in his other hearing, waiting. He sensed it when Jake distributed two of them to the other pods, and he knew when the pods had departed. They'd surround the asteroid, allowing him greater reach.

The fourth one hovered by his side. It was coming with him.

With them.

Kit was standing with one hip cocked. It was the bored posture of someone waiting outside a coffeeshop, checking their messages. The spacesuit ruined the illusion, but still. Kit didn't seem terribly solemn about, or interested in, noble self-sacrifice. Nor did he radiate optimism, which was good, since Solomon would have found that unbearable.

Solomon liked him, he realized. They didn't have much in common, and their history was complicated, and maybe they'd never be close—walking into the breach together guaranteed that they'd never be close—but Kit was weird, and irreverent, and while his outfits were all garish eyesores, Solomon respected his commitment. As usual, this realiza-tion came far too late. Kit wasn't going to make it to twenty-five, and it was Solomon's fault.

"You don't have to do this," Solomon said. The pods might have departed, but Kit was a runner. He could be safe on the surface in an instant. He didn't have to go back into the Nowhere with someone who'd attacked him. "I don't understand why you'd want to."

"Well, obviously I don't *want* to. I hate going near that thing. But give me a little credit—I also don't want you to die for no reason. You're trying to save the multiverse; I'm not a complete asshole. We don't have time to call someone more heroic."

"Yes, ah, just one question. When you said 'meet me at Zin's' to Emil, what—"

"Oh my *God*," Kit groaned. "The world is ending, I don't wanna waste time indulging someone else's fan fascination with Zinnia Jackson. Yeah, she's my mom, okay? I've lived with her and Louann for ten years."

"That would explain why you seemed familiar even though we'd never met," Solomon said. "It's been twenty years since I saw Zin in person. My mother is Evelyn Holland."

"Oh," Kit said, recognition dawning. "I—uh—weird. We going or what?"

Solomon nodded.

They entered the darkened lab, where the lights in their suits illuminated the walls pulsing with the organism. Even in its solid form, it dripped now. A thin film of its slick, quicksilver-like secretion coated the floor.

Kit recoiled. "You didn't tell me it was gonna be *gross*."

Solomon suspected that was a joke, but nothing seemed funny, so all he said was, "Apologies."

The vibrations were so overwhelming that it was like being tumbled inside of a drum. The room had constricted. It would only take a dozen steps to cross from where he stood into the breach.

The distance daunted him, but he strode forward anyway. It was easier to concentrate on taking steps than to think about the cacophony of pitches in his head and wonder how he could possibly sort through them, or to look forward into the jaws of the breach and know, in every particle of his being, that this was going to hurt.

He remembered, on the day he'd tried to run away from Jake, having to think through every motion of walking. Movement came more naturally to him now, but he wished it didn't. He wished walking occupied all of his thoughts. He wished he hadn't made it this far. He wished Jake would tackle him from behind and tell him not to do this.

Except he didn't wish that, because he didn't want Jake anywhere near this place.

"Can I help or is this like, a *you* thing?" Kit asked, picking his way carefully across the ooze-slick floor.

"The latter," Solomon said. "But if you can get us out alive, that's more help than I had hoped for."

"No problem. How will I know when it's time?"

"I don't know," Solomon said. "I'm assuming either it will be obvious or we'll be dead."

"Great."

"If I... relapse," Solomon started, and then had to take a deep breath and try again. "That is to say, if I lose control and hurt you, get yourself out."

Kit held his gaze, searching, and then said, "Yeah, okay."

Even through the roar of the room, Solomon could tell his voice quavered. It was the first time Kit had shown any fear, and it stung that it had nothing to do with the breach or the alien or the Nowhere and everything to do with Solomon.

A moment later, Kit said, "I don't think you will, though."

Solomon couldn't speak.

"The first time, all you wanted was for me to get you out," Kit continued. "And I'm gonna do that, I promise."

He smiled, and Solomon offered him a tentative nod in return.

They'd reached the edge.

Solomon didn't know what Kit could see, but this close, his own vision blinked between the grey, dirty floor and a shifting, lightless gash in the world. How could he ever have thought he wanted to go back? He swallowed down acid.

"Would you laugh if I said 'once more unto the breach'?" Kit asked.

"No."

"Just checking," Kit said, then wrapped his arms around Solomon and hurled them both in.

———

JAKE AND EMIL distributed the devices and saw the others safely on their way. There was only one pod remaining. Mercifully, the craft hadn't been squashed or fused with something else in all the tremors.

Jake checked it methodically anyway, just to have something to focus on. When he crouched down, he realized it was the same one he and Sol had flown down to Alaska. He could still see the tiny seam where he'd repaired the heat shield.

If they got hit by another micrometeoroid on the way down, Sol wouldn't be there to hold things together. He and Emil would die in a fiery crash.

That should scare him, but it didn't.

"Jake?"

Jake shook it off and stood. He popped open the canopy and started to boost himself up, but Emil put a hand on his arm and stopped him.

"No offense, Jake, but I'm gonna fly us."

"What?"

"I said your name four times and you didn't hear the first three," Emil said.

"Oh."

"I think I'm like fifty percent less fucked up than you right now, which is saying something, because I'm not doing great. But after all that, I can't let you crash us into the surface because you're crying too hard."

"Fuck you," Jake said, and it sounded listless even to him. He wasn't crying. He sort of wished he was.

He got into the back seat without further complaint. Emil pressed the little machine into his hands.

"I have anti-anxiety meds, if you want," Emil said as he got into the cockpit. "Including some that'll knock you right out. You can be unconscious for this."

"No, I... I need to see it," Jake said. Sol deserved a witness. He deserved a million witnesses, or more, but he wasn't gonna get that. So Jake would watch.

They departed the asteroid that housed Facility 17. It was the last time he'd ever see it, and he didn't care. Jake had lived a lot of places in his life and he'd been glad to leave most of them. He wasn't given to nostalgia and he didn't have any particular love for this place—except that Sol was in it.

Or maybe by now he wasn't. Maybe he'd jumped back into the breach.

Kit was with him, and Kit had been so easy about the whole thing, like it was a quick trip to the grocery instead of a plunge into the unknown. Jake hoped Kit had the right of it, not Sol.

Emil positioned them according to whatever coordinates Sol and Dax had provided. They had a clear view of the asteroid, the long side of its roughly flat, oval form.

Nothing was happening. Despite the shock of all those contractions that had warped the inside, the outside looked the same.

The machine in Jake's lap was inert. He laid his hands on its sides. Unable to hear or sense whatever it was that Sol could—some higher-dimensional vibration—Jake wouldn't know when Sol was using it. He touched it anyway, wishing he wasn't wearing gloves so he could feel the cool metal growing warm from his hands.

Outside, the asteroid flickered.

No, it hadn't. That was his brain trying to make sense of something that didn't, couldn't make sense. The asteroid had shrunk. Unevenly, and only a little, but unmistakably.

"What the fuck," he whispered.

"Yeah," Emil agreed.

That wasn't good. From what Sol had said, it wasn't supposed to shrink in sudden, noticeable movements. What they'd witnessed was another tremor.

His palms were damp inside his gloves. He clutched the instrument. Time seemed to take forever, an age between each beat of his heart.

The day he and Sol had crawled close to the breach, back when Sol still thought he wanted to follow the call of the void, Sol had experienced such a spike of fear that he'd fainted. The breach terrified him. He'd suffered in there in ways he still couldn't talk about.

And he'd gone back in.

It was an insult to his courage to wish he hadn't. Watching the asteroid, suspense stretching his whole body to the point of pain, Jake couldn't help it. A treacherous little part of him wished Sol had just run.

But there'd be nowhere to run. Jake knew that. The breach was unstable. New space would spill out of it, old space would get sucked into it, and it would grow until it ripped everything apart. Its existence rendered the future unlivable.

Sol's absence would render the future pretty fucking shitty, though.

Not unlivable. Jake had made it thirty years on his own, and he had better friends now than he'd had for most of that time. He could go down to the surface and make a life for himself. It would hurt a lot, remembering Sol—and every day would be constructed out of reminders—but he could do it. And he'd rather have those memories than not. So few other people would know what Sol had sacrificed so everyone else could live. Jake would have that knowledge, at least, even if he couldn't have Sol.

Being alive is like that. It hurts, but it's good.

Ah, fuck, it sucked to cry in zero g.

———

SOLOMON only barely remembered to push the last instrument into its position directly outside the breach.

The Nowhere flooded his senses, its viscous, impenetrable fluid pulling and pushing him in every wrong direction. It crushed him. Freezing and burning, it hurt in impossible, familiar ways. His body did not belong here. He knew every equation that proved it, and he knew it far more intimately than that. He wanted to curl into a ball and whimper, to scream and spasm, to kick and cling to Kit until Kit got him *out*, everything else be damned.

But he could feel Kit holding him, and that one solid, real sensation broke through his panic. He knew where he was and what was happening. This time, there was a chance he'd get out. But even if he didn't, he'd come here with a plan, and he didn't intend to die without trying it. He owed the world at least that much.

Being in the Nowhere was agony, but he had lived this agony for days. All he needed now was a little time.

Solomon could not recall if it had been so loud last time. Constant high keening like he'd heard in the lab, a cluster of pitches jostling and elbowing each other. Tumbling down the scale, there were bigger, blunter sounds. Thunder everywhere. Muffled booming, like being dragged underwater and hit with wave after wave. The organism had upended everything, and they were caught in its chaos. How could he hear what he needed to hear in this?

He focused instead on the quiet of the untouched device sitting just outside the breach, a short but impassable distance away. The small machine that Jake had assembled with such steady hands. The three others just like it, far from here, tranquil in the silence of space.

The noise diminished.

The organism had noticed him, he thought. He never knew if he was ascribing too much sentience to it. But it had responded to him before, and he suspected it was doing so again. In answer to his silence, it had ceased its work.

Maybe it was fanciful to think of a creature so alien as doing anything like waiting. Listening. But he'd brought himself to the edge of death for this. A little extra absurdity was harmless.

A flat, he thought. G. C. E flat.

All four devices, positioned perfectly, rang out with the chord. Pitches that shouldn't fit together but did. Pitches that sounded *better* together. The whole transforming the parts into something unexpected, a little bit crooked, just right. Dissonance shimmered at the heart of the chord, haunting and alive. It overtook him. He swam in it, this sound that wasn't a sound, this feeling of resonance everywhere.

The organism answered him with a sound powerful enough to drown in, but it was the same chord.

The organism probably thought it was the only chord he knew. He'd thought nothing was funny earlier, but he could almost laugh at that.

Yes, just like we did before, he wanted to say. Carefully, slowly, together. But the only communication they had was in music, so instead he played quietly, drawing down the rumbling chaos into something calm and patient. The organism followed him, and as it did, the violent sloshing of the Nowhere lulled.

The alien had grown in size so rapidly and abruptly after they'd repaired the distortions. Perhaps it didn't know its own power.

His heart squeezed in sympathy. Solomon hadn't understood his ability at first, either. It had terrified him. He'd hurled things on impulse. The new hearing and the telekinesis had struck him as separate skills, but they weren't. Everything moved to its own music.

Out in space, the devices orbited, their distant harmony pulling taut the ragged edges of the breach. The sounds around him ebbed.

He'd closed his eyes, he realized. When he opened them, there was silver streaming everywhere.

The alien, going home.

———

JAKE HAD RESOLVED to bear witness, so he blinked until he could see again and trained his vision on the asteroid. It hadn't flickered again, not after that first one, but he couldn't put much stock in that. The tremors had been coming every thirty minutes or so, and it hadn't been that long, even if it had felt much longer.

He stared at it like he was the one who could move it with his mind. Move it, turn it inside out, whatever. He stared like he could make it give Sol back.

"Jake, look," Emil said.

"I'm looking."

"It's getting smaller."

"Is it?"

Jake held up his hands, keeping them as steady as possible to mark the boundaries of the asteroid in his vision. The process was so gradual that it was imperceptible, but the asteroid shrank away from his palms.

"Holy shit."

Sol had succeeded. He'd communicated with the alien, gotten it to stop thrashing around. They were working together.

If that was working, then maybe...

Jake couldn't hold his breath. The change was too slow, and he didn't want to pass out. He kept breathing, and watching, while hope ran through him like caffeine.

The black void surrounding the asteroid grew and grew until the asteroid was a tiny point at its center, and then it was gone. No matter how gradual, the ultimate disappearance shocked him. He'd left Sol in there, and now it didn't exist.

Sol is in the Nowhere, he reminded himself. He'd never expected that thought to be a comfort. It wasn't much of one.

"Is it gone?" Emil asked, and it took Jake a moment to parse that he was talking about the breach, not the asteroid itself. "How will we know if it's gone?"

"I could see the breach after I got stuck," Jake said. "Like a big, rippling, warped gash. It had kind of a shine to it. There's nothing like that now. I think it worked."

The uninterrupted darkness of space should have eased the tightness in his chest, but it didn't.

[23]
A SURE THING

WHEN KIT HAD SAID "MEET ME AT ZIN'S" BEFORE walking into the lab with Sol that afternoon, Jake hadn't known that "Zin's" referred to either a rundown dive bar in Nashville owned by retired pop star Zinnia Jackson and her wife Louann or the apartment above said bar that was inhabited by the two of them and, apparently, Kit. Jake didn't know Kit very well. And he couldn't recall either Kit or Emil ever mentioning that one of Kit's adoptive moms was global icon Zinnia Jackson.

Zinnia Jackson, crossword clue. Zinnia Jackson, whose hit songs had been written by Evelyn Holland. Sol's mom.

Neither Sol nor Kit was present at Zin's.

It was the middle of the night, so the bar was shut down. Jake and Emil were in the apartment above it, and nothing felt real.

"Meeting her freaked me out, too," Emil told him, handing him a pillow so he could sleep on the couch. "But it's definitely not a 'never meet your idols' situation, don't worry. She's actually better in person."

Jake didn't idolize her. He didn't know any of her songs.

What he knew about Zinnia Jackson fit into a very short list: she was famous, but judging by her modest apartment, either not rich or not ostentatious about it. The dizzyingly bright decor in her apartment suggested the former. It had been a couple decades since she'd been arena-concert, weeping-crowds-of-fans famous, so she was probably fifty or older, but she was round-cheeked and youthful-looking, her brilliantly purple silk robe and matching bonnet setting off her light brown skin and deep red eyebrows. She'd let them into her apartment in the middle of the night, hugged Emil, made them both tea, shown distress but not surprise when she learned that Kit wasn't with them, offered Jake the use of her couch, and then yawned and excused herself back to bed.

And she had probably known Solomon Lange since he was born.

Jake wanted to ask her about that, but it was late and she was already back in bed.

"Everybody checked in," Emil said, looking up from his tablet. "Everybody except, you know."

"Yeah."

"I bet we'll hear from them soon," Emil said. "See them, even. Kit said to meet them here. All we have to do is wait."

"You make it sound easy," Jake said.

For a born runner like Kit, travel through the Nowhere was instantaneous. The breach had been closed for hours. They should be here by now.

"I'm gonna go upstairs to Kit's," Emil said. "Let me know if you need anything."

"Night," Jake said, and settled in for a long, restless one.

———

IN THE MORNING, Jake had coffee with Zin—she insisted he call her that—and her wife Louann, a calm, unassuming white woman in paint-spotted coveralls with grey in her short brown hair. Louann said a grand total of five words over breakfast. (Morning. Coffee? No problem. Thanks.) She still managed to make him feel welcome, which he appreciated.

"I can't say I'm sorry to hear that place is gone," Zin told him. She had said a lot more than five words. Her dark red curls were free this morning, but she was still wearing her purple silk robe. "I don't know what was going on up there —all secret, I know—but I never liked it."

"Your instincts are good," Jake said. He picked up his mug and discovered it was empty.

Louann poured him a refill without being asked, and he nodded in acknowledgement. It was a strange little scene, him in his half-zipped spacesuit, taking up too much space in their narrow kitchen.

"I didn't like Kit being involved, but he's grown and he never listened to me anyway," Zin lamented. "You know how hard it is to raise a child who can teleport?"

"It sounds hard," Jake agreed.

"It's the best thing I ever did," Zin said, a wobble in her voice. Louann patted her hand on the table.

Jake wished he could say he was sure Kit and Sol would both show up soon, but he wasn't any good at lying, so he nodded in sympathy and cautiously turned the conversation away from the present and toward the past. "I don't know if you were aware, but one of the people working in the facility was the physicist Solomon Lange."

"Oh, Solomon," she said, clasping her hands around her mug and smiling. "Evelyn and Tom's baby."

Jake had prepared more things to say, nothing invasive,

just a prompt or two to see if Zin remembered Sol. He didn't need any of it.

"A real bright kid. A serious one, too. Evelyn and I kept in touch over the years even after we both retired, but I haven't seen him in person since he was about fifteen—you know that age, all legs and arms, braces and frowns, so shy it made me melt. He was very polite, though, Evelyn made sure of that. Even though we're not in touch, I see him in the headlines whenever he wins an award. I'm not surprised at all, you know. Evelyn is the smartest songwriter I ever worked with, and Tom is quiet, but once you get him talking, you realize he could think circles around anybody. They must be so proud."

She dabbed at her eyes.

Shit. Jake had thought he wanted this—had lain awake longing for it—and now his throat had closed up. It was too much. Learning anything new about Sol made him feel like he'd pressed his thumb directly into the center of a bruise. Tender. Aching. He'd wanted to know more about Sol, a whole lifetime's worth of more, and now this casual sketch of Sol as a coltish, awkward teenager might be the last new thing he ever got. And thinking about his parents being proud—fuck. Jake had to look up at the ceiling and blink until he wasn't in danger of crying in front of two people he'd just met.

To be fair, at least one of those two people was on the verge of crying in front of him.

"Oh, look at me," Zin said, straightening suddenly like she'd been nudged under the table, which maybe she had. "You didn't even ask me a question and I said all that. I'm sorry, honey. I get carried away. Is Solomon a friend of yours?"

Jake managed to say, "Yeah."

She studied him. "He's with Kit, isn't he?"

He nodded.

"The waiting never gets any easier," she said. "You let us know if there's anything we can do."

"This might be a weird question," Jake said, as it dawned on him that there was another stretch of miserably empty hours in front of him. "But is there anything around here that needs fixing?"

Zin burst out laughing. "Have you *seen* this place?"

Louann smiled, stood up, and gestured for him to follow her. Jake spent the rest of the morning with her, moving between the tiny bar kitchen and the dark basement, figuring out where the clog was in the pipes. Nasty, necessary, hard work. It was almost enough to make him stop counting the hours since the breach had closed—sixteen—and wondering how long was too long, and at what point did holding out hope become irrational.

He was on his back under the kitchen sink when he heard Emil say, "Jake? They're here."

Jake sat up and nearly smashed his forehead into a pipe.

"They got thrown off course and ended up somewhere else, that's why it took so long," Emil said. "They didn't have any way to contact us. But they're okay."

Jake wiped himself off as best he could, took the stairs to Zin and Louann's apartment two at a time, and careened into the living room.

Sol was there, enveloped in Zin's ample embrace, tears streaming down his cheeks. He raised his head, laid his bloodshot gaze on Jake, and smiled. It hit Jake like a malfunction in the gravity generator, pinned him right to the floor. There was so much power in his presence. Of course Solomon Lange could reshape reality according to his will. Nothing made more sense.

Jake was wildly in love with him. The feeling was too big for his chest, but it fit there all the same. His face split with a smile. A couple tears leaked from his eyes.

Zin let go of Sol and he turned toward Jake, and then they were hugging. Jake didn't remember crossing the room and maybe he hadn't, maybe he'd floated, maybe Sol had pulled him in, and nothing mattered but the way their lips met, the small, closed, intimate space of their mouths, how warm and wet and alive they were.

There was a trace of salt to the kiss. Sol had been crying, and fuck it, Jake was crying, too.

"You smell," Sol told him and then hugged him tighter.

Jake laughed wetly. "So do you, but it'll take more than a little stale sweat to make me let go."

"I love you. Come home with me."

"Yeah, I'd like that."

The short fuzz of Sol's beard brushed Jake's cheek and neck as Sol sagged against him, letting Jake take all of his weight. Jake was happy to carry him.

———

FOUR DAYS LATER, Solomon lifted his head from Jake's chest and announced, "I am tired of lying in bed and doing nothing."

"Mm?" Jake said.

Usually it was Solomon who dozed off while they were lying together—cuddling—since the Nowhere had leeched all the energy right out of him. But this morning Jake had removed a dead tree from the drive by hacking the fallen trunk into firewood. Then he'd restacked the entire store of wood. Solomon knew all these things because he'd sat on a camp chair and watched. So it was only logical that Jake had fallen asleep when Solomon had demanded company in bed.

Solomon poked him in the chest. "I want to lie in bed and do *you*."

That woke Jake up. Solomon estimated his reaction was half lust and half worry. The worry was obvious—Jake surveilled his every movement, lest he carry a bowl of soup to the sink and faint from fatigue—but then again, so was the lust. Jake had refrained from asking for sex, but he'd taken a conspicuous number of showers over the past few days, and Solomon knew he was not conditioning his hair.

Jake said, very carefully, "You sure you're ready to, uh, exert yourself?"

"You can do the exerting, if you insist," Solomon said, like this was a magnanimous compromise.

"Oh, I see," Jake teased. "You're gonna make me do all the work."

"I could fuck you while you fuck me, if you want," Solomon said.

Jake scrunched his nose in confusion. "Is this some kind of higher-dimensional math shit that can only be seen with a computer simulation?"

"No, it involves a dildo."

Solomon rolled over and opened the top drawer of his nightstand, where there was a colorful array of lube and toys. Mostly dildos, a couple of butt plugs, a prostate massager. As with everything he owned, they were all objects that would function for solo use.

Jake sat up to get a better view of the contents and his eyes got round. "That's... a lot."

It was only one drawer. Still, it tickled him to make Jake stare. All those years of only having no-strings-attached sex with experienced partners, Solomon had been missing out on moments like these. "I don't think you should be scandalized, considering how quickly you repurposed essential safety equipment for sex in zero g."

Jake reached around him and lifted a dildo out of the drawer. It was medium-sized, dark red, flexible, and ridged down to its flared base. He'd grabbed it by the base, and above his fist, the length flopped back and forth. "Who says I'm scandalized? I was deep in thought."

"About?" Solomon asked. He stripped off his pajamas. That was another nice thing about having sex with someone who lived with him and liked him. It didn't have to be a show every time. Not that he minded a show, but he'd never had the option of this kind of sex before. Easy, comfortable sex.

"This can't move by itself," Jake said, pointing the dildo at him. "Which means you're intending to move it telekinetically. So when I asked if you were propositioning me with some higher-dimensional math shit, you should've said yes."

It was impossible not to grin back at him. Another thing Solomon couldn't recall doing with previous partners, or anyone else ever: being silly. "Are you registering an objection?"

"Hell no," Jake said. He pulled his shirt over his head and then shucked his underwear. "Based on past results, you can put pretty much anything you want up my ass, with or without the use of your hands. But promise me that if you don't feel good, you'll tell me so we can stop."

"You worry too much. Of course I would tell you. Can you imagine me keeping my opinion to myself?"

Jake pursed his lips. "Good point."

Solomon pushed him flat on his back and sat between his spread thighs. He slicked his fingers with lube and pushed in. Jake relaxed beneath him, his eyelids fluttering shut. It seemed a waste that they'd spent four days not doing this, but then again, it had been four days of Jake cooking for him, bringing him food in bed, and then kissing and holding him, all things that made Sol feel squishy and vulnerable and cherished. It felt a little unreal, to be given so much and to give nothing in return, but every time Solomon mentioned it, Jake kissed him on the temple and said, "For a genius, you sure do need this concept explained a lot. It makes me happy to do things for you. Because I love you."

Solomon understood it perfectly when he thought of himself doing things for Jake. It was the asymmetry of their circumstances—the nagging worry that he might always be the one taking, never the one giving—that troubled him. But perhaps the two of them formed a shape whose contours could not be so easily described.

He slid the toy into Jake and savored the sound Jake made as he did. Preparing himself required less time, and he was eager to feel Jake rather than his own fingers, but when he crawled forward and made as if to straddle Jake, Jake put a hand on his chest to stop him.

"Save that for later. I want you in kissing distance," Jake said. "Lie down on your back."

There would be a *later*. He believed it. He felt too good not to believe it. And what did later matter, when there was *now* to contend with? As requested, Solomon lay down on his back while Jake moved—slowly and gingerly, very aware of the toy—over him. His arousal hung between his legs, thick and heavy, and Solomon couldn't wait for Jake to bear down on him, into him, until he could lose himself in feeling Jake all over, inside and out.

"God, when you look at me like that—" Jake said and then groaned as he entered in one long thrust. "Fuck."

The fullness of it burned through him, pushing away all other thoughts. Jake kissed him hard. Sol wanted this—the long, hot slide of it, the in and out of it—and nothing else, forever. He wanted Jake to feel it, too.

Concentrating through the onslaught of sensation, he moved the toy. He was cautious with his first few strokes, delicate, and then Jake grunted and said, "Would you *please* fucking fuck me?" and Sol laughed and did as he was asked.

It was easy to fall into the same rhythm. They moved together, and after a while, it felt so right Solomon no longer had to think about it, like they'd fallen into each other's orbit and this was the natural state of things. Here, there was symmetry. The same sensation passed between them, a closeness that intensified with every shift and stroke and kiss. They accelerated together, Jake speeding up and Solomon matching him. Jake reached between them and wrapped his hand around Solomon's dick, which was slick and dripping, and brought him off with a couple of rough caresses.

Solomon arched into Jake's touch and shuddered through his orgasm, a burst of sensation as sudden and all-consuming as lift-off, and he felt Jake come inside him in a few long pulses.

"Fuck," Jake said, then kissed Solomon's cheek, slid his cock out, and collapsed on top of him. "That was so good," he said, his words muffled by the pillow.

"Agreed," Solomon said. He wrapped his arms around Jake, who was pressing him into the mattress, and kissed the side of his head. "You're getting good at that."

"Oh, I'm *getting* good at it?"

"Mm," Solomon said. "I think you need practice. A lot more practice."

"Uh huh," Jake said. He removed the toy, set it aside,

then rolled onto his back and stared up at the ceiling. "Then again, I do have a lot of free time now that my workplace has been obliterated from existence."

"I'm sorry about that," Solomon said. "I didn't mean to overturn your entire life."

"Well, I'm not sorry about it," Jake said. "There are other jobs in the world, but there's no other you."

"Actually—"

"Yeah, yeah, multiverse, I know," Jake said. "I don't want a knockoff alternate-universe version. I want the original."

"I want you, too," Solomon said. "You know that, right? I want you to stay. To live here, if you're willing, or I'll move to be with you, or whatever you want. I want to make it work. Even if the rest of your living space is as chaotic as your workshop. Even if you sometimes drop your wet towel on the bedroom floor, which is horrifying beyond comprehension."

"I'll stop the towel thing," Jake promised. "And if we stay here, which I'd be happy to do, I'll get a separate workshop to protect your delicate sensibilities. We'll figure it out."

"You're sure you want to live out here in the woods with me? You really think this can work?"

"Yeah, I do," Jake said. "Somebody really smart once told me that in an infinite multiverse, even a one-in-a-trillion chance is a sure thing. That's us."

ACKNOWLEDGMENTS

I am grateful to Ryan Boyd and Tasha L. Harrison for their editorial insights. Their suggestions made this book so, so much better.

I would also like to thank Valentine Wheeler and K. R. Collins for their early reading and cheerleading. Thank you to the members of the Liscord, whose friendship and conversation helped me get through the loneliest parts of the pandemic.

These books would not be possible without my live-in Science Consultant, for whom no question—be it about electrical wiring, space flight, or telekinesis—is too trivial or too bizarre to be considered carefully. He is indispensable to me both as a physical chemist and as a human being. His reading of an early draft left me with a dozen margin comments that just said "GRAVITY?" I did my best to address them, but any remaining errors or nonsense in this book are my own.

ALSO BY FELICIA DAVIN

THE NOWHERE

THE GARDENER'S HAND

ABOUT THE AUTHOR

Felicia Davin (she/they) is the author of the queer fantasy trilogy *The Gardener's Hand* and the sci-fi romance *Nowhere* series. Her novel *Edge of Nowhere* was a finalist for Best Bisexual Romance in the 2018 Bisexual Book Awards. Her short fiction has been featured in *Lightspeed*, *Nature*, and *Heiresses of Russ 2016: The Year's Best Lesbian Speculative Fiction*.

She lives in Massachusetts with her partner and their cat. When not writing and reading fiction, she teaches and translates French. She loves linguistics, singing, and baking. She is bisexual, but not ambidextrous.

She writes a weekly email newsletter about words and books called *Word Suitcase*, which is available at feliciadavin.com. You can also find her on Twitter @FeliciaDavin.

Lightning Source UK Ltd.
Milton Keynes UK
UKHW010628090621
385201UK00001B/88

9 780998 995755